# THE ISLAND

ALSO BY NATASHA PRESTON

*The Cellar*

*Awake*

*The Cabin*

*You Will Be Mine*

*The Lost*

*The Twin*

*The Lake*

*The Fear*

# THE ISLAND

NATASHA PRESTON

DELACORTE PRESS

GetUnderlined.com

Educators and librarians, for a variety of teaching tools, visit us at RHTeachersLibrarians.com

Library of Congress Cataloging-in-Publication Data is available upon request.
ISBN 978-0-593-48149-3 (pbk.) — ISBN 978-0-593-48150-9 (ebook)

The text of this book is set in Janson MT Pro
Interior design by Jen Valero

Printed in the United States of America
10 9
First Edition

For Ash. Love you, buddy.

# Prologue

I upload my latest trailer to TikTok advertising my new YouTube video, *Killer in the Family,* and I sit back. Within seconds the numbers under the little heart start climbing as if Jeff Bezos were watching a livestream of his bank balance.

He's building rockets. Malcolm Wyatt, a rich dude who invited *me* to his amusement park, is building islands.

Tearing open a packet of Hershey's Kisses with my teeth, I wait. Chocolate passes the time. I get a bunch of comments telling me how awesome it is that I've posted, but it'll take about thirty minutes for people to head over to my YouTube channel to watch the full video, then come back to TikTok to let me know what they think.

My hard-core followers comment on both. Then on Insta too.

I can wait. If I go downstairs right now, I'll just hear my parents arguing over Malcolm's invitation.

That invitation might just be the single coolest thing that has *ever* happened to me, without exception, and they're not certain they're going to let me go.

Not. Going. To. Let. Me. Go.

When Dad initially said no, I thought I was going to pass out. I was light-headed and everything.

There is no option: I *have* to go.

Things got so desperate I even had to send an SOS to my brother in college to call Dad and fight from my corner. Blaine is much better at wrapping our parents around his little finger. It helps that he's a literal genius and gives them excellent bragging rights.

If anyone can convince them, it's him.

How will I be able to look at myself in the mirror if I have to stay home that weekend while someone else takes my spot?

Nope, it's not happening.

I'm getting on that island, even if it kills me.

Only six of us have been invited. Six influencers. An exclusive weekend on a new island resort. An amusement park so remote that you can only reach it by boat.

It's a freaking dream come true.

The owner, Malcolm, wants us to endorse it. Influencers are taking over the world. If I hadn't accidentally made it big, I might be in a little despair over that fact.

People listen to someone online they've never met more than they do to their parents, teachers, doctors. It's tragic, really, but I'm not complaining. I'll be able to go to a top college and leave without any debt. I can buy a house when I'm done.

I've already got a brand-new BMW that my brother was *so* jealous about. It was glorious. His was two years old when our parents bought it.

I lean back in my office chair and peel the wrapper off a chocolate.

The count climbs. When it reaches more than one hundred thousand in minutes, I lock my phone and go to eavesdrop on my parents.

I'll come back in a bit to see what people are saying.

When I leave my room, Mom and Dad are still debating, as I expected. It's been two days and my trip is all that's been discussed. I tiptoe along the hallway and listen to Mom tell Dad that spending a weekend with other successful influencers who aren't focused on murder might "do me good."

Mom's not a fan of my content.

"She might start blogging about makeup like that girl Ellie's obsessed with, Gregory."

Ellie is my thirteen-year-old cousin. She's constantly glued to her phone watching some TikTok-er named Ava dance and vlog about beauty tips, hacks, and tricks.

"I don't think that's going to happen, Cheryl. She's obsessed with this death stuff. We don't know anything about this place or this billionaire who's invited her. It's perverse. Who does he think he is, asking my seventeen-year-old daughter to his island for the weekend?"

"Oh, Gregory, be real. Malcolm Wyatt is completely legitimate. And this trip? This is what being an influencer is. There's a group of them, all around her age. And a woman . . . Camilla something, will be their chaperone while they're there."

Camilla Jenkins. She's Malcolm's personal assistant and is apparently the one who's coordinating everything. She'll be watching out for us until the boat picks us up on Monday at lunchtime.

"Don't you see an issue with the fact that you're only pushing for this in the hope she'll come home and start doing dances online . . . or whatever it is these kids are posting?"

I close my eyes and cringe. Lord, shine a light.

"Even Blaine agrees with me," Mom says. She's smug; I can hear the triumph in her voice. Dad will be rolling his eyes.

See, Blaine is their golden child. He's the one not reporting on crime in his spare time.

He's at Princeton studying biochemistry.

"Oh, you know he can never say no to her. He'll agree with whatever she wants to do. Besides, this isn't up to Blaine."

Oh yeah. My brother might be their golden child, but he's always had my back and let me get my way.

"Forget Blaine. This is about Paisley. It's a great opportunity for her, Greg. It's no secret that I don't love what she does, but we can't argue that it's taking her places. She'll make some good connections."

She's probably referring to the billionaire.

There are a couple of millionaires on our street, but anything beyond that is blocks away, deep in the posh suburbs. This kind of money isn't part of my world. At least not yet.

Dad's sigh travels up the stairs. That's his sigh of resignation.

I know it well. It's the same one I heard after Blaine and I spent a week pestering him for a puppy. Bailey, our sweet Lab, is asleep on my bed.

*Yes!* I leap into the air in silent celebration, punching the air above my head.

I take out the invitation from my hoodie pocket and leap again.

At the end of the month, I'll be spending a whole weekend on Jagged Island.

# 1

## THREE WEEKS LATER

From the mainland, Jagged Island looked tiny, but as the boat speeds toward the rocky cliffs, I see that it's much larger than I thought.

It must be, to fit a whole amusement park, hotel, and restaurants on it.

Large hills and hoops of wooden roller coasters jut out of the ground and stretch high into the sky.

Sharp black rock that looks as if someone has carved vertical shards from the surface frames the island. The amusement park sits high off the water. Waves crash against the cliff face and white foam races back into the sea.

Trees are sparse on the island but the few there are full of bushy green leaves. From here, the park is dark, wooden, and void of color.

Even with the blue ocean and clear, sunny skies, the island appears more gloomy than glamorous. I kind of like it. The Magic Kingdom isn't my thing.

Our boat jumps over choppy water as we hurtle toward the jetty. I grip the side of the boat as my butt leaves the padded seat I'm trying to sit on.

"This looks creepy as hell," Ava says. Ava as in BeautyFulAva. The TikTok girl who my cousin is obsessed with and who my parents want me to be more like. Absolutely not going to happen. Before I left, Ellie made me promise to ask for her autograph, but so far, Ava's been a total brat.

Her contoured face twists in distaste as she stares at the island. Her glossy blond ponytail whips behind her in the wind. She's as sharp as in her videos, savagely rating brands that don't live up to her expectations. Her reputation for brutal honesty gets her a lot of attention.

Here, it might just get her hated.

We're not her followers.

When we arrived at the harbor, she dragged three large bright pink suitcases on board the boat and acted offended when Gibson, our rather hot driver, questioned if she needed it all. I'm trying to not judge her too harshly, but she's referred to Gibson as "the help" twice and we've only been on the boat for fifteen minutes.

He looks ready to throw her overboard.

"Nah, this looks awesome," Liam replies. Liam is a gamer, though from his appearance and muscular physique he seems like more of a jock. He has a dominant personality and perfectly styled brown hair. I focused on him straightaway. It's hard not to.

His YouTube channel is massive and he's TikTok-famous—his TikTok has exploded. He's a big fan of any game with violence and hits back at negative comments in the way a jock would—with complete and utter annihilation of his opponents.

He's gorgeous and probably wouldn't give me the time of day if we went to the same high school.

"No," Ava says more forcefully. "It's *creepy*. Who's going to look at an ad for this place and want to come here . . . besides goths, freaks, and serial killers?"

I wonder how much trouble I'd get in if I shoved her into the water. I doubt Gibson would care.

James wraps his arm around her shoulder. "I'll look after you."

It won't be the rough sea that makes me hurl.

Ava smiles up at him with her flawless bat-winged eyes. James is a movie buff. He reviews them, makes them, dissects the continuity, and rarely rates anything higher than three stars—his only five-star review last year was for *Squid Game*. He's tall and on the skinnier side, but you can tell he works out between all that movie-watching. He has striking features. His jaw is squared, his eyes are a very dark blue, and his hair is blond and curly. He's the only guy wearing aftershave. It's strong, woody.

And he makes Ava giggle a lot.

I don't know what she was expecting. The invitation was black with intricate red and gold gargoyles etched into it. All gothic and perfect and authentic.

The aesthetic is so on brand for me.

A couple days ago, I covered the tragic, historic story of

five-year-old Maggie, who was murdered at the Rocky Point Amusement Park in Rhode Island. It created a buzz among my followers. Half of them are saying a private island is the perfect place for murder and the other half thinks I'm crazy to stay somewhere I can't leave immediately if I want to.

It's only perfect if no one but you and your victims know you're there.

I'm sure I'll find an edge to the resort; the gothic vibe will help.

We're almost there now. I have to tip my head up to see the island. A few birds circle above like they're searching for prey.

This weekend we get to check out the park, spend time on the rides, and hang out at the hotel spa and pool. Then Malcolm is hoping we shout great things and send all our followers to the island.

The invitation described the resort as unconventional and extraordinary. One of a kind.

The boat leaps over another wave.

My stomach flips.

Gibson is the only one who doesn't look slightly green as we rock over choppy water. He steers the boat and smiles into the sun as we cut through the sea. His eyes are hidden behind dark aviators.

I think he's around our age, maybe a year or two older. His earlier use of "sup" when he helped us onto the boat threw me a bit, but he's fresh-faced and dressed in jeans and a white T-shirt. His light hair is cut quite short with a shaved line down the side.

He looks happy. Like he could race around on the ocean all day and never get bored.

Beside me, a girl named Harper grips the edge of the boat. She's a book blogger. She reads at least one book a day and posts so much on TikTok I can't keep up with her. But her reviews are awesome, and we had a short conversation a few months ago when she raved about a true-crime novel that I later devoured.

Her skin is dark, and her Afro is tied on top of her head. She smiles at me with her bloodred lips and pulls a well-read thriller paperback out of her bag with her free hand. The pages are so curled at the edges that it's not a surprise she doesn't mind the odd splash of water on the cover.

I'm not convinced reading's going to help her nausea.

"It's funny," Harper says. "I've swam almost every day of my life. We spent two years living in the UK, where I swam the English Channel. England to France—not all at once, like some more hard-core swimmers. But you spend all that time in the water and a boat still makes you feel sick."

"Impressive," I say. "How old were you?"

"Fifteen. We moved back to the States soon after. My dad did the swim too."

"Wow. I love swimming, but I wasn't good enough to make my school's team," I tell her.

"My parents don't accept anything less than impressive. Or, rather, perfection." She rolls her eyes and clings harder to her book.

"Why does it look depressing?" Ava says, her voice grating.

She's gripping her long ponytail and twisting it around her hand. "I'm supposed to be living it up in luxury, not slumming it on a grim, run-down island."

"It's not grim," Gibson says.

Will, who's mostly remained silent, finally speaks up. It's not surprising that it's a reply to the very hot Gibson. "Nothing weirds me out."

Ava mutters something inaudible, but from the look on her face it probably wasn't kind.

Will's a rival beauty blogger with a slightly larger audience than Ava's. That must be killing her. He has shiny brown hair, a fake tan, dark eyes, and smooth skin I would *literally* kill for.

I snap a picture of the ominous setting for a TikTok I'll post after Malcolm takes us on the island tour. Which the itinerary boasted would happen right before we check into our rooms.

The top of the hotel comes into view. Constructed from stone with sharp points, two turrets, and carved gargoyle, the hotel is stunning. The six of us get it all to ourselves for a long weekend. We hit the jackpot.

Each of us has more than 500,000 followers. Liam is at 499,900, so he'll be joining us soon—probably by the end of the weekend.

The second I found out who else was coming, I did my research. I'm probably most like Harper and Liam. Though we're from wealthy families, our follower counts are higher than our bank balances.

"So, is this rich dude a psycho or something?" Will asks casually.

Ignoring the strong urge to push him off the boat too, I reply, "Just because he appreciates Gothic architecture doesn't mean there's something wrong with him."

He flashes his fluorescent white teeth. "Course not, crime girl."

He's done his homework too.

If I wanted to be petty, I would tell him his foundation doesn't match his skin color, but one, I'm not petty, and two, it's as perfect a match as Blake Lively and Ryan Reynolds.

Instead, I look away. It's not the first time someone has insinuated that I'm strange. My mom regularly tells me to blog about something else. "You're too cute and friendly to cover such a dark topic, Paisley." As if you needed to be hideous with boils all over your face and a missing front tooth to report on crime.

News flash: plenty of serial killers are good-looking and act friendly.

There is no "type."

Gibson slows the boat and throws the rope to a man on the jetty who's so gorgeous he doesn't look real.

This is a resort for wealthy *and* beautiful people.

"Welcome to Jagged Island!" says the man, easily catching the rope. "I'm Reeve, head of maintenance. You'll see me more this weekend since the island is running a skeleton crew until we open to the public."

Reeve is tall with dark skin, and his muscles have muscles. He has the darkest eyes I've ever seen in my life and cheekbones so sharp they could cut through steel. He's sort of a slightly older version of my ex-boyfriend, but I won't hold that against him.

"Thanks," I say as he helps me off the boat. He gives me a Hollywood-worthy smile, and I trip over my own feet.

Smooth.

Ducking my head, I focus on tugging my suitcase out of the way of the others getting off the boat and not on my burning cheeks.

Why do I blush when every cute guy looks at me? I am such a loser.

At least Reeve has made more than just *my* head turn. Will, Ava, and Harper also do double takes and smile at him hopefully. We're all sixteen and seventeen, so I don't think he's going to give any of us a second glance. He'll probably forget we even exist when we leave on Monday.

He claps his hands. "If you all want to follow me, I'll take you to Malcolm."

I guess Malcolm doesn't come to greet his guests.

We walk up the ramp next to the steps. Both are long, winding, and carved into the island. Sweat beads at the nape of my neck as I wheel my suitcase behind me.

Ava has Reeve pulling two of hers. She just handed them off to him. I could never be so bold.

Even Reeve's irritated expression is cute.

Ava had asked Gibson to take her stuff, but he has to take some staff back to the mainland. Something about orientation this week but them not being needed over the weekend. She brightened when he said he'd be back in around an hour; James just sulked. I got the feeling he was used to girls falling all over him.

"At least I don't need to go for a run today," I say as we climb the slope that seems to stretch on forever. My bag gets heavier with each step I take.

Harper grunts. "I brought books with me. This *hurts*."

"What do you set your Goodreads challenge to?"

"Three hundred and fifty a year."

"Wow. I can only manage about fifty."

"Are they all crime?"

"Mostly. Lots of nonfiction."

"Hey, I run too if you want to go out together tomorrow?" she asks.

"That sounds good. I lost my running partner when my brother moved to college." I grin over at her. "How incredible is this place?"

"Right? I didn't want to say anything in front of the princess. Can't be bothered with the drama."

I like Harper already.

I switch hands and tug the case to the top. That's when I get my first real look at the park. It's exactly what you'd expect of a theme park, except it went heavy on stone and dark wood.

Reeve unlocks a large gate with sinister-looking gargoyle heads carved into the pillars. On the other side of the gate is a white cart professing the best ice cream in the world and largest choice of toppings.

A little bit of fun to lighten the darkness.

The roller coasters are all on thick wooden tracks that conceal the metal ones so the aesthetic of the park isn't compromised.

A group of staff members passes us, heading to the boat. They're all wearing dark navy shorts and red polo tops. They look us over as if we're a circus act.

My parents weren't happy that the island wasn't fully staffed, but it doesn't need to be. You don't need hundreds of people working for six guests.

Blaine convinced them to be happy that the owner and his assistant would be with us. And that this was an opportunity that came once in a lifetime—and that I'd managed to get all on my own.

I wish I had his powers of persuasion.

"It's cool, but this place is kinda weird," Harper says, looking around.

I open my mouth to reply but Reeve beats me to it, explaining that Malcolm wanted an exclusive park with a unique angle. A theme park for the rich, but he didn't want it dripping in gold and diamonds.

No glass and mirrors and caviar.

That was overdone, apparently.

"Malcolm grew up traveling the world, but it was his visit to the Burgos Cathedral in Spain when he discovered his love for the Gothic era," Reeve explains as they walk up the cliff.

I get the feeling that his speech is rehearsed. Part of the orientation. Watch a video about the new boss's life.

I can imagine how enthusiastic the staff was to learn about a billionaire's private-island dream while they're probably getting paid twenty dollars an hour to serve guests and control rides.

Reeve leads us around a corner, past the entrance to a rather adult-looking poltergeist train. "I'm *definitely* going on that later," I mumble to myself.

And then I look up and, *holy hell,* that must be Malcolm. Standing at the thick double-pointed-arch wooden doors of the hotel is a tall, lanky man with curly black hair and a pipe. He's wearing a long burgundy coat—despite the summer heat—and a black turtleneck.

He spreads his arms wide. "Welcome to my island."

# 2

Malcolm floats into the hotel, pointing things out as we follow along behind him.

Harper nudges me with her elbow and rolls her eyes as Malcolm boasts about his incredible resort.

I look up at the tall ceilings framed with ornate wooden designs weaving in and out of each other like a bowl of spaghetti. Every archway is peaked and reaches almost to the ceiling. It looks like it was made from just one piece of wood.

"Ah, magnificent, isn't it?" Malcolm comes alive when he talks about his island. "You wouldn't believe how long it took to complete. Worth every cent."

How many cents did it take?

"The hotel is huge," I say.

"For the number of guests. How astute of you, Paisley. Yes, the hotel is big, but so are the rooms. We could fit plenty more in, but I opted for quality over quantity. Don't you hate it when you arrive at a hotel and your room is tiny? No room to even swing a cat. Here you can swing lions."

It's impossible to tell how literal he's being.

I'm about to ask how much the resort cost, how long it took to build—things my followers would want to know—and when he expects the island to make money after what I imagine was a *huge* outlay, but he interrupts my train of thought by bringing us to his "masterpiece" in the lobby: a long glass-fronted cabinet that spans the distance between two tall, arched windows.

We all stop and stare.

It's full of short-length swords, axes, labrys axes, and even a mace.

Comfortable soft leather armchairs are dotted between archways. Each set of two chairs faces each other, giving a private feel in a public place.

"Why would anyone have those?" Ava says. She tries to keep her sneer quiet, but it doesn't work. Malcolm ignores her. Everyone besides James does.

He whispers something in her ear that makes her laugh.

If I were Malcolm, I would put them back on the boat and send them home.

"Are these weapons real?" I ask.

James pushes past me and Harper. "Can we take them out?"

"Absolutely not," Malcolm replies. His tone is scolding, but James isn't fazed. Nothing about him makes me think that he listens much to authority.

Liam steps up close and smiles at me—and my face flushes—before addressing Malcolm. "So, *are* they real?"

"Unfortunately, no. A few of the swords are, but most of what you see here I've had made. They're authentic to the era and work just as they would have been, though."

So they're real enough. Which I'm sure he paid an eye-watering sum for.

"What's the fascination with all this . . . stuff? I thought you built a luxury resort on a luxury island," Ava asks, raising her eyebrows.

Malcolm looks at her, his eyes unreadable. "Well, young lady. How many resorts have you been to like mine?"

"None." Her reply is another ugly sneer. For someone on a free trip, she sure isn't acting very appreciative.

"There we are. I don't want to be another Disney. This place isn't for little children."

Harper and I grin at each other. Ava blushes a deep shade of pink and glares at Malcolm.

He deserves a high five for that subtle insult.

The island, according to our information packet, is aimed at wealthy people ages thirteen and older.

Now, the info pack didn't *actually* say *wealthy,* but three nights here costs six thousand dollars per person.

It's an expensive weekend.

Even though my parents would be able to afford it, I couldn't see them dropping twenty-four grand to bring our family here. Not for three nights, anyway.

There will be a lot of trust-fund kids booking rooms the second the website goes live. A different type of spring break.

Blaine will come here with his friends, I have no doubt.

Malcolm continues the tour, taking us past the lobby, around a massive fireplace that's taller than me. The other side is the bar lined with every type of alcohol and soft drink imaginable.

"Kenna, our cook, will be here later with Reeve to prepare cocktails." He raises a finger. "Apologies. *Mocktails.* This weekend is strictly alcohol-free."

"Note how he said that last part directly to James and Ava," I whisper to Harper and Will.

"Does that mean *we* can sneak a few beers?" Harper replies, winking.

I smile because I really don't think so, given the fact that there are coded locks on the row of fridges.

"I can break those locks," Will says, peering over the bar as we're led along a corridor.

I nod but my focus is back on Malcolm, who is breezing right along. "The entire east wing of the hotel is our wellness center. Treatment rooms, swimming pool, sauna, hot tub, steam room, and organic juice bar. If you would like a fresh-pressed juice, you can ask Kenna and she will make you one." He smiles. "Highly recommend the beet-pineapple blend."

Malcolm pushes open the high double doors to the wellness center. It's amazing.

"Wow," I say, gazing around in awe. "I'm spending a lot of time here."

The pool is huge, the lighting low, and the aroma of lavender and eucalyptus floats around the center. The classic luxury doesn't clash with the Gothic aesthetics of the resort. High ceilings, intricate carved designs, and archways are carried on throughout.

Each arch has a subtle door that must lead to the treatment rooms. A hot tub is set into the ground. It looks like it's part of the stone floor too. It wouldn't surprise me if Malcolm made the builders dig the pool and hot tub out of the stone floor.

Either way, it's stunning.

"Now I'll show you down in the basement where we have the game room. Arcade, pool, air hockey, interactive tennis, and another bar. Feel free to use it whenever you like this weekend."

"I might check it out," Liam mutters, his eyes saying much more than that. He's probably spotted the game consoles by a massive U-shaped sofa.

"Do you play pool?" Harper asks.

I smile. "Oh, you're going down."

She laughs and links my arm with her own as if we've known each other for longer than an hour.

"Think Ava and James will be too cool to hang out with us?"

She nods immediately at my question. "Without a doubt. Who cares, though? You, Will, and Liam are the only ones I'd want to spend any time with anyway."

"Same," I reply as we follow Malcolm back up the stairs and into the lobby again. He points out a restaurant on the way.

"Now," he says. "Camilla will give you your key cards and you can get settled in your rooms. I'll be back in thirty minutes to meet you for lunch before we take the tour of the park."

Camilla jumps into action, flying behind the reception desk. "All right, Paisley, you're room 237." She hands me a key and is telling James his room number before I can thank her.

Two thirty-seven. The number sounds familiar and then I remember. Wasn't that the number of the room in *The Shining*? The one where the dead woman was in the bathtub.

I wait a minute and take the elevator with the others.

Ava and James laugh as they call for the second elevator.

"They should get married," Liam says as he tugs his suitcase into the car.

"They're definitely perfect for each other," Harper says, shrugging.

I press the number two on the board. "We should team up a little this weekend. Use our platforms to introduce each other. There are a lot of crossovers between all of us."

"Not much between me and Liam," Will points out.

He wasn't being unkind. Liam plays video games where he commits crime and Will blogs about beauty.

"That doesn't matter. We all share this park and this weekend," I reply.

Harper is the first out of the elevator. "Paisley's right. We can all help each other."

We start walking down a long hallway. "This is me," I say. My room is close to the elevator, but there aren't a lot of doors in the hallway. If this were a normal hotel, my door would be much closer to the elevator, but as it is, it's a bit of a hike.

Malcolm did say the rooms were bigger.

"See you downstairs in thirty!" Harper says, skipping ahead to her room. She's in 239 next door. The boys are farther down.

I unlock my door and step inside, parking my suitcase next to the wall.

Whoa.

My room is sick.

It's a large suite. To my left is a marble bathroom with two sinks, a round black bathtub, and a double shower. There's a mirror spanning the length of the wall and a TV set into it.

I'd never get out on time if I turned that on.

I continue into the room past a wall of wardrobes and large mirror. In the main room is a sofa, table and chairs, large TV, and mini fridge.

I poke my head around the door to the bedroom. A massive four-poster emperor bed takes up most of the space. The floor is dark wood with a large soft rug with a red and gold twisty pattern. There's a slight scent of lemon and something else I can't name, but it smells . . . rich.

How much did all this cost? I know Malcolm's net worth thanks to the internet, but I don't have any idea how much it took to build this. The island cost close to ten million dollars when Malcolm purchased it a few years ago. Back then it was just rock and dirt and trees.

I walk around my suite with the four-poster emperor bed and black bathtub. In the main area is a wide window. The peaked archways continue, spanning the height of the room and house large panes of glass.

Stepping forward, I peer out the window. From here I can see half of the jetty and a lot of the ocean.

I texted my mom when we arrived. Now I snap a few pictures and text them to my family.

Mom:

Wow! The hotel looks amazing. But also—strange?

Paisley:

It's 16th century gothic, mom

Blaine:

Surely you recognize it from your era?

I chuckle. Is my brother looking to ditch his golden child title? I'll happily take over the throne; it'd be much easier not to have to go through a middleman to get what I want.

Mom:

You can do your own laundry when you're back home.

Paisley:

We're going to ride the coasters now!! I'll check in later. Love you all!

I toss my phone on my bed and start to unpack my suitcase. I packed pretty light, so once everything that needs to be hung up is, I decide to go on Instagram and post a quick video with the gargoyles carved into the bedpost in the background.

The comments are unanimous.

My followers think the island is haunted.

I'm leaving the bathroom light on.

If anyone's in the bathtub, I'll f*reak.*

# 3

"I saw your video," Harper says. "I just posted one too. Our followers have reached the same conclusion."

I sit down on a plush chair in the lobby. We're the only ones down here so far. Both of us are impatient for the rides.

"The haunted thing?" I ask.

"Yeah. Some comments on mine are even telling me to leave now."

I laugh. "That's slightly over the top. There's nothing paranormal here."

She shrugs one shoulder. "You never know."

"Really? Do you believe in ghosts?"

She takes a second to think about it. "I'm undecided. I've never witnessed anything spooky, but that doesn't mean it's not out there. I do know that I will never mess with a Ouija board. What about you?"

A shiver runs the length of my spine. "I don't believe in ghosts.

There are enough monsters in human flesh. I think I would go crazy if I started to believe there are some I can't see, too."

"Does blogging about murder mess with your mind?"

"The active cases do more than ones that have been resolved. It's still super sick what people do to each other, but it's easier to detach when it's something that happened years ago." That sounds kind of wrong—death is death. But that's how I feel.

And there is no way anyone can learn all the gruesome details about a murder and have it not bother them. Unless you're the one committing those crimes, of course.

"I get that." Harper nods. "And it wasn't your brand, but I loved all your Britney stuff. Her family is . . ." She trails off, shaking her head.

"The Britney posts brought a lot of new followers, but my murder stuff is what keeps people watching. Everyone loves a good killer." I roll my eyes. "Not that I'm judging. I've been fascinated since I was about thirteen."

Harper raises an eyebrow. "What happened when you were thirteen?"

The one case I will never cover. The one that kept me awake, hidden under my blanket after my parents went to sleep, trawling articles online about the murder.

It was close to home and my parents didn't want me to hear anything about it. But I live in a small town, and it was always going to get around.

"Um." I clear my throat. This has never been an easy one to talk about and it's why I'd never cover it. "Did you ever hear about Elliana Delaney?"

Harper shakes her head. "No. Who is she?"

"Elliana was my neighbor. I was eleven and she was eight, so we didn't hang out. The Delaneys lived in a massive house two doors down from us, manicured gardens, pool out the back, you know the type. Her parents seemed perfect, and she seemed perfect. Then, her mom went missing one summer. Elliana and her dad went on TV begging for information about her."

Harper's mouth parts. "Let me guess, the dad did it?"

"Yeah, that's the story about her mom. We don't know for sure what happened, but five days later, Elliana was murdered. The cops think her mom was killed and she knew all along and couldn't keep her mouth shut any longer. He slaughtered his own daughter to stop her from talking."

"No way! How did they find out it was him?"

"His DNA was found under Elliana's fingernails. He was charged and found guilty."

"What about her mom's murder?"

I shrug. "No body and no evidence that he did anything to her. He was never even charged with anything to do with her mom."

"Tell me he got life."

"He did. No chance of parole. Elliana was just a kid. I read the transcripts from court, and the judge came down hard on him. As she should have."

Harper presses her hand to her heart. "God, that's awful. And that's when you started to vlog?"

"No. I started researching crimes, murder, kidnappings. Anything and everything. I had notebooks on cases. It wasn't until about eighteen months ago that I started my podcast. Elliana and her mom were something else. I had to find out everything, but I knew them, you know?"

She nods.

"Ah, my two favorite influencers," Malcolm says, floating into the lobby. It sounded like he was in physical pain when he called us influencers.

"We're just waiting for the others," Harper says.

"Very good. We still have time." He checks his watch. "You're welcome to go through to the dining room. Camilla is already there with drinks."

I stand. "Thanks."

Harper and I head into the hotel restaurant. We're the only ones here, which feels a little weird. But the good thing is our food doesn't take long. I opt for a cheeseburger and fries with ice cream for dessert; Harper gets a chicken Caesar wrap and a fruit cup. Everything is served on white china plates rimmed with silver. And our drinks are in heavy crystal goblets.

After lunch, we head out into the park. There's a gate separating the hotel and courtyard from the amusement park. For insurance purposes, I suspect.

"This is awesome!" Harper nudges my arm, her dark eyes sparking in the sun as the others appear. "Where to first, Paisley?"

Reeve is waiting and smiles at us. "Who's coming with me?"

Me. Absolutely.

Harper, Will, Liam, and I volunteer to go with Reeve. Gibson is the unlucky one stuck with Ava and James now that he's back from the mainland.

"Haunted house!" I say. "I need that." It's always the first ride I go on when I'm at a park.

"All right," Reeve replies.

"We're all coming with you," Gibson says, slapping Reeve on the back. "I'll throw myself off the cliff if I have to spend the day with those two."

The rest of us laugh while Ava and James make out under one of the live oak trees.

Reeve thumps Gibson's arm. "I get you, man."

"How scary is it?" I ask, as we walk along the dark asphalt, passing entrances to a roller coaster and drop tower.

"You'll see," Reeve says, winking. Since we're the only guests in the park, we won't have to wait in any lines. Each ride has an attendant at the ready, in case we decide we want to try it out.

Everything is made from wood and stone and has a similar Gothic carved design. All natural material, likely sourced from the island itself. There's so much to see—intricately carved buildings and benches, signs that are hand-painted, beautiful gardens filled with burgundy tulips and covered walkways. I'm never leaving this park ever.

After four hours of riding and re-riding almost all the thrill rides, we all seem to drift apart to different areas of the park. Will is doing a video with the gargoyles by the entrance. Liam says he is going to catch up with Gibson, Ava, and James, who are heading toward the log flume.

I have so much footage. We've barely covered half the park since we've all stopped about a thousand times to take photos, selfies, and videos.

Reeve takes me and Harper under a shelter, and we board a dark train carriage. The seats are in twos, so Harper and I head for the first one.

"Enjoy," Reeve says as the ride attendant, a young woman with glasses and long black hair, presses a couple buttons. I catch a glance at him grinning at me before we disappear past a black sheet.

Harper tugs the bar lower into our laps. The metal digs against my thighs.

"I don't think we're going to go upside down." I've never been at a park without knowing a little something about the rides. This is all uncharted territory—we're some of the first people ever to ride these rides.

"Can you guarantee that here, though?" she asks, arching a dark brow.

"Fair point, but we'd have a harness if that was the case."

The train rolls noisily on the tracks and wobbles slightly as if it's been used every day for a hundred years. Harper tightens her grip on the bar as we descend into darkness.

The car rocks again as we slowly make our way without even a slither of light. I blink but I can't see a thing. My heart beats faster with every second of nothing.

The only other sound I can hear is Harper's breathing.

We swing sharply around a corner, and I gasp. If we'd been going any faster, I might have bumped into Harper.

It smells like wood and rubber.

"Paisley," Harper whispers. She sounds scared.

I squeeze her arm. How long have we been in here in the pitch black?

A low hiss like an aerosol can cuts through the tunnel and something tickles my face. It's cold and unscented, but loud.

Harper and I both jump and shout out at the same time.

"What the hell was that?"

"Air," I reply, ducking my head. "It's okay."

This is all very creepy and too subtle. The calm before the storm.

Above us something drops from the ceiling with an animalistic squeal. This time Harper and I do more than shout. We scream louder than the hideous gargoyle-looking thing as it's illuminated by a soft blue glow that accentuates its wrinkled features and large eyes.

Harper and I laugh.

"My heart!" I say, sitting straight again.

We don't have any time to recover before something else pops out from the wall. We get no break as another terrifying character launches itself toward us. I leap over to Harper's side of the car, and she laughs her ass off.

Low lighting glows all around us, making it even harder to see than before, and some birds drop from the ceiling, hanging far too close to our heads for my liking.

Harper ducks. "Are those bats?"

I look up and strain my eyes. "Blackbirds, I think," I reply.

The ride creaks loudly and "people" spring out from nowhere again.

We both laugh and huddle together in the middle of the car. Harper points one of them out, a creepy-looking hunched-over old man with no teeth. Air sprays from above him, making us both jump again.

I scream when something touches my shoulder. Spinning around, I see nothing but the shadows of birds cascading on the walls.

We then finally poke back out of another sheet, and we're in the daylight again.

"Oh my god!" Harper says. "That was awesome."

"Yeah," I reply, looking over my shoulder. "Did something touch you in there?"

"What?"

The ride comes to a stop and Reeve looks up, laughing at what I assume were mine and Harper's squeals.

"Back there, near the end. I thought something touched my shoulder."

"It was probably just the air. I felt it on my face."

The bar rises up and I step out of the car, Harper behind me. "Yeah, probably."

Only it felt very much like a hand.

# 4

Will and I are the only ones not drinking whatever mocktails Kenna, Jagged Island's chef, and Reeve have made. They all smell far too sweet, like cotton candy on speed.

Gross.

So, we're drinking water. Will sparkling and me still. Harper and Liam are drinking the mocktails. Liam said he needs the sugar hit after a busy day. Harper says she usually eats and drinks a strictly healthy diet thanks to her doctor parents, so while she's here without them, she's living it up.

If she's not used to a ton of sugar, she probably won't sleep at all tonight.

After a day in the park, we've reconvened at the hotel restaurant, where we just finished an amazing meal of jerk chicken, coconut rice, potato salad, and cake. I don't know how anyone has room for another drink.

"I've listened to some of your podcasts," Will says next to me. "Found myself more interested than I probably should've been."

I'll take that as a compliment. "If you're not interested in murder, why did you listen?" I ask him.

He grins. "I checked everyone out when Camilla sent the list of attendees."

"Ah," I say, nodding. "I did the same."

"I like your eyebrows," he tells me, and I think that's the highest compliment from people in the beauty world.

"Thanks. I followed one of your tutorials."

Makeup isn't something I've ever been good at, and I don't have the energy to do all that contouring crap that confuses your phone's face ID, but Will posted a video about a quick everyday look that only takes me ten minutes.

That I can do. Besides, if I don't wear anything, I look too much like my brother.

"You're all right, you know, angel."

*Angel* is what Will calls people in his videos. The ones who do their makeup along with him or fans he does shout-outs to. Somehow he doesn't sound patronizing.

"What do you think of the park now that we've seen it all?" I ask him.

"Well, when I heard Malcolm was a billionaire who built an exclusive park on a remote island, I kind of thought we'd be in for some sort of modern luxury heaven." He shrugs.

"As opposed to this luxury hell?"

Will laughs. "Well, kind of. I'm not going to lie: this is going to create a much bigger buzz. Everyone is going to want to come here. This must be heaven for you."

I'm sure my eyes light up. "I absolutely love it! All the gargoyles and the sense of being here completely alone. There's only *one* way off the island."

I smile again because Will looks like he wants to run away.

See, I'm friendly.

"This place is probably haunted. My followers think that. They want me to do a dead makeup tutorial."

"Like, making yourself look dead?"

He nods. "I've done some Halloween stuff. Blood and gashes. Skin hanging off, bones showing. That kind of thing."

"Nice." I look up at the ornate Gothic carvings on the ceiling. "Ghosts sure would add to the ambiance he's created at the resort. Who were they? How did they die? There could be a history here that we just don't know about."

"Wow, you really do love all this death stuff."

"I don't love death. I'm fascinated with what people can do to each other. I want to know why and how. My parents say I always ask too many questions. I'm too inquisitive. And my brother, though he's supportive, thinks it'll get me into trouble one day."

"Or maybe it'll lead to a job with the FBI."

I roll my eyes. "Try telling my mom that."

That would freak her out more. Chasing murderers would be a huge, scary leap from reporting on them.

"All right," Malcolm says, drawing our attention as he stands at the head of the table. "I want to thank you all for being here. It's an honor to have you as my guests this weekend. Please feel free to document your time here as you wish, and if you have any issues, I trust you'll come to me first. There's nothing that can't be rectified."

Basically, if we find a tiny, curly hair on the sheets, we should call him instead of posting a picture online.

"I hope you all enjoyed the meal. I'm going to retire to my room and leave you to enjoy your evening." He picks up his sugar-coma-inducing cocktail. Camilla gives us a little wave and follows him out of the room.

"Do you think those two are together?" Will asks.

"I don't know, but she follows him everywhere."

"She's a doormat," Liam says. "I would've poured my coffee over him by now."

He's sitting on my other side, but I barely spoke to him throughout dinner. When we first met, I didn't think I'd ever be on his radar. He'd always be on mine because he's one of those people you can't help noticing. A tall, hot jock who can make you blush with a sweeping glance.

Or he could make me blush like that anyway. I'm so uncool.

We've already split into high-school cliques. Liam looks like he'd be with James and Ava, but so far, he's been with us.

"Malcolm is her boss," I say. My defense isn't a good one. "She probably has to be nice to him," I add.

Liam shrugs. "Maybe. I think he's power hungry. Did you see him barking orders at her all evening?"

Will and I nod.

"I haven't heard him utter a single *please,* either," Harper says.

"He's a sleaze," Will says. "There's just something about him that I don't like. But the guy knows how to design a park, so I'll let it go."

"Can you believe how much it costs to stay here?" Harper asks. "My parents want to come when it's open. They just love anything exclusive."

There's a tone to her voice that tells me she doesn't feel completely comfortable around all this money. A girl transferred to my school after her parents won a ton of money and she hated how much it changed her life.

Sometimes you just want what you know.

I can barely remember the time when we had to count pennies. I was seven. My parents took a leap of faith on a business, and it paid off *massively*.

It's left me with a gift. Being able to notice who was born into this life—Ava for sure, Will, Malcolm, and Harper—and who wasn't. Liam, James, and me.

Camilla is a hard one to read. She walks around with super straight posture that's right out of my private school, but I can tell her outfits aren't as expensive as they look.

Malcolm definitely does not pay her enough. I don't think there's a sum large enough for me to be Malcolm's servant. Now that he's gone, everyone feels free to talk.

"Did you do the ghost train?" Harper asks the others. "Me and Paisley nearly died!"

Liam's eyes dance. Dammit, he really is gorgeous. "I didn't get on that one yet. Hey, Paisley, maybe me and you could do it tomorrow?"

He asked the question in a totally normal tone. No sign that he's joking.

I don't dare look over at Harper and Will. It's not necessary, anyway—I can f*eel* the look they're giving me. They'll have goofy smiles for sure.

Um. He really asked me that. Liam wants to spend time with me. *Calm down, he's probably just being nice.* "Sure," I say, trying not to sound like a complete idiot.

"Cool." Liam nods and goes back to his chocolate fudge cake, joining in a conversation about a new video game with James and Ava. Ava's eyes look bored as hell, but she's smiling like it's her job for James's sake.

Harper pulls a thriller from her lap and opens it on the table. Her napkin falls to the ground as her focus is on the book. I've done that more than once.

"I have an idea," Will says, leaning over and whispering so that no one else can hear. "Let's sneak into the park when everyone's asleep tonight."

I jolt and raise a brow at him. "Seriously?"

"Why not? We're alone. How much trouble could we get into?"

A lot, actually. "It was a rule."

The safety information sheet clearly states that we cannot go into the park or be on the jetty alone. There was nothing stating the consequences of breaking those rules.

"Where's your sense of adventure, angel?"

I smirk. "Oh, I wasn't saying no."

Will laughs. "Let's meet by the fireplace in the lobby at midnight. Everyone should be in bed by then."

It's only nine now but everyone looks dead tired. We've all had a full-on afternoon in the park and walked thousands of steps. I feel my bed calling me, but I want to see the park at night more.

"Okay."

After dinner, we hang out in the game room a bit. I play a couple games of pool with Harper, Will, and Liam.

Liam hits the ball into the pocket. We're on our last game, best of three. So far, we've both won a game.

He looks up at me and grins. "You ready to lose, Pais?"

"I'm not out yet. Do your worst."

Chuckling, he hits the white again and this time misses.

"See, that's what happens when you get cocky," I tease.

"I'm just giving you a chance," he replies, stepping back.

Rolling my eyes, I walk around him and lift a brow. I don't know where I got the confidence from, but I can't say that I'm not enjoying it.

The attention from someone like Liam is flattering, though I'll only ever admit that to myself, but I'm not stupid enough to think that it's more than a little flirting.

I pot the next three and miss the fourth, but then we're neck and neck. Liam lifts a brow.

"You thought this game was yours," I say.

To be fair, he has the advantage now. If he gets the next two in, he's onto the black. I lean against the table and watch closely as he lines up his cue.

"Paisley, distraction is cheating."

"I'm just watching."

"Sure, you are."

Why would me standing here be a distraction? I'm not giving that a second thought. Nope. Don't think.

Liam hits the ball but misses.

He looks up, playfully scowling.

"My turn."

He watches with crossed arms as I win the game.

"Fine," he says. "Well done."

"How hard was that to say?"

Laughing, he replies. "Very. I think everyone is splitting."

Stifling a yawn, I say, "Yeah, I should get to bed."

We all drift up to our rooms at the same time.

There are a lot of videos about to be uploaded on TikTok as we all will probably try to get content out there. I have footage from dinner and playing pool, but I haven't had time to post.

I say good night to Liam and Will, whose rooms are past mine, and go to get ready for bed.

Well, that's what I should be doing.

In an hour, Will and I are sneaking out. I spend the time messaging my parents and Blaine, telling them that I'm safe and having the best time. I send a few more pictures, but only my brother gets the torture equipment ones.

Ten minutes before midnight, I can't wait any longer. Opening my door quietly, I slip out and tiptoe along the hallway. Will might be early as well. I can't wait to see what the park looks like at night.

Will is only a few doors up but I'm not going to knock. We might be caught, and he told me to meet him by the fireplace.

I take the stairs and try not to let the complete silence freak me out.

The lights are turned down low, a soft orange.

It would be comforting if it wasn't for the grotesque characters carved into the ceiling staring at me, watching my every move.

I slide through the door and into the lobby. My Converse-clad feet are light on the dark stone floor. The only real noise I can hear is my own breathing.

Along the far wall of the lobby, the medieval weapons shine against the artificial light in the case. One catches my eye and I walk up to it to get a better look.

It's a crescent-shaped weapon that looks sharp enough to take off a head in one swing. The craftsmanship is phenomenal.

A second thing catches my eye. Wait a second . . . Maybe I just missed it before, but there are two sets of hooks along the large knife section of the cabinet that aren't holding anything.

I guess Malcolm's collection isn't complete yet.

# 5

The lobby feels too quiet, particularly when you're alone with a bunch of medieval weapons. I've not even seen it in full life yet, but I know this isn't what it's supposed to feel like. There should be people behind the desk, the odd person milling about, laughter in the bar, and the clattering of plates and cutlery in the restaurant.

Shouldn't I hear Will's footsteps by now?

The information packet said the reception desk is staffed twenty-four hours a day, but no one is there. We've all been given Camilla's and Reeve's cell numbers for off hours this weekend.

I noticed that Malcolm didn't give his up for emergencies. We have it from some of the paperwork we were sent. But the fact that he's not on the emergency card makes me think he doesn't want us to call him under any circumstances.

I do another lap, not that I need to get the steps in, while I wait for Will. The lack of any noise is starting to make me nervous.

My eyes seek out every frightening-looking gargoyle around the arches and up toward the ceiling.

My heart thumps harder. This quiet feels like the start of the ghost train . . . and that doesn't make me feel any better.

The doors in the lobby are never locked. There's no reason for them to be, I suppose. It's not like someone could walk in here off the street. And the sea has gotten progressively rougher. A storm will hit tomorrow night.

By Monday it's supposed to be back to normal, but I'm sure Gibson's boat can handle a choppy sea. We might just get more seasick than we did during the ride out here.

We're lucky that while we're here we'll only catch the tail end of the storm tomorrow night. It would suck if we had to spend all day inside.

I do another lap of the lobby and ignore my watch telling me to take a minute to breathe. It must know I'm anxious.

There's a door for staff only to the left of the reception desk. I can see from a thin arched pane of glass in the door that there are more rooms down there. Probably the kitchen, staff room, service room, and things like that.

Malcolm went that way when he headed to his room. I bet he has a massive suite out of the way of guests. Of course, that wasn't part of the tour.

I can see my worried expression in that little slice of glass. Okay, if Malcolm, Camilla, Gibson, Kenna, or Reeve comes out of their room, I'll be busted. Time to be a bit more discreet.

As I turn, I spot someone along the staff corridor. They're

wearing a long, dark robe. They're too short to be Gibson or Reeve and I can't see them walking around in pajamas.

Malcolm.

His head is bowed as he walks from one room and disappears into another.

I back up, my heart in my throat at nearly getting caught. Stepping behind the large fireplace that separates the restaurant from the bar, I decide to hide and wait for Will to make an appearance.

This is all over if I'm caught. I can't believe I was doing laps as if I'm damn invisible. Not that anyone seems to be awake.

The park probably has a much different atmosphere after midnight. If my followers are right and there are ghosts of tortured victims here, maybe we'll feel their presence.

Or maybe that's all rubbish and we'll just spook ourselves. I'm really good at getting inside my own head and convincing myself that a creak in the night is a murderer sneaking along the floorboards.

It's a gift.

Blaine would laugh at me for even thinking I could sense ghosts.

I check my watch for the millionth time. The first thing I notice is that I've walked fourteen thousand steps today—no wonder I'm being told to take a calming breath—and the second thing I notice is that Will is currently seven minutes late. Unusual since he told me he's always on time. This was his idea and he's the one leaving me hanging.

I walk the length of the fireplace. Once. Twice. Three times.

The opening is taller than me. I could walk right through it without ducking if a bucket of chopped wood wasn't in the way.

*Come on, Will.*

After another ten minutes I figure he's probably fallen asleep. Will's not coming, and I have a choice to make.

What I should do is go up to my room, but if I don't go out there, I might not get to see the park late at night. Liam might be up for sneaking out with me, but tomorrow night the storm hits, and then there's only Sunday night left.

The last time I left something until the last minute, I got a C and my parents acted like I ripped up the test and spat at the teacher.

So, I'm going for it.

Before I can change my mind, I step around the fireplace and walk straight out the door without looking back. My skin prickles as the cool air hits my bare arms. The temperature has dropped a lot, but it's not unbearable.

It'd still be hot at home, but there's not a lot of protection from the elements on this little island.

I peer around the corner of the hotel. It's dark out but the sky is clear.

Thousands of stars sparkle above my head.

Some of the tracks from the coasters at the other side of the park have disappeared into the dark.

What else could be hiding in the dark?

*Nope, don't think of that.* I briskly move toward the park. I walk past the poltergeist train, step over the tracks, and try the door. It rattles as I tug but it doesn't budge.

Locked.

Good call, really.

Maybe I could convince Reeve to bring me out here at night. By the looks of it he has a key to practically every lock on this island.

Walking through the tunnel would be awesome. I could get up close and personal to that ghastly-looking killer who jumped out of the wall and made me scream.

I would *love* to whack him.

A shiver rolls down my spine, and I let go of the handle. Big mistake. It creeped me out before, and I was with someone during daylight hours.

Harper said the thing I felt was just a gust of wind.

A few blasts hit us along the ride, so that's not impossible, but this was different. I felt fingers curl around my shoulder. It was only a second, but it was there. I know I didn't just imagine it.

One of the horrible characters that pops out could have a curled hand, designed to make people think a person was grabbing them.

It's a good and effective trick.

Blaine would laugh his ass off if he knew I was skipping walking a ghost train because I'm paranoid.

He'll never know about this.

I take my phone out of my pocket and snap a few pictures of the park at night as I walk away from the ghost train.

A gust of wind sweeps my hair in front of my face, and I don't know why I jolt like I've been seen because there's no one else out here.

*Dammit.*

I'm *so* over wind.

Looking over my shoulder, all I see are rides and darkness.

Being alone in the dark already has me paranoid and I've only been out here for five minutes. I'll be certifiable in an hour.

Note to self: don't stay out longer than an hour.

The live oak trees lean to the side. The stupid wind is picking up a little more now; we're too high up from the sea to get wet from the spray, but I bet it would be different if a storm rolled in. I guess I'll find out tomorrow night.

Malcolm must have something in place for that.

No one would want to come here if you were constantly drenched.

I'm kind of looking forward to the storm. I'll be snuggled safely in the hotel and watching the rain from the window. Footage of a storm will create an awesome atmosphere for my videos too.

Large gray clouds begin to circle the island above me. I watch as they roll in and steal the stars away. The sound of the ocean crashing against the cliff is oddly calming but also like a warning.

I shudder, the skin on my arms bobbling, and look over my shoulder.

Is someone there?

I open my mouth to call out and instantly decide against it. I'm not supposed to be out. Malcolm was still awake, but why would he come out here?

Unless he saw me. But if he did, why wouldn't he call me out for breaking the rules? *His* rules.

No one else is here. If Will had snuck out, he would come to me. If Malcolm was out here, he would scold me.

Against my better judgment, I walk toward the jetty. The closer I get to the cliff's edge, the more the air stings my skin.

Gibson did say the temperature drops considerably at night, but I didn't expect it to get so cold so soon. It must be ten degrees cooler than when I stepped outside just minutes ago.

There's something beautiful about being here alone at night. The island is quiet and sleeping. I take in the view of moonlight bouncing and rippling off the ocean. It won't be long until the clouds steal that too.

Behind me something scrapes on the ground.

I jolt and spin around. What the hell was that?

My heart lurches as I scan the immediate area.

Empty.

What could that have been?

Or who?

"H-hello?" I say, mentally kicking myself.

Blaine, the guy who doesn't believe in coincidences, ghosts, or anything that science can't back up, would say that there's an explanation for everything. He'd tell me that it was a gate rattling in the wind or a flag flapping. *Anything* that would put his mind at ease.

The world just isn't that easy.

*Yes, Blaine, that noise could be an axe-wielding murderer who sailed over while we were eating dinner.*

Someone on Reddit worked out, with some mathematical formula that made my brain hurt, that statistically we will walk past thirty-six murderers in our lifetime. Give or take, depending on lifestyle.

It's quite fascinating in an absolutely frightening way. How many have I been close to already? Have I said thank you to one for opening a door or bumped into one at the mall?

I could have served one during my summer job at the Olive Garden.

Here's a breadstick to go with your homicide.

Sometimes even the briefest encounter could imprint on a killer, and they could come after you. A small smile, a simple gesture, could be enough to seal your fate as some crazy's next victim.

That kind of murder is rare—usually victims know their killers personally—but it does happen.

Thankfully, there doesn't seem to be anyone here. No Malcolm catching me out at night or murderers wanting to chop off my head.

I'm not sure what made the noise but there is nothing else here. It's just me, the wind, and my overactive imagination. It was probably just the rattling of a gate. Like my brother would say.

Despite the dark vibe of the resort, this is the first time I've actually felt afraid.

I'm alone, one of eleven on the island, and I'm as freaked out as that time when I went for a solo run at night.

Time to return to the hotel and hopefully convince Will, James, or Reeve to come out with me on Sunday. Or maybe Harper. I'm sure I can trust her. I think more than anyone else on the island, to be fair. We're not supposed to go into the park at night, but she was the one asking if we could steal some beers.

I turn around and follow the path toward the hotel gate with a gnawing in my stomach. Snapping more pictures, I get a couple of the sea as I retreat.

Another gust of wind takes my long hair and blows it in my face so that I'm momentarily blind. It's at that exact moment that a flash of black whips past in my peripheral vision.

"Will?" I call. He could have come out to find me and is now having some fun.

Wouldn't it be hilarious to scare the one fascinated with murder? Out of everyone in the group, I would mess with me too.

It has to be him. He's the only one who knows I'm out here.

"Okay, that's funny. You got me," I say, lowering my phone. "You can come out now, Will."

It's completely silent besides the wind, but I don't feel alone.

Clutching my hair in my fist, I glance around. What explanation would my brother have for this?

My stomach cramps.

A bird. He would tell me it had to have been a bird. Definitely not a person running. And I feel like there's someone else here because I'm freaked out.

I spin again, my breath catching in my throat.

"Will, you've had your fun. I'm going back in now. This was only amusing for two seconds. . . ." I look over my shoulder. Nothing. "Are you coming with me? Will?"

In the back of my head, a little voice is screaming that it might not be him. But why would anyone else want to scare me?

Ava and James, maybe.

If Malcolm or one of his staff saw me, I don't think they would walk on and pretend I wasn't there. I feel the first drop of water on my nose as I scan the area, making a note of the places a person could hide.

Trash cans, rides, food stalls, to name a few of the places a murderer could be watching me from right now.

God, maybe I *should* take a break from the crime podcasts and vlogs.

Enough of being ridiculous.

It was a bird.

I turn my back on the paranoia and walk away. The sky darkens further as the clouds claim it all. My instinct is to look over my shoulder, but I know I'll only sink back into my imagination.

The hotel is still deserted, but I feel much safer as I walk through the lobby door.

My shoulders slump. I shoot him a quick text.

**Paisley:**

Thanks for standing me up. You missed all the fun 😉

No reply.

I'm tempted to go knock on Will's door so I'll know for sure if that was him out there, but he's between Ava's and Liam's rooms. Knocking could potentially wake up two more people and then I'd need to convince them to not tell on me.

Liam would be fine, but it wouldn't surprise me if Ava tried blackmailing me. Despite the fact that she sweats money.

I creep along the lobby and take the stairs back up to the second floor. The oak carvings look more sinister at night, despite the low glow of soft lighting. Shadows of claws cast on the walls up high. I walk under two archways before I reach my door.

The lock clicks, yielding to my card, and I let myself in. Unfortunately, I'm not as quiet closing the door as I was opening it. I feel like the echo of it ricochets across the whole floor.

I cringe and close my eyes, as if not being able to see will somehow stop everyone from waking up.

Even if I disturb anyone, they won't know it was me. I brush my teeth in the bathroom big enough to house a family of four and change into pajamas. It's late but I'm still not going to skip my skincare routine. I just do it fast instead and scrub my face, splash some cold water on, and then dry. That'll have to do tonight.

I can't wake up looking like I have two black eyes or I'll be questioned on whether I slept well.

I'm not great at lying.

Hitting the light switch in the bathroom, I'm descended back into darkness. I use the light from my phone to guide my way.

Now that I'm locked behind my door, a rush of excitement replaces the fear. My heart has returned to a steady beat. Before getting into bed, I walk to the large window in my room and peek out of the window facing part of the park.

My view only covers the entrance and the first smaller roller coaster, so there's not a whole lot to see, especially at night.

The park is still. It's sleeping—like I should be—and there is no evidence that anyone was out there with me.

Because there was no one!

Drawing the thick black curtains, I get into bed and sink between the soft white sheets. The pillow instantly molds to my head.

It makes me wonder how much Malcolm would charge me if I slipped it into my suitcase.

I was hoping to switch straight off and fall asleep. Doesn't seem like that's happening tonight. I plug my watch and phone into their chargers and resist scrolling through TikTok. That's never helped me sleep before.

*If* there was someone out there, I doubt they would hang around.

Will is a dead man tomorrow if that was him.

# 6

Breakfast is served starting at eight a.m. this weekend, but I've been up since six a.m., excited for a full day in the park.

I'm not leaving this island until I've ridden everything at least twenty times.

So far, I've edited five TikToks ready to post throughout the day, recorded a short vlog, and started making voice notes for my next podcast. I've also made notes on the sixteenth-century Gothic era Malcolm is obsessed with and the weapons in his little chest of horrors.

Were they used for torture and murder? I mean, what else would you need a mace for?

There are lists for days in my notebooks, and as long as I take enough footage and pictures, I'll have content for weeks.

I'm not even tired after being up until one a.m. That might also be because I've had two coffees from the Nespresso machine in my room already.

I'm anxious to see Will. I need to know if he was following me to freak me out last night. At the moment, he's a frenemy. I flit between thinking he fell asleep and being sure that he was outside.

Why, though?

It's not like we've known each other for that long. In my experience, a prank like that is something you save for a good friend. Or a sibling.

Since it's morning and I don't need to sneak around, I take the elevator and head to the restaurant. I can smell the food before I even get inside and almost drool.

Everyone besides Will is drinking coffee and helping themselves to an array of colorful food laid out on the table. The room smells like coffee and cinnamon.

Actually, I wouldn't mind the storm hitting now. I could eat this food all day long.

Kenna has outdone herself again.

"Morning," I say, taking a seat next to Harper.

She smiles brightly and puts a slice of cantaloupe on her plate. "How cozy are those beds? It was like sleeping on a cloud. What ride are we hitting first?" she asks.

It would seem I'm not the only one making use of the Nespresso pods this morning.

"How many cups of coffee have you had?"

"Oh, I don't drink coffee, but today I've had *three*."

Her dark eyes are wide. She's rebelling against her parents with copious amounts of caffeine. Today her hair is bound in a tight bun on the top of her head and she's wearing matching sage joggers and a T-shirt.

I'd look like a toddler in that, but she's flawless.

"Maybe make that the last one for a while. We can start on whatever you want today."

Liam did ask if I wanted to hang out with him, but I'm not going to ditch Harper.

She rolls her eyes. "James and Ava have already made their own group and we're not invited."

After the way they were flirting yesterday, I'm not at all surprised. What I am surprised by is the fact that in her more recent videos, Ava has a boyfriend.

But that's none of my business.

"Anyone seen Will?" I ask.

"He hasn't come down yet."

"I heard him moving about in his room around midnight," Liam says. "Real loud. I was trying to record. Rude." He takes a large bite of toast, ripping it like a lion shredding flesh.

Well, there's my answer. Will wasn't asleep. He was getting ready to spook me.

He is *so* dead.

"He's probably trying on his outfits to get the perfect Saturday look," James says.

It isn't funny, but Ava still laughs.

Harper, Liam, and I ignore them. "Looks like it's us and Will today," Harper says more to Liam, who's scowling a little behind his smile. "Is that okay?"

"Yeah, sounds great," Liam replies. He sounds like it's anything but great.

Harper grabs another cinnamon roll, determined to make the most of her sugar-fueled weekend. "Whenever Will gets his ass down here. I can't believe he's missing these pastries. And the coffee. Have some coffee, Paisley."

"I will," I say, laughing at her caffeine buzz.

Will was up right before he was supposed to meet me, according to Liam. I can't believe he didn't message me to gloat about scaring me outside.

I would have.

Malcolm, who's been floating around the lobby and restaurant since I came down, finally sits with us. Camilla closely follows him and puts a cup of coffee and bowl of oatmeal in front of him.

I guess he's too rich to get his own breakfast.

Despite the money I'm now making, which isn't billions like Malcolm, my parents would never let my ego inflate that much. They would tease the crap out of me if my head grew by even a millimeter.

Blaine would probably throw things at me.

"Good morning. I hope you're all rested?" Malcolm's voice is silky smooth. Dark shadows hang under his eyes, like he didn't sleep well.

It makes me wonder if he heard or saw me.

When he barely glances in my direction, I figure I'm probably okay.

Ava and James laugh at Malcolm's question. Did they not sleep well?

Ew, I do *not* want to know.

"The bed is amazing," Harper offers. "And huge. I could fit all of my paperbacks lined up on there with me."

I love this girl.

"How many did you bring with you?" Liam asks.

"Eleven."

"Eleven!"

She scowls. "What? I don't always know what I'll be in the mood for, and I had plenty of room in my suitcase. I've been up since five, sitting in the lobby reading."

I'm half listening to the conversation and half watching the door for Will.

I take a hair tie off my wrist and make a high ponytail. My long, black hair hangs down the middle of my back.

"No one's seen Will. I thought he would be down here by now."

"Not yet," Malcolm replies. "He's a seventeen-year-old boy. As I recall, we didn't used to rise so early. Your posts yesterday drove up traffic to the website by three hundred percent. Do eat up, all. We're getting started in twenty minutes."

His eyes are glowing with dollar signs.

"Would we leave without Will?" I ask.

Ava scoffs. "As if I'm wasting this weekend waiting around for him."

How nice.

"Will can join us whenever he likes. The whole day is yours to explore the park and hotel. I recommend the hot beds in the spa after a long day of rides." Malcolm grins wide at the mention of the spa.

Once I've finished eating, I'll go to Will's room and knock. He won't want to miss anything.

I settle on a cinnamon bun and almond croissant with a large coffee since those are the smells that are making me drool most.

Harper grabs a helping of fruit in what feels like a futile attempt to balance good and bad, so I pop a slice of melon onto my plate. It'll help with the guilt I have for eating only sugar.

"Kenna and her team are the best in the world, as you tasted last night," Malcolm says.

The jerk chicken yesterday was out of this world.

"She was born in the Caribbean and came to the US with her family when she was three. She learned how to make those during a year studying pastry in France," Camilla adds as she picks up a croissant.

That must be why they're so good.

I finish eating fast and put my silverware and napkin on my plate. "I'm going to go wake up Will."

Malcolm waves a hand. "All right, but be quick. We leave in five!"

He says *we leave* as if we have to catch a bus to the park. There's only us on the island, so it's not like we couldn't catch up. Reeve and Gibson are going to split between both groups again.

I'd like to come back when the park is fully functioning.

I take the elevator and it's only when I reach our floor that my stomach drops with unease.

There's something wrong here. Will was so excited for this weekend. He wouldn't just sleep in and miss everything. And he didn't mention feeling sick yesterday.

Liam catches up to me halfway along the corridor. "Hey, are you worried about Will or something?"

I stop. "Well . . . kind of."

"Why?"

Can I trust him? I don't think he'd tell on me. "Okay, you *can't* tell anyone this. I mean *anyone.* Promise me."

He shrugs, only looking half interested, and holds up one hand. "On my life."

"Last night Will and I were supposed to sneak into the park. It was his idea. He told me to meet him by the fireplace at midnight but didn't show. I figured he just fell asleep, but when you said you heard him last night . . ."

Liam nods once. "Whoa. Okay. You think he ditched you?"

The words sting. I bite my lip and avert my eyes. Will ditched me.

"Yeah, I guess he did."

Maybe I should just leave him the way he left me last night.

There's more to this story, like me going out there alone and getting freaked out. I don't tell Liam that part because he might think I'm a massive baby.

The crime reporter scared of the dark.

Yeah, no. I'm not owning up to that one.

"You really think he just wouldn't show? It's not like he'd never see you again," Liam asks. When did he join team Will?

We start walking again. "I've known the guy a day, I get that. He doesn't seem like he'd do that, but I guess . . . he did."

Liam shrugs. "Will's decent. It was late and we'd had a long day. He probably fell asleep."

That's what I hope.

I'm not going to admit this to Liam, but it wouldn't be the first time someone has ditched me. My best friends in junior high did the same thing. One day we were meeting outside the cafeteria to go in for lunch and the next they went in without me.

They never said one word to me again.

It still hurts, as much as I pretend it doesn't.

I *hope* Will's different.

Liam knocks on Will's door, and we wait.

For a second at least, and then Liam gets impatient. "Open up, Will! Come on, we've gotta roll."

I knock too. "Will, it's Paisley. Are you okay?"

I press my ear to the door, but I'm met with silence on the other end.

"Could he really be sleeping in?" I ask.

"A seventeen-year-old guy?" Liam asks with a hint of sarcasm. "Like Malcolm said, yeah, he really could be."

"Yes, but *here*? And you and James managed to get up fine."

Liam knocks again. "I never sleep for long."

"That sounds awful."

"I'm used to it. I get a lot more done. My coach loves the extra training I can get in before sunrise."

I knew he played sports.

"How much sleep do you get?"

"Six hours if I'm lucky. Usually five. I'm used to it now. My mom wouldn't survive with anything less than eight."

"Is it just you two?"

He does a double take, and I'm sure I've put my foot in it.

"I'm sorry. That was a pretty invasive question."

His dad might have died. I'm such an idiot.

"No, it's okay. It's only ever been us. My grandparents are selfish assholes, and my uncle has his own life. My mom's done everything for me. What about you?"

"My parents are together, have been since they were in college. I have an older brother. He's at Princeton."

I can never say that without sounding like I'm gloating. I'm not. I'm just so proud of him and hoping Ivy League genes run in the family.

"Wow. Princeton."

"He's annoying as hell but he's also my best friend. That probably sounds lame."

He shakes his head. "It doesn't."

We smile at each other. Him casually, me like an absolute fool.

I should come with a warning.

Liam nods toward Will's door. "He's going to be pissed at us if we wake him. We've got the next two days here, so he's not going to miss anything. Let's come back in an hour if his lazy ass still hasn't surfaced."

I bite my lip, not loving that idea but not really able to do much else. When people—my mom—wake me up, I want to scream. "Okay."

If he was running around scaring me last night, then he likely didn't get much sleep either. He's been quite vocal about getting his eight hours in. Something to do with his skin care.

"Come on." Liam nudges me and laughs. "Race you to the lobby."

Are we seven? "Race you?"

Liam bolts. It takes me a second to make up my mind. I'm on the track team at school. I catch up to him quickly and he shouts "Hey!" as I dash past.

Will is momentarily forgotten.

# 7

Malcolm sends us off with a wave of his hand at the entrance of the park. Liam and I catch up to Harper and Reeve, who are waiting near the main gate.

"Took your time," Harper says, giving us both a smile. She stuffs a paperback into her backpack and throws it over her shoulder.

Ava and James are up ahead, almost tiny dots in the distance. Gibson, poor Gibson, is slightly behind them, shaking his head at their massive egos.

Reeve claps his hands. "Since I won the coin toss and got you, can I recommend starting at the service entrance side of the park?"

"There's a service entrance?" I ask.

Reeve smirks. "It's around the side of the island, closer to the staff quarters in the hotel."

I'd ask why we'd want to see that, it sounds kind of boring, but I have to admit I'm curious. This will be our only chance to see it. I can't see it being accessible to guests when the park is open.

Maybe he'll also show us the staff wing. Malcolm's room with his coffin for a bed.

Harper shrugs like she doesn't really care where we start. We don't go home until lunchtime on Monday, so it's not like we'll be missing out on anything.

Today we should be able to finish going on everything. Tomorrow and Monday morning are all about riding our favorites as many more times as we can.

Liam's frowning at Reeve as if he's trying to figure out why anyone would want to see where deliveries are brought to the island. We weren't shown that side of the hotel.

"Okay, fine," Liam says, knowing he's on his own at this point.

Reeve and Liam walk ahead and start talking about football. Apparently they're both Giants fans.

"I wonder if we'll go into the hotel that way," Harper says. "That wasn't a part of the tour."

"Oh my god, I'd love to spy on Malcolm," I tell her. "He only seems to appear when there's food involved. I bet he sleeps in a coffin."

Harper laughs. "Why would you build all this and not enjoy it? He and Camilla are . . . strange."

"Uh, yeah."

She waves a hand. "I mean, beyond the usual. Why doesn't she tell him off? If some guy kept barking orders at me . . ."

I nod. "Same. There's something about them that's off. Have you noticed?"

"Maybe they are together?"

I shake my head. "No, I don't think that's it. The way she looks at him sometimes, it's as if she's confused how she got here."

Harper's eyes widen as we walk around the back of the hotel. Reeve punches a code into a keypad on a gate.

"Paisley, are you saying he kidnapped her?"

"No." I can't help laughing. "I can tell you're a reader, though. I'm not sure what's going on. Maybe she never meant to stay working for him as long as she has."

"That's boring."

"We can pretend it's the kidnap thing if that makes it more exciting."

Harper grins. "Thanks."

The part of the hotel that's hidden from guests is just as polished in a creepy Gothic way as the areas accessible to guests. It's nice to know that they make the staff areas nice too.

There are a couple of tables and chairs, a little hut that I assume is for smokers, and a vending machine.

We walk down a slope like the one at the main entrance. This one is wider and longer. The gradient is subtle. I almost died pulling my suitcase up the last slope, so this was a good idea.

There's a larger jetty and deck chairs.

Reeve looks over his shoulder. "We call this The Beach. Malcolm doesn't care if we hang out here and swim on our breaks and between deliveries. When the water's calm, obviously."

I watch waves crash gently against the side of the cliff. The sea is calm right now, but that will change tonight.

The sun is strong overhead, and the wind has died almost completely. Up top there's no breeze at all. Today would be a great day for a swim.

"I'll bring you back later, if you want," Reeve tells us, but he looks at me.

My face catches fire, but I try to be casual and smile.

Maybe he would sneak out with me after all.

"Isn't it supposed to storm?" Harper asks, glancing up at the sky.

"Due to hit us just around eight p.m.," he replies. "Plenty of time to ride and swim."

Harper looks at me, asking a silent question.

"Well, I'm in," I say.

"Yeah, whatever," Liam replies. He hasn't been the cheeriest so far today.

Reeve turns his back to us when his phone dings.

"Did anyone bring a bathing suit?" Harper asks.

"Of course! I have three bikinis. There's a pool!"

She purses her lips. "I have books."

"You can wear one of mine or just lounge on one of those deck chairs and read while we swim."

She points her finger at me. "That is why I like you."

"All right, guys, let's split. I'll bring you back here after lunch." Reeve looks up at the hotel and back.

"Does Malcolm nap after lunch, then?" I ask.

Reeve laughs. "Something like that."

"Maybe he can't come out in the daylight," Harper whispers in my ear.

"You think that message was Malcolm telling Reeve to bring us back?" I ask.

"Yep."

Liam trails behind us, looking back at the jetty and all the carved stone with a scowl. "This man has too much money."

"He's one of the top ten richest people in the world," I say over my shoulder.

Liam scoffs. "Have you seen all his companies? He has loads. The man gets bored easily and moves on. I bet he never steps foot on this island again after this weekend. He'll be rubbing shoulders with Bezos and building his own rocket."

"You don't like him?"

Liam is not exactly short of money himself. He rolled up in a brand-new Range Rover yesterday. His clothes are all designer, he's got the latest phone and earbuds.

"I don't know him. But does anyone need *billions* when so many are hungry?"

"No," I reply. "They don't."

In my old school I saw kids skip meals and wear shoes until their toes popped out.

I was only seven, but I remember. Malcolm has the money to help end that.

"Is that what you would do if you became a billionaire?" I ask.

He catches up to me and nods. "Yeah. Too many people sit back while others suffer."

"Who have you watched suffer?"

"Um."

I snap my teeth together. "I'm so sorry. I shouldn't have asked that."

"No, it's okay. I wasn't born into money."

"Same," I say, giving him a smile of solidarity.

Reeve follows us as we zigzag the park to get the five roller coasters done before lunch. There are a lot of loops, and I don't want to lose any of the food Kenna makes for us.

By the fifth coaster, I'm feeling ready to take a break. My stomach rolls upside down as we loop again and then gently glide to a stop.

The harnesses lift and we get off. I smooth out my long hair and Harper chucks her bag over her back.

"We should go check on Will again," I say, looking at my phone. I stopped texting him after about ten texts and no answer. "I'm starting to worry about him."

Liam nods. "I'll come with you."

Harper hesitates. "Do you mind if I don't come? I wanted to check out the Waltzer again." She waves to Reeve, who's sitting on a bench.

"Sure, no problem," I tell her.

We say goodbye and jog back to the hotel. We take the elevator up to our floor and in minutes we're rapping on Will's door like there's a fire.

"Will, open up!" I shout through the wood.

Liam thumps the door with the side of his fist. "Dude has gotten serious rest. He can't still be asleep."

No, he can't be.

"Something isn't right." I take my phone out of my pocket and call Camilla.

"Hello?"

"Hi. It's Paisley. Liam and I have just come back to check on Will. He didn't answer my texts and he's not responding to our knocking on the door. He wouldn't be sleeping this long."

She's silent for a few seconds. "Hmm, all right, I'll come up. Stay there."

I lower my phone.

"She's coming?" Liam asks.

"On her way," I reply, knocking again on the door. "Will, Camilla is going to come and open the door if you don't let us know you're okay. Can you open the door?"

"All that crime has made you suspicious, you know," Liam tells me.

I'm very aware of that fact. I see crime and murderers everywhere now, even when nothing's there. When you've spent long enough listening to experts tell you anyone is capable of crime, you believe it.

"Pretty much," I reply. "What do you think's happened to Will?"

He shrugs as if he's not thought about it.

I've already gone over about fifteen different scenarios. Most of them horrible.

I'm about to knock on the door again when Camilla appears, walking toward us down the dark carpet.

She holds up a master key card and the light on Will's door turns green. She opens the door and walks in, calling his name. I hesitate for a nanosecond; a lot of my scenarios involve finding Will dead in the room.

I step over the threshold and glance around. The room feels cold and empty.

"He's not here," I say.

# 8

Where would he have gone?

"His bed is made," I say, frowning at the neat corners of the sheets and plump pillows. "It's never made in his videos."

"So?" Camilla says.

"So maybe he never slept here last night."

Camilla and Liam exchange a glance as if I'm not here and can't see it.

Then Liam chuckles under his breath and turns to me. He shakes his head to clear away his amusement.

Camilla's thin lips pinch and she frowns. She looks stressed.

"I'm glad I get to see the detective's live show. Even more impressive than a vlog. Maybe he changed rooms," Liam says.

I glance into the bathroom. There are two large green toiletry bags sitting by the sink. "And left all his stuff here?"

Liam shrugs again and follows me into the bathroom. "He might be exploring the hotel, getting footage. We've all done that."

"Possible, but all his products and makeup are still zipped in those bags. He's either a total neat freak and put away all his stuff completely before leaving the room or he's not wearing makeup." I meet Liam's gaze in the large bathroom mirror. "There was this video he posted a couple days ago when he said the only time he'd leave his house without a 'full face on' is in an ambulance."

He could have been exaggerating, but somehow I don't think so.

"Perhaps he doesn't feel the need to wear it here," Camilla says as Liam and I walk back into the room.

"No, Paisley's right. It's unlikely." Liam looks around Will's room again, searching with fresh, now suspicious eyes. He pokes around inside the closets. I'm glad he's backing me up, because I know that something is wrong here.

I crouch and peer under the bed. Nothing. Of course.

"I'll try his cell before we start to worry," Camilla says, sounding an awful lot like my mom. Her words don't match her slightly panicked expression.

It's too late for that. I'm already stressing.

"That's not going to work," I say, getting up from my knees.

"Why?"

"Because his cell is charging over here on the nightstand."

I tap the screen. There are a *lot* of notifications, starting from last night. He hasn't checked his phone at all today.

Camilla's face falls. Liam frowns. We're now on the same page, believing Will is missing.

She can explain the bed and even the makeup, but no one

leaves their phone behind. Especially not an influencer about to explore an exclusive, invite-only weekend on a new amusement park island.

None of us wants to miss a thing. We all have our phones on, ready to capture something cool at any second. A quick TikTok or an Insta post. My battery is already half drained from today.

Will is *super* active online. He's not leaving his room without his phone. He wouldn't even go to the bathroom without it.

"I'm going to radio the team," Camilla says, her voice wavering as she walks out of the room to speak privately.

The fact that she's worried makes me more nervous.

"You think he's hurt or sick?" Liam asks.

"I don't know. I can't see any other reason why he would leave his room and everything in it."

Liam blocks me as I try to pass. "Hey, do you think he went out after you did? We would've seen him." He swallows. "God, what if he fell into the sea."

I shake my head. "Don't go there. I don't think that he would've gone past the fences. We have to find him, Liam. He could be hurt."

Liam and I walk out of Will's room and follow Camilla, who beckons us with a wave.

"We'll find him, don't worry." Liam wraps his arm around my shoulders and gives me a squeeze. I dip my head so he doesn't see the blush sweep across my cheeks.

I appreciate that he's trying to comfort me but it's not working. He doesn't sound very confident. We really shouldn't panic, though. We have no idea what could have happened.

"Will could've slept in late, then woken up and decided to go to the gym or the pool for a workout. Though that doesn't explain the phone or that he's suddenly very neat," I say, desperately trying to make sense of this.

"He might not want Kenna or Camilla to see a mess," Liam offers.

The two female employees are the ones who have to clean the rooms. That fact made my eye twitch and had me being extra neat. Will might have thought the same.

We take the elevator down to the lobby.

My heart thumps harder, and there's no sign that it's going to calm down anytime soon. "Where could he be? We're supposed to be riding roller coasters and posting videos."

When we reach the lobby, everyone has congregated by the doors, a buzz of conversation and theories. Ava and James are whispering, Reeve and Gibson are looking at something on a phone, and Malcolm is being questioned by Harper.

The speed of her questions almost makes me smile.

Malcolm has changed his outfit since this morning at breakfast. He's dressed from head to toe in black, with a thick red ring on his pinkie finger.

"All right," Gibson says. "We did a quick sweep of the spa and basement. We're going to split into groups and search the hotel and park. Will probably just wants to check things out for himself, but we need to make sure he's okay. I don't like that we don't know where he is."

"The island is surrounded by water," James says. "He easily could have fallen in."

That's the second time drowning has been mentioned, but I don't think he could have fallen in.

I bite my fingernail and then stop myself. I'm not supposed to do that anymore.

Malcolm holds his hands up. "Whoa. Let's not talk like that, James. This place is secure. I made sure of it. You've seen the fences separating the park and the cliff edge. No one needs to be saying that Jagged Island is dangerous."

Liam scowls at James and then Malcolm. Unimpressed with them both.

James and Liam look as if they'd be best friends. Both play football, dress impeccably, and are popular. Real-life popular, not only online like me.

"All right," Reeve says. "Liam, Harper, and Paisley, you're with me. Keep in touch."

My mind spins as I try to catch up with the current events. I should be eating lunch soon and then swimming. Will should have caught up with us and screamed all the way through every ride.

I step outside and the loss of air-conditioning makes me want to turn straight back around again. The sun is almost directly over us now.

"We're starting from the jetty," Reeve says.

I catch up with him. "Which one?"

His reply is a smirk.

That was a genuine question. But he walks us closer to the main entrance to the island.

He punches in the code for the gate and takes two more steps before stopping dead and making me almost walk straight into him.

"The boat's gone," he says.

My jaw almost hits the stone beneath my feet. "What the . . ."

The boat stays here. Gibson needs to take us back to the mainland on Monday. Was it there earlier this morning? I didn't notice.

Harper scoffs. "Oh my god, is he for real? Will took the boat! What a jackass . . . Kind of a cool one too." She adds the last part as an afterthought.

"That doesn't make sense. If he wanted off the island, why wouldn't he just say so? Why wouldn't he take his things?" I ask.

"Maybe he's playing a prank. Taking it out for a joyride," she offers. "Wasting all our time while he's at it."

Reeve is on the radio telling them what we've found. He sounds angry, calling Will "the damn kid." Will is only a couple years younger than him and Gibson.

Malcolm's and Gibson's responses are a long string of curse words that overlap each other. Malcolm sounds furious. Their voices crackle a little through the speaker that Reeve has to his mouth. Malcolm barks something again that gets lost with Ava and James shouting in the background.

"How would he have got through the gate? Unless he climbed the fence . . . ," Liam says.

"Or memorized the code. But I just know he didn't take the boat," I say.

"Paisley, I know you want to see the best in him, but—"

"No, Liam. Think about it for a minute. Would you leave without your things? Without your phone? If you took a boat for a ride as a prank or just because you wanted to, you'd take your phone. That's the exact sort of material he would want for his channel."

Liam frowns, but Harper nods like I've got a point—because I do.

"Even if he wanted to mess with us, which doesn't seem like him—"

"You don't know him," Liam reminds me, cutting me off.

"I get that, but is there anything you've seen from him, in his videos and since we met him, that makes you think he'd do this?" I ask. "That he'd think it's amusing?"

"Well, no, but that doesn't mean he hasn't. I say we get on with our day and leave him to his boat trip."

I gesture toward the water. "Remember the waves yesterday?"

"She's right," Reeve says, taking charge. "No one would have taken a boat out in those conditions. We even thought about doing three trips to get you all here with the helicopter, but Gibson said the water would hold until after you arrived."

"Back up. You have a helicopter?" Harper asks.

"Two of them. Anyway, point is, it's more likely the boat sunk than that Will took it out for a joyride."

"What the hell is going on?" Malcolm shouts as his and Gibson's group runs toward us. "Where is this punk and where is my boat?"

Reeve takes a deep breath and explains what he's found. "Did the boat sink? Possibly. In any case, I think that's a lot more likely than this kid committing grand theft on the sea."

The boat isn't massive, and it's certainly not a yacht, but it is big enough to fit sixty people on at a time and probably crazy-expensive. They expect to use it throughout the day, taking people to and from the island. It will always be kept here overnight in case of any emergencies.

Except now it might be at the bottom of the ocean, and someone is missing.

"Did you find any sign of Will?" I ask.

"Nothing, but we haven't searched very far," Malcolm replies, looking over his shoulder as if he's expecting someone.

Does he think Will is going to stroll over and tell us he's parked the boat back at the jetty?

"I don't like this at all," I murmur.

Liam is the only one who hears me. "We're not panicking yet, Paisley. Okay. This is probably his strange idea of fun. He's not a prankster, so he clearly didn't think it through. He might have a second phone. Recording us freaking out right now."

His voice is low and soothing and his eyes stare deep into mine. A similar look has passed between Reeve and me. I don't know if either one of them is serious or if they just like a bit of flirting while away.

Last night I thought I sensed someone else outside. But if it was Will, why would he let it go on for this long? If he's playing a game, he's been doing it since midnight. And I'm the only person who knows that.

Malcolm might let me into the security room to watch the

CCTV if I tell him what I saw last night. The rules on sneaking into the park were very clear. It's a safety breach, and if we're caught doing it, we'll be on the next boat home.

Plus, it might have been him. He was the only person I saw or heard when I was out.

There currently is no boat, so they can't kick me off the island just yet. I haven't seen a helicopter either. I'd assume they're not easy to hide away, but they could be here somewhere. On top of the hotel, maybe.

That's a point: why haven't they checked the video footage yet?

As if he's reading my mind, Malcolm instructs Reeve to go check.

"See, Paisley, Reeve is about to find out where he's hiding," Liam says.

I clear my throat and smile. At least I think I'm smiling. For all I know I could look as worried as I feel. My heart is beating too fast.

"I could come with you," I say, trying to sound casual. "I mean, two sets of eyes are better than one, right?"

Malcolm waves his hand, but the rest of him is frozen. He doesn't even move his head or look at me with those dark, vacant eyes. "Take the crime girl."

He knows my name. Robotic asshole.

He's not allowing me to go out of the kindness of his heart. This is a tactical move. I'm a crime vlogger, and although there is no crime, he knows that searching CCTV for a "missing" person is exciting for me.

Little does he know, I have an ulterior motive too. Reeve is an employee, and I'm hoping giving a crap about me sneaking around at night is above his pay grade.

I figure the best way to get him to keep my secret is to explain and plead. He's been a little flirty, so I think I have a solid chance at getting him to agree.

Reeve leads me into the hotel and punches in a code for a staff-only door. I turn my head so he thinks I'm being polite, but my eyes dart in the direction of the keypad. I store the code in my head for another time, just in case.

Maybe they're all the same.

"Will this be on a podcast? I'm surprised Malcolm let you come down here."

I laugh but don't commit because this probably will end up on one of my platforms. "I assume he's going to ask me to twist the truth a little. Like, tell my subscribers and followers that it was part of my tour."

Reeve chuckles. "Now, *that* sounds like Malcolm."

"Is he always like that?"

"Like what?"

"I'm not sure how to say it without being rude."

Reeve grins and gives me a wink. "Go for it, Paisley. You're not going to offend me."

"Intense. Creepy. Like he's constantly thinking and plotting. When he's around it's like his mind is half with you and half elsewhere."

"Well, I don't know about all that other stuff, but I see what you mean about the creepy thing. The dark clothing and the stare don't help. That's just him."

"How long have you worked here?" I ask as we walk along a corridor.

"I've been on board since the hotel was up. I've known Gibson since we were kids. He was recruited to drive the boat."

"Where did Malcolm find you guys?"

"Gibson at the docks in LA. Gibson said he took him out on a day trip and by the end of the day Malcolm offered him the position. He told him he'd only accept if I could get a job too."

"That was nice of him."

*Weird of him* is my first thought. Was Reeve finding it hard to get a job? I understand wanting to help your friend out, but for that to be a condition of employment is strange.

"He's a good friend."

"Were you working on the boats with him?"

Reeve hesitates, his hand gripping the handle to the security door. "Not exactly. You don't touch *anything* in there. Got it? I don't want to lose my job."

"Yes, boss." I smile, but he doesn't.

"I'm serious, Paisley."

Raising my palms, I nod. "I won't touch anything, I promise."

I mean, I might another time if I have to come back. The code to the door is stored nicely in my mind. But I'll be good for now, not wanting to be the reason Reeve loses his job.

"Good." He opens the door and I follow him inside.

It's relatively large in here for a security room, not the poky little things you see on TV. There are two chairs, a small sofa, a vending machine, and a large desk with six screens and other equipment.

Reeve sits down and types away on a keyboard. I take the other chair. The screens are currently live. I can see the two groups have now formed into one and are currently in the game room. They move quickly through the basement level since it's already been checked.

It won't take them long to finish there and get outside.

"What time are you rewinding back to?" I ask. "He went to bed at the same time as me. There was only Malcolm, Camilla, Ava, you, and James up past that."

"Yeah, I went up at two a.m. and was the last."

What?

My heart skips a full beat.

Two in the morning. That means he was up when I was sneaking around.

# 9

Despite being on solid ground, my stomach flips like I'm on a roller coaster.

When I was in the lobby waiting for Will, I didn't see or hear another soul.

The hotel is big, so Reeve could've been in the basement, and we just missed each other. It's not like I can ask him without making myself look guilty. He might find out soon anyway. I'm probably going to pop onto the screen soon looking shifty and sneaking out.

He might already know that I was out there . . . because it could have been him sneaking around and scaring me.

I clear my throat and try not to let him know I'm spooked. "You were here alone until then? Didn't you get bored?"

He shakes his head, runs his hand through his short hair, and clicks a few buttons. "I did a final sweep after the last of them went to bed and then headed up."

Okay, odds are he was somewhere else in the hotel, then. How close did I come to being caught?

"So, we're thinking he got up early and snuck out. Liam heard him in his room in the early hours. Are you checking from this morning?" I ask, planting the seed that we can skip last night.

"Sure. I'll start at six a.m. for speed. If we don't see him, we'll try earlier."

I don't realize how much of a relief it is hearing him say that until the tension leaves my shoulders. I roll my neck and slide my chair closer to the desk.

My heart rate returns to its seminormal rate. See, this is fine. No one will know that I've broken the rules. I won't have to ask Reeve to cover for me, and I won't have to lie.

"You take those two screens and I'll do the other four," he tells me.

"I can cover three."

"Take the two, Paisley. . . . Wait, that's weird." He taps again and again. His dark brows pull together. "What the . . ."

"What's weird?" I don't know what I'm supposed to be seeing. The team is still walking, opening their mouths occasionally to, I assume, call Will's name.

What the hell is he seeing that I'm not?

"Reeve, what's weird?" I press.

He taps again, harder like he's getting frustrated with it. "The footage is gone!"

"Gone? How is that possible?"

His fingers hit keys furiously. "This is crazy. How? There's nothing here to suggest the cameras malfunctioned. We have alerts for that."

"Hold on. You're telling me that it wasn't a glitch but someone erasing it?"

"Yeah," he mutters, still tapping away as if there's a chance he'll recover the footage. His fingers hit the keys harder. "This is . . . Dammit!"

"Can you get it back? There must be backup for this, right? Like the cloud?"

He shakes his head. "No, I don't think so. Well, yeah, there's a backup, but it's gone too. Shit, Paisley. Everything's gone."

"From when?"

He looks at the files and then, very slowly, to me. "From the second you guys stepped through the gate to the park on the first day."

I grip the edge of the seat and try to ignore the pounding in my ears. "Will, the footage, and the boat are all gone."

It's a grim summary of our current situation.

His head turns slowly toward me. "Is one or all of you behind this?"

I recoil, almost falling back off my chair. "What? No, of course not. Well, I can't speak for everyone else, obviously. How would we even get access to this room to delete that stuff?"

His eyes tighten as he realizes that *he* is the one with the access here. Gibson does the boat and rides. Kenna cooks. Camilla is Malcolm's servant. I mean, assistant.

"Can anyone do this remotely?" I ask.

"I don't know. I can work this system because I've been trained on it, but I'm no tech wizard. Hackers can get into most systems, right?"

"There've been cases of people hacking the FBI."

"You sound almost happy about that," he says.

"I find it impressive, that's all. I can't even get into my email some days."

He turns back to the screens, and after tapping a few more times, his shoulders slump. Gone is his anger. It's replaced by fear. I can see it glowing in his eyes.

"They're going to blame me. I don't know how to do this, Paisley. I can view them, but I don't have the clearance to alter anything. I can't even download anything. I don't know how hacking works. I didn't do this."

What is going on here? One minute he's calm and the next he's so uptight he might snap. "No one will blame you. We'll figure it out."

"That's not true. *He's* going to blame me," he repeats.

The way he says it makes me shudder a little. He's resigned himself to being the fall guy. Other staff members have access to this. A bunch of them were leaving the island as we were arriving, right as the cameras stopped recording.

"Goddamn it!" He thumps the desk and presses the button on his radio. "Malcolm, it's Reeve. Come in."

There's no way of knowing what time Will left his room last night. I can't even be happy that the evidence of me sneaking out is gone.

This is serious.

"Reeve . . . ," I say when he clips the radio back onto his belt.

"Malcolm wants us to meet him in the hotel restaurant."

"Why there?"

"Because that's where they are."

Ask a silly question.

He shoves the mouse away, stands up, and runs his hands down his face. "All right, let's go and find out what the hell's happening here."

I grab his sleeve as I get to my feet. "Wait. Do you think we're in danger?"

The silent answer hangs in the air like a bad smell.

"Come on, Paisley. Stay beside me. Okay."

Yeah, as if I'm about to go off on my own now. Reeve strides out of the security room, and I have to double my steps to keep up with him. For someone who wants me to stay right with him, he sure does move as if he wants to ditch me.

In the restaurant, Malcolm is pacing, his face red and a vein on his forehead like a bolt of lightning. I bet he's calculating the losses of getting bad reviews from us. He pins his eyes on each one of us for a second before moving on.

Camilla is preparing coffee, spooning beans into the machine, her face ashen.

Who's thinking about taking a coffee break right now?

"Is this part of the weekend?" Liam asks. "Are you messing with us? Because I'm all for a good mystery, but I want to know if this is real."

I hadn't thought of that. But I'm not sure Malcolm is the greatest actor and there's something about his face that makes me believe this is very real.

"This isn't a game!" Camilla snaps, spilling coffee beans on the counter.

Liam scowls at her.

In the corner, Gibson shakes his head, looks at his phone, and then holds it to his ear. He repeats this three times.

Something else is wrong.

"What's up?" I ask him as he swears at the phone.

"It's not working. Everyone, check your phones."

I check mine and I have no service or Wi-Fi. Battery has dipped under half now.

Why wouldn't the Wi-Fi work?

I clear my throat. "Nothing," I say, flashing them my screen to prove it.

One by one, we all acknowledge our lack of service.

"How could this happen?" Malcolm asks. "We have a cell tower on site and generators in case the power goes down and takes the Wi-Fi out."

Camilla crosses her arms, waiting for the coffee to brew. "This *shouldn't* be happening."

"Reeve, what did you find out?" Gibson asks.

"Err, the CCTV is working but not recording. Which makes sense since we need the Wi-Fi to back it up. But the really weird thing . . . Yesterday's footage has been erased."

"We need to get help," Camilla says. "I didn't sign up for this. The isolation is one thing, but now we can't contact anyone or leave. No. No way."

"Camilla," Malcolm says, leaning in and whispering something in her ear. She doesn't completely relax, but her shoulders lose some of their tension.

Liam and I exchange glances, both seeming to think the same thing. Camilla is being weird. It's an overreaction.

What's he saying to her now?

Maybe he offered her a big bonus. I might need one after this. Ava probably already has a figure in mind for keeping quiet.

"I think everyone should stay in the hotel. Gibson and I can do a sweep of the park for Will," Reeve says.

"No, you need to try getting us back online," Malcolm says. "Gibson, James, and Liam can do a sweep of the park and continue looking for Will. I'll try to reach a couple of contacts."

"I'll come," I say, not loving the "women stay inside and men do something worthwhile" thing.

"Actually, I could use your help, Paisley," Reeve says. "You've been in the security room, after all."

"Um. Okay."

I wasn't allowed to touch anything, so I'm not sure *what* help I could be.

"All right. Reeve, you take Paisley. Camilla, you stay here and keep an eye on Harper and Ava. Call for Kenna too. We'll all meet back here. James and Liam, stay with Gibson. Everyone needs to keep their radios on." Malcolm nods, almost to convince himself that his plan is the best way forward.

"No one is to go anywhere alone," Camilla says. "Not after Will . . ."

My stomach twists into a big knot at the thought of something happening to him, but it must have. He wouldn't still be hiding if he was playing a prank.

So where is he?

James and Liam mentioned falling into the sea. There's a wooden railing around the perimeter for safety. He couldn't have stumbled into the water accidentally.

"Maybe you should check Will's room again, Camilla, while you're getting Kenna. It's a long shot, but I don't want the boys running around the park if Will is back here," Malcolm says.

She gives me a small, pitiful smile. Camilla has written Will off already. I won't give up hope that he's okay until I see evidence that he's not.

"You really think he would've gone back to his room?" Ava says. "And what, be sitting there watching Netflix and eating peanuts?"

I'm glad Camilla only made coffee for Malcolm, because I would have thrown mine all over Ava's perfect pale-pink outfit.

"Maybe he went back for his phone," I say through gritted teeth.

"That's a good point, Paisley . . . and Malcolm. We'll check," Camilla replies.

I smile at Ava—sarcastically, of course—and she turns away.

"Let's all get going," Reeve says. "Paisley, I just want to run out and check the jetty first."

Our three groups split up again. Camilla's heading for the staff side of the hotel. Gibson's going East. Reeve and I walk toward the lobby door.

"What do you want to see down there?" I ask, hesitating. "We already know that the boat's gone."

"We do, but I want to figure out if the boat sunk or was stolen. We know that for sure, and we've at least solved one mystery."

He makes it sound fun. Like we're at a murder mystery party. I've not failed at one of those yet.

I start walking again. We take long, purposeful strides and reach the jetty fast. "You think if we can raise it, it'll work again?"

He shakes his head. "There's no way we'd ever get something like that out of the water."

"So, we're trying to work out if this was someone on the island trying to hurt us or a series of events brought on by the high wind last night? The boat sinking after being caught in rough waves and the wind knocking out the service?"

"Precisely."

"There must be another way out of here," I say.

"Rowboats. Six of them in storage near the service jetty. Weather isn't good enough for that. We'd be catapulted back against the rocks in seconds."

"Are you serious? That's our only option? What about the *helicopters*!"

"Not on the island. Malcolm decided to keep only the boat here. Helicopters can be here fast, but only if we can get a message to Ramesh."

"Who's that?"

"The pilot."

Of course.

Reeve and I walk down the slope. I run my hand along the jagged rock of the cliff face. We walk along the jetty.

"The rope is gone," I say, crouching down. "No fibers around the post, so it was removed, not ripped."

Reeve glances up at me. "Good work, detective."

I ignore him and lean over the edge. "No marks against the side of the wood, so it was probably pushed to the side. If it was sunk it might have scraped and left a trace. Water's too deep to confirm, though."

"You're right. We can't be certain, of course, but it looks like it was taken," he agrees.

"You can't steal a boat and stay on an island at the same time."

Reeve dips his fingers in the water. "I wish I knew what's going on. If we're in danger. Let's get back and see if we can figure out why we're cut off."

On the walk, Reeve radios the others and tells them what we found and our theory behind it. Malcolm seems relieved that the boat was stolen, said it means that whatever group of "random dumb kids" came out here left with his boat and theirs.

He thinks the fact that his boat was taken is proof that no one else is on the island.

I'm not so sure.

Why would anyone take a boat and just leave us here?

# 10

I laugh as Reeve opens the door to the service room. It leads to stairs . . . and a dark basement room. This is nothing like the basement with the game room.

He has got to be joking.

"I'm sorry, have you lost your mind? You want me to go down *there*?"

He grins and it lights up his whole face. He's carefree. It makes him look cute, but I'm not paying attention to that. Or I'm trying not to. "Are you scared, *crime girl*?" he asks, using Malcolm's name for me.

"Um, I'm not scared. I'm just thinking, if anyone else *is* here, a basement is a good place to hide out."

"How would they get in there without the door code?"

"Maybe they have the door code. How many members of staff work here? The ones who aren't due to start until the official open?"

Reeve's eyebrows shoot up as if he hasn't already considered this. Surely employees are the most likely suspects? They have security codes, know the layout, the routines. Who else could have done this?

"What are you thinking about the lack of phone service?" I slap his arm playfully as I have an aha moment. "It's a cell jammer?"

His face is the picture of shock for about a second. Then he comes to the same conclusion. "It must be."

"They're ridiculously easy to pick up. I've thought about leaving one in my brother's dorm and sitting back to enjoy. Would that take out the whole island?"

"The cheap ones certainly wouldn't. Some of the better ones have a wider range and certainly could. You'd splash out a bit if you wanted to . . . do whatever is going on here."

"Are we getting ahead of ourselves?" I ask. I have a habit of doing that; it's why I spend longer on research now rather than reaching straight for my camera to record.

Lack of accurate facts and knowledge can really screw you over. No one will continue watching your videos or listening to your podcasts if you can't even do basic research.

"The storm has already hit the mainland. Could that have knocked the Wi-Fi and service out?"

Reeve looks over his shoulder as we walk down the stairs. He takes a second to think about my question. "We've never lost service before. It wouldn't be down for this long when the storm hasn't even reached us yet."

I straighten my shoulder and follow him down.

"Given the fact that Will's missing and the boat's gone, I don't think we should just explain this away."

"I agree. But we also shouldn't panic."

At the bottom, Reeve switches another light on, and the room brightens further.

He stops and turns toward me. Down here couldn't be more different from the hotel. Light concrete floor, clinically white walls, and long tube lighting overhead. "You think I'm panicking?" I ask.

I almost bump into him again. He's one of those awful people who just stops with no warning.

"What? Oh, no I don't. I'm just saying that I think it would be easy to let paranoia take over. Let's not do that."

He turns away and radios Gibson.

Okay. I take a breath and follow him deeper into the room. There's a massive boiler and rows and rows of electrical switchboards. It reminds me of a modern version of the control room in Jurassic Park.

At least we don't have to worry about dinosaurs.

"Is this all for the hotel?" I ask.

"And the park," he replies. "There are other smaller electrical hubs around the island, for the rides, but this is the only place where everything is right here."

"What are we looking at or for?"

He stops at one of the boards and opens the glass doors. "This one is for the island's internet connection."

"Reeve . . ."

"Yeah, I see it." He looks over his shoulder. "Someone's been in here."

I nod. "Oh my gosh."

The rows of wires marked *Internet* have all been vandalized, snipped neatly.

"I don't like this," I whisper. "Someone came down and cut the wires."

"Neither do I," he replies. "We need to check the rest before we leave."

"Shouldn't we get in touch with the others?"

"Yeah, we'll go find them when we're done. We all need to come up with a plan. First, look for anything else that's been tampered with. The rest of these are electricity, and we know that's working. I doubt there will be anything else, but we have to be sure."

I'm flustered, dashing along the wall of wires, looking for any that have been cut.

"I can't see anything," I say, my fingers shaking against the glass cabinets.

The room feels thick, like it's full of smoke. I can barely take in enough oxygen.

Reeve grabs my hand. "Paisley, breathe. You're safe."

"Will is missing, the boat is gone, someone's done—"

"Hey, it's going to be okay."

He sounds so sure of himself in a way that eighteen-year-old guys with no fear have. I recognize it from Blaine. Fearless and able to conquer the world. Or at least whoever is messing with us.

"I'm fine now," I say, holding on to some of his strength and keeping it for myself.

I take a long breath and mentally slap myself for being such a baby. When has freaking out ever helped any situation?

Reeve and I spend the next few minutes meticulously checking each board for cut wires, but like he thought, they're all intact.

"Can we go now?" I ask. As calm as I am now, I have no desire to stay down here longer than I absolutely have to.

"Yeah, we've seen enough. I'll need to get Gibson down here. We might be able to repair these and get us back online," he replies, tapping the glass in front of the snipped wires.

Reeve and I make our way upstairs, this time much quicker. I want to get far away from this creepy basement room. Reeve holds his hand to my back as if he's frightened that I'll have another meltdown.

That's not going to happen. I've had my minute, and now I'm going to figure this thing out.

"There must be another way to contact people off this island."

"Not that hasn't been destroyed," he replies. "That I know of, anyway. Malcolm will know more." He laughs. "Or he should."

That doesn't fill me with confidence.

In the lounge, we find Camilla pacing. Ava and Harper are huddled together, whispering.

"What's wrong?" I ask, wondering if what Camilla is about to tell us is as bad as what we have for her.

She freezes and turns her head to us slowly. She's pale and her wide eyes look too big. "Kenna is missing. We can't find her in the hotel."

So, yes, what she has to say to us is worse.

"Dammit," Reeve says, running his hand over his hair. "Someone's cut the wires downstairs. We have no internet connection. We're not getting back online unless we can wire it up again. And we think there's a jammer somewhere, which would explain why we can't get service even with the Wi-Fi down."

Camilla's mouth drops. "I—I can't believe it. No. This can't be right. Are you sure?"

"I wish I wasn't sure. Paisley and I are going to catch up with the others. Do they know about Kenna?"

"I radioed. They told us to stay here and keep trying the phones, but . . ."

"Yeah, they won't work. Are you coming with us?" I ask.

Harper stands. "I am."

It comes as no surprise that Camilla and Ava make an excuse to stay. In case Kenna or Will come back, apparently.

I don't want to voice my suspicions, but what if they *don't* come back?

Reeve, Harper, and I leave the hotel and agree with Gibson to meet by the haunted house. Not a great omen, I'll admit.

"Malcolm with you?" Gibson asks as our group merges with his.

Reeve glances at me. "No. I figured when he wasn't back at the hotel, he'd be with you."

*This is great.*

Gibson is straight on the radio.

I take a minute to glance around, and Liam stops beside me.

"How're you doing, Paisley?"

"Well, we're stuck on an island with no way of communicating and no way of leaving. And no cook."

Clearing his throat, he replies, "When you put it like that . . ."

"Did you find any sign of Will or Kenna?"

"Nothing. Some trash in some of the trash cans, but I think that was from us yesterday."

We all eat a bunch of Hershey's Kisses and KitKats. Even Ava, who is supposed to be a vegan.

"There was a can of Pepsi in one of them, though. That was weird," he says.

I lift a brow. "Right. Because they only have Coke here."

"Exactly. But someone could have brought it with them."

"Will or Kenna, you mean."

"They're the only ones missing . . . unless you count Malcolm too."

Which I currently do.

"Dammit. Malcolm's not responding," Gibson says. "He has an office underground. He could be there."

I do a double take. "He has an underground office?"

"It's an apartment, really, off the staff quarters," Reeve replies. "It's directly under the lounge."

"How do you get to it?"

"First door on the right through the staff area."

My brain hurts. "What's our next move?"

"I'm going to radio Camilla and Ava to knock for Malcolm and get back to us. I can't imagine that he'd leave the hotel. We're going to keep searching."

"What are we searching for, exactly? We've been out here for hours and we've found nothing but a can of Pepsi," James says, rolling his eyes as if this is all such an inconvenience for him. He seems oblivious to the fact that people are missing and that this is a bad thing.

"James, shut up," Gibson says, sounding exasperated.

"Gibson and I need to try fixing these wires, so Paisley and Liam, can you walk the park and do a sweep clockwise? And James and Harper, go counterclockwise." Harper turns her nose up at Reeve's instruction. "At no point do you split up. Keep the channel on two and stay in contact with each other and Camilla."

Reeve hands radios to me and Harper.

"We're really splitting up?" I ask him.

He gives me an amused smile. "Better than being underground, right?"

"I guess . . ."

"You all right?" he asks.

"Fine."

"Okay. I want you back in the lounge the second you've completed the sweep. Got it?"

We all agree to meet back in exactly two hours.

# 11

A thin mist rises from the ground with every second we get closer to the storm. Waves crash loudly against the cliff as Liam and I walk the perimeter.

We've been walking for a long time. My feet are aching.

It's still warm, and the breeze is welcome as the sun scorches my shoulders above me.

If the park was open the mist would add to the atmosphere, it would be electric. Right now, with Will missing, the boat gone, and cell service down, it's just plain creepy.

"Splitting up from Reeve was a mistake," I say, goose bumps pinching my skin.

I look over my shoulder.

"Why?" Liam asks. His voice has an edge of hurt as if he believes I only feel safe with Reeve.

"Safety in numbers and all that."

"We don't need anyone else with us. We're on a deserted island."

Only it's not deserted. There are eleven of us here. Ten if Will really has left . . . or worse.

"Will!" I call out. "If you can hear us, please shout! This isn't funny anymore!"

Liam's thorough in our search. He looks around, up, and down. Does he think Will could be hiding in a tree or under a table? He checks every inch of the island as we go.

"Paisley, do you think he's dead?"

"Why would you ask that, Liam? Jeez."

"Hey, don't be a hypocrite. You've thought it more than once. Hell, you thought it before we even knew he was missing. All I've done is voice it." He ducks, looking under an ice cream cart.

Will couldn't even fit under there. He's not a toddler.

But he's right. I am being a hypocrite; I've been through dozens of scenarios. The best one being, Will is pulling some elaborate prank, filming his own episode of *Punk'd.* The worst one being that he's dead.

"Sorry. You're right, Liam. It's just saying it out loud makes it very real, you know? I cover this stuff all the time but it's always things that have happened to others. No one I know, no one I've met. It's easier to detach."

"Hey." He pulls me to a stop, his hands resting on my pinking shoulders. "How about we both stay positive unless there's a reason not to."

"Sounds good."

He drops his hands. "Okay, this is useless. We've not seen him anywhere and we've spent almost two hours walking the perimeter. We need to get back soon."

"Where else could he be?"

"You think every room in the hotel has been checked?"

I shrug and lean against the ice cream cart close to the entrance where we started. "Who knows. That wasn't our job. What else can we do?"

"Think his phone will reveal anything?" Liam asks.

"Not sure we could even get into it. He'll have a password." I push off and startle as a panel in the side of the cart falls to the ground.

Liam shouts, his eyes wide and mouth open in horror. He grabs me, yanking me toward him with a fistful of my shirt.

I gasp as I hit his chest and my heart stops at his reaction. "Wh-what?"

"*Don't* look, Paisley."

I don't listen because I *have* to know. I cling to Liam as tightly as he's clinging to me and turn my head.

A deafening scream rips from my throat as Will's body dangles half out of the cart. His bloody hand rests on the asphalt. Palm up, holding a small pool of his own blood.

Liam spins us both around so our backs are to Will, but it's too late. I've already seen the long gash in the center of his chest and his large, vacant eyes.

I suck in long, deep breaths and try not to faint as my lungs burn and my head spins.

He's dead.

"Oh my god, oh my god."

No. He was *murdered.*

"It's okay, it's okay, it's okay," Liam chants. I'm not sure if he's talking to me or himself. His body, wrapped around mine, shakes almost violently. I manage to wiggle free enough to grab the radio attached to my jeans and call the others.

I tell them we've found Will's body, going into slight detail so they're not as shocked as Liam and I were when we found him. I tell them that it's clearly murder.

"It's okay," I say, pressing my palm to his cheek. Crap, he's really freaking out. "Liam, look at me."

His haunted eyes make contact, and he swallows. "I'm sorry. Jesus, I'm sorry, Paisley. I—I've just never seen . . ."

"It's the shock," I say.

"I should be looking after you." His voice is hollow.

"We're taking care of each other. They're coming," I say as Harper and Camilla answer my call for help. "We're going to find a way of getting off this island."

The others are outside in a matter of seconds.

"What's going on?" Camilla asks.

They're breathless as they run toward us.

I step forward. "He was murdered. He's been in that cart. They put him in there. It's not . . . nice to look at."

Camilla rears back and turns around, not looking. She retches, bending over and resting her hands on her knees.

Gibson and Reeve do look. Both shout out in shock even though they know what they're about to see.

When did they even get here? They didn't mention anything on the radio.

"We need to get out of here. Right now," Reeve says.

"Kenna and Malcolm are in a lot of trouble," I mutter.

Reeve puts his hand on my burnt shoulder. "If they're not already dead. How many more carts are there around here?"

I squeeze my eyes shut. "Don't."

I've seen so many dead bodies since I started my crime channel. But I've always been separated by a screen. I'm safe in my room, surrounded by my fluffy pens, posters of my favorite bands, and photo of my dog, Bailey.

This is the first time that I've seen one in real life.

Harper holds back, staying by the gate to the hotel. She has her arms wrapped around herself and she's furiously biting her lip.

I leave the rest of them and walk to her. Behind me I hear Reeve take over, giving orders to Gibson and Liam. Camilla's heels click as she follows me.

Harper wraps me in a hug when I reach her. We hold on to each other like we'll break if we don't.

"It's okay," I whisper.

"I can't believe he's dead."

"We're getting out of here."

She sucks in a ragged breath. "Too right we are."

"Into the hotel, girls," Camilla says. She looks over her shoulder three times as we go. Her face is deathly pale.

I hold my stomach as we walk into the hotel, still not sure that I don't need to throw up.

In the lobby, Harper, Camilla, and I take a seat. No one has anything to say, so silence stretches for what seems like hours. It's been minutes.

We're all trying to process what's happened in our own way.

For Camilla, that's tapping at a hundred miles an hour on a phone that doesn't have any service.

For Harper, it's reading. She has her backpack by her feet and a book sitting on her knees. She's hunched over as she reads like she's having to force herself to focus by fully facing the pages. I don't see her eyes move once, so I don't think she's actually taking anything in. It's more like a comfort having a paperback in front of her. A safety blanket.

For me, it's watching out of the window as Gibson, Liam, and Reeve pick up Will's body and carry him . . . somewhere. They disappear from sight, and I don't know what to think. I didn't hear them mention taking him anywhere in particular, but of course they will have to. The storm is coming, and we can't leave him out there. The birds of prey that I've seen circling the island might land if we don't move him. There is no way we can allow anything as horrific as that to happen to Will.

His parents will need to bury him. All of him. And the cops will want as much forensic evidence as possible. Water and animals can really screw with that.

I watch out the window with bile rising in my throat, but they don't come back. I suppose they won't wander through the lobby with blood on their clothes.

Ten minutes later, they resurface. Liam just after. Each one with slightly damp hair and new clothes. They must have taken another entrance and gone to clean up in their rooms.

No one says a thing, but we acknowledge each other. A small nod, half-smile, a worried glance.

I wait and observe, wishing I could get into everyone's head.

Reeve hands me a mug of coffee. "Are you okay?" he asks, kneeling in front of me and breaking the silence.

"You probably think I'm ridiculous. I spend all day talking about murder, and here I am, shaking in an armchair."

I sip the coffee and welcome the slightly bitter taste.

"There's a big difference between talking about murder and witnessing one. We're all scared here, Paisley."

"Did you manage to fix the wiring?"

He dips his head. "Not yet. We're doing that next."

"Do you guys know how to fix it?"

"Yes."

There's something he's not telling me. Usually, I want all the answers, but I'm happy to remain ignorant on this one.

Instead of asking what I should ask, I reply, "Good."

His dark eyes blink slowly. He knows that I don't believe him. He doesn't believe him. But neither of us admits it.

"What on earth is going on?" Malcolm erupts into the lobby, throwing his hands up. "I've been in my office trying to make contact and then I hear that Will is *dead*. How can he be dead?"

"Murdered," I say. "He's not just dead. There was no accident. Someone stabbed him and stuffed him in a cart."

Shoving his hands through his curly hair, he blows out a long breath. "Jesus. What are we going to do? I can't get hold of anyone. Nothing is working."

I press my lips together to stop myself from crying. Nothing is working.

"What the hell kind of resort is this?" Ava snaps, leaning on James. "There has to be an emergency way off this island."

Malcolm straightens and his eyes cloud at the accusation that his island is completely unsafe. "There is. Of course there is."

James throws his hands up. "What are we waiting for, then?"

"The wind is too bad. Has been all day," Gibson says. "The only way off the island are the rowboats, but the water is far too rough for that."

"He's right. And rain was forecast for any second. Our best chance is to stay here, stick together, and try to repair the emergency radio or Wi-Fi," Reeve says.

Malcolm looks like he wants to remind his employee who's in charge. But he's not offering many solutions. He's very good at being the owner, showing off, and watching people revel in what he's created. He's not so great in a crisis.

He takes a seat next to Camilla and puts his head in his hands. His dream of having the most talked-about, most successful independent resort is slipping away.

"I'm going back downstairs. Gibson, you ready?" Reeve says.

"Shouldn't we try to find Kenna?" Harper asks. "She could be hurt."

"She's probably dead," Ava says. "Why would we risk our lives going out *there* to look for her?"

Lovely.

"You think we're safer in here, but this person has been in the hotel. Last night, while we were sleeping, this guy was snipping wires and kidnapping Will."

Ava narrows her eyes. All right, I didn't need to say that and make her worry more, but who the hell doesn't want to try to help another person who could be in trouble?

"I'll go," I offer, draining the last of the strong coffee. I'm so over being scared in this place. At least I can be scared and useful at the same time.

"No," Gibson says. "We can't have anyone else going missing. Reeve was right: we all have to stay in the hotel."

"So we just write Kenna off?" Harper snaps. "We can't do that."

Gibson's exasperated. "We'll drop like flies if we don't stick together."

She folds her arms. "Fine."

I don't feel good about it, but I can't say I disagree with them.

No one has seen Kenna since last night.

I can't ignore the heavy feeling in my stomach that tells me she's already dead.

# 12

Hours pass in relative shocked silence. Harper reads—this time she turns pages. Camilla and Malcolm whisper almost constantly. Something is up with them, beyond the obvious. Ava and James are in their own little world.

I sit by the window, watching the rain pelt the glass, waiting.

The storm is here.

Reeve and Gibson have been back in the control room, trying to rewire the internet connection. It's been almost two hours, and nothing is fixed, so it doesn't look good.

I can hear the wind howling, even over the roar of the fire Malcolm lit. That was a strange moment. Without a word, he got up from where he was sitting with Camilla, lit the fire, and returned to her.

It's not cold inside.

I guess he's trying to make us feel more comfortable.

Wind and rain batter the hotel. We're completely stuck here

tonight. Even if we could get word to anyone off this island, no one would risk coming here.

These sorts of storms aren't typical. We just got very unlucky. I look around the lobby at the other unfortunate humans trapped here with me. We're missing two. Will and Kenna.

Our earlier decision to not search for her still haunts me.

We're all scared, though no one will say it.

We didn't try hard enough to help her.

How do we live with ourselves?

"What're you thinking of?" Reeve asks, sitting beside me. He has a bowl of chips and salsa that he places on the table in front of me. "None of us are that hungry after everything, but we have to eat."

I sit up straight, my mouth watering despite my stomach churning over. "How's it going? Did you fix the wires?"

He winces like it hurts to deliver bad news. "We're looking for some new wires to replace the old ones. They're unsalvageable. Gibson's checking storage. I'm sorry."

This feels like a waste of time. They're not electricians. I understand the desire to do something, though, to at least *try*, even if it's a long shot.

I'm going out of my mind sitting here waiting.

"It's not your fault. There's no spare wire here at all? That seems . . . suspicious for an island. You'd have supplies, surely?"

"We have some, but we can't keep a replacement for everything here. There's not enough room and no one thought we'd have so much damage. We have spares for realistic events, not massive sabotage."

"Right. Well, that's a stupid idea."

Reeve laughs, nodding, and nudges my arm playfully. "I agree. How are you doing?"

"We don't have enough time to analyze that one. I just want to go home."

"I'll do everything I can to get you there, I promise."

I smile and hope that he can't see through the doubt in my eyes. "I know you will. I can't stop thinking about Kenna."

He ducks his head, and it's nice to know I'm not alone with my guilt. "Yeah, she's not been far from my mind either. She was nice. Great chef. Her burgers are to die for."

I lift a brow.

His face falls. "Sorry, bad choice of words. Forget I said that."

The choice of the word *die* isn't what I reacted to.

As I dip a chip in salsa, I wonder if Reeve caught his use of past tense when he spoke about Kenna.

He keeps his head bowed and sighs.

He said that she *was* nice. Then again, he also said her burgers *are* to die for.

I'm overthinking. He probably just misspoke.

Reeve *couldn't* have done this. He wouldn't. As much as I don't want to believe that I've made friends with—and crushed on—a killer, I have to remind myself that I don't know him.

I don't know anyone here. It was only yesterday that we met. The only one of them I had any previous contact with is Harper, and that was only a few messages on Insta.

Reeve was the last one to go to bed. According to him, he was still up when I came down. We just missed each other. Unless we didn't and he was hiding from me.

What if Will was just late and Reeve murdered him after I went into the park?

Would he have had enough time to do all that—hide Will's body and get back inside before I returned? I only waited by the fire for, like, ten minutes before I briefly went outside. Then I was walking around the park. It's super risky.

Was he the person I thought I saw when I was out there? He could have been running to get back into the hotel first and avoid being seen.

There are holes in the story, though. Like, *why* would he kill Will? He didn't know we planned to sneak into the park.

Maybe I should check Will's and Reeve's social media to see if there's a link.

Reeve doesn't seem like the kind of guy who spends much time on TikTok, but someone with no socials is totally sketchy.

And what if I stop speculating and deal with facts?

"What're you thinking, Paisley?" Reeve asks.

"What?" I plaster on a smile and look into his eyes.

"You've been holding that same chip for about fifteen seconds and the salsa is about to drop."

"Dammit!" I hold my palm under the hand that's about to let bright red salsa drip on Malcolm's expensive sofa. I take a bite and we're clear. I won't have to pay for anything to be professionally cleaned.

"What's your angle?" he asks.

"Oh. No, I have no clue. It's annoying, actually."

His eyes narrow a fraction. "Really?"

Clearly a sudden change in my personality isn't something

that he's going to buy. I've got to be smarter than that. I'm usually fast on my feet, quick to think and make excuses that sound legit.

"Sorry, the trauma of seeing Will . . . It's all so crazy. My mind is a little frazzled. I'm not on top of my game." I back up my speech with a smile, the same one I use when I lie to my parents about where I've been.

The "please believe me" smile.

It has a sixty-forty success rate.

"Understandable."

"What's *your* angle?" I ask. "You work here, you've been around all the staff. The ones who left when we got here and the ones who've stayed."

He lies back in his seat and crosses his legs at the ankles. "Hmm. Well, I was thinking. Just because those staff members were scheduled to leave, doesn't mean they did. They have a room. They know the island. It wouldn't be too hard to slip away and get back to the staff quarters. Or there could have been more on the island from the previous week."

"You mean since more people were on the island to begin with, someone could have stayed much longer, preparing for *this*?"

I want that to be true. It's easier to handle thinking it's a complete stranger and not someone I've spent time with here.

"The CCTV stopped recording from when we got off the boat, right?"

He points at me, smiling. "You're good."

There will be footage of everyone who arrived *before* we did. We can figure out from there who didn't leave.

"Do you have a full staff list?" I ask, my eyes casting over the lobby.

Malcolm is by the weapons cabinet, staring at it. He's put on his long coat despite it being warm in here. Camilla hasn't moved.

"Yeah, of course. It's not something I've seen or would need, but it's on the server. I can pull it up. People have been coming and going for the last three weeks, though. Things are ramping up now that we're getting ready to open. We've had orientations, practice runs, *get-to-know-you* days. Those were particularly awful."

I hate forced games. They're always so awkward.

"We'll go back from Monday and tick off everyone who left yesterday. Then go back further if that doesn't give us anything."

Reeve nods in agreement. "I need to let Gibson know what I'm doing while he searches for wire we'll likely never find."

Malcolm's spindly shadow casts over Reeve's face. He folds his arms over his chest. It's unnerving. I didn't see him move toward us. "You two look rather serious."

"Paisley had an idea."

Malcolm sits at the end of my sofa. He presses his fingertips together like he's hatching a plan to take over the world. "Oh?"

It's hard to tell what Malcolm thinks of me. It's hard to tell what he thinks at all. He's got a great poker face.

I know I'm not here because he's a fan; he proved that by not bothering to use my name. We're all on this island because he thinks we can convince wealthy people to spend their cash here.

Up until last year, I personally wasn't that wealthy. It was just my parents. Now I can afford to put myself through college all on my own. I've gotten tons of messages from rich college students who are studying things like law, crime, and forensic science. People with important parents—successful attorneys and business owners, hedge fund managers and even a few celebrities.

Those are the people Malcolm would *love* to have here most.

I explain my theory about the perpetrator, Reeve backs me up, and Malcolm finally agrees. It took Reeve to convince him but at least it's done.

"We do need to know who's doing this. We can't just sit here until someone realizes they haven't heard from us," Malcolm says, rubbing his lightly stubbled face.

"These guys spend so much time online. Surely someone will start questioning the radio silence soon," Reeve says.

And people say screen time is bad for you. It might just save our lives.

"Well, wouldn't that be something," Malcolm says, raising both brows.

"You don't like social media?" I ask.

"I don't like the side effects."

"Like people knowing about your business?"

"I'm talking about the negatives. Everyone and everything look so perfect online. In reality, people have issues, skin has texture, teeth don't glow, and stomachs have rolls." His voice is almost angry, but he controls himself and grins a little too wide.

Okay, he has a point there, but it's not very helpful to our situation, and his tone was also a bit creepy.

"Do you want anyone else to go with you and Paisley?" Malcolm asks.

The security room isn't far from the lobby and it's, thankfully, not underground. Not that my phone works anyway.

"No. Gibson is busy. I'm going to ask Liam to help him," Reeve says. "Paisley and I know exactly what we're looking for. Anyone else might just slow us down."

That's not strictly true. Wouldn't it be better for Camilla to go with him? She knows the staff too. But once I've seen the staff's photos, I'll recognize them. Still, Reeve's not picking the best sidekick.

Actually, this is my theory. He is *my* sidekick.

I'm not going to tell him another member of the staff would be more helpful because I want to be the one down there.

"I'm going to grab a coffee before we get started. Want one?" he asks as we stand.

"Er, yeah, thanks."

Malcolm floats away in the direction of Camilla. He's always so controlled, moving swiftly and purposefully. It's weird as hell.

At the bar, Camilla is still a little hysterical, shaking her head and tapping at her useless phone. Malcolm hangs back, completely out of his depth. He has no clue how to handle someone so emotional.

It's kind of amusing, really.

Someone needs to take that thing off her. It's not going to work. Mine's dead after taking a lot of videos this morning. I've not had the courage to ask someone to come to my room with me to get my charger. With everything that's going on, that seems a bit heartless. Our phones have no service anyway.

Since there is absolutely no way I'm going to go alone, I

follow Reeve toward the bar and take a seat. He goes behind and starts to prepare two coffees.

Malcolm and Camilla don't even look my way. He's moved closer to her and they lean in, huddling together and whispering. They haven't even noticed that we've moved closer.

Camilla shakes her head. Fear flickers in her eyes so acutely that I feel a bolt of dread ripple down my spine.

They're too far for me to hear what they're saying, but I can read Camilla's lips.

*Robert.*

She's scared of someone named Robert.

Who the hell is that?

No one here is named Robert.

Malcolm shakes his head, his eyebrows pinched together, but she repeats the name two more times.

Whoever it is, Malcolm doesn't think he's in danger . . . or that Robert is dangerous.

Why wouldn't they share their concern with us? This Robert could be the person who killed Will and took Kenna. We should all know who this guy is and what he looks like.

"Ready?"

Reeve's voice makes me jump. I didn't notice him walking around the bar holding two takeout cups of coffee.

He hands me one. "Thanks. Yeah, I'm ready."

Reeve leads the way and the second the door clicks shut behind us. I ask, "Who's Robert?"

"Sorry?"

"At the bar just now, I heard Malcolm and Camilla whispering.

She looked *petrified* and she said the name Robert. Is there someone here with that name?"

"Maybe. We'll have to check. You said she was worried?"

"No, I said petrified. Whoever Robert is, she's more than just worried about him. Way more."

Reeve puts his coffee down and fires up the computer.

I sit in front of the screens and wait as he clicks a bunch of icons and inputs passwords.

He does a quick glance my way. "Whatever you see in here, you need to forget."

"Got it," I reply, rolling my eyes.

Sure, he shouldn't be showing me staff details, but I'm hardly going to publish this information. All I care about is finding this sick asshole and getting home.

Reeve taps on the keyboard and a folder named STAFF opens. I take a sip of coffee and pray that it wakes me up a little. It's not even late but I feel like I've been awake for days.

There are folders within that one for each staff member. One of the folders that I see as he's scrolling reads CONVICTIONS.

"There! No, scroll back up." I point to the folder. "That one. Who here has a conviction? Is that what that means?"

He shakes his head. "I can't show you that."

"Why not?"

"Look, I get where you're coming from, and I know what's happening here. But I need this job, Paisley. I don't have a lot of money, and Malcolm's taken a chance on me."

What does that mean?

He doesn't want to share that information or . . .

"Reeve, are *you* in the folder?"

"Dammit," he says, putting his head in his hands. He looks so defeated, hunched over and ashamed.

Okay. What's going on?

I don't move for a minute. He's still, as if he's trying not to be seen.

"Hey, it's okay. Reeve, you can tell me."

"I didn't do anything to Will," he says, sitting back up. This time his shoulders are back, squared. He's ready to fight. "I'm not the person doing this. I promise you."

Of course that's what the killer would say.

My heart thumps harder. I want to believe him. "Please just tell me. I bet I'm imagining something worse than it is."

He blows out a long breath and looks so sad it breaks my heart. What happened to him?

"Your whole life can change in an instant. One day you're on track toward college and working your ass off to be an engineer. The next, *everything* is gone. One mistake, one second, and your world can be turned upside down."

"What are you telling me?" I ask.

He reaches over, squeezes my hand, and quickly retracts it. "Okay . . . I got into a fight. In high school I'd hang out with some guys. We'd hit bars and be idiots. One night, this guy was giving us some grief. He started on Gibson and got him to the floor. He was about to get another punch in, but I got there first. The guy hit his head hard when he went down."

I grip the edge of the chair. "He died?"

"No. He was in the hospital for a couple weeks, but he made

a full recovery, thank god. I was charged with assault and spent nine months in juvie."

What the . . .

"How old were you?"

"Sixteen. Seventeen when I was released. It's not been easy to rebuild my life. Not many people are willing to take me on. I was trying to protect my friend. I never meant for the guy to get that hurt."

I clear my throat. "Okay."

"You can stop looking at me like that, Paisley. I'm not going to hurt you."

"Sorry."

"I'm *not* dangerous."

I stare into his eyes. They're honest, scared, and searching for something that looks an awful lot like acceptance. Reeve has probably spent a long time having people turn him away because of a mistake he made.

He trusted me with his biggest secret and now he wants to know if I'll turn my back on him like so many others did.

It's a lot to ask of someone you've known for a day.

"Reeve." I let go of the chair and put my hand over his. This time I feel a jolt at the contact. "I believe you. My brother has gotten into fights before. It would've ruined his life if he was charged for them. Did anything happen to the other guy?"

"His parents were rich," Reeve replies, patting my hand with his free one. It's all the explanation I need. Money can fix almost any problem. "Shall we get on with this? I'd really like to get you off this island."

I sit back, breaking our contact, and wave toward the screen. "Let's get that list and find this guy."

He scrolls past the CONVICTIONS folder and we start to look for names.

"All right. Where are you, Robert?" Reeve mutters, his eyes darting over the screen.

"Check for a Rob, Robby, and Bobby, too."

He smiles but doesn't stop clicking and scrolling through names.

It takes less than five seconds to find him. Robert Jenkins.

Jenkins.

That's Camilla's last name.

# 13

"Well, detective. Are you thinking what I'm thinking?" Reeve asks, looking between me and the name screaming at us on the monitor.

"You know I am," I reply. "Camilla's hardly been levelheaded, but you should've seen her eyes when she said *Robert.* Wild. Afraid. She suspects him, and her reaction is *exactly* what you'd expect from a family member. I'd be that scared if it was someone I love, too."

"You really think she believes it's him? Maybe she's just scared for him. He might be staying on the island without permission."

"No way. If she thought he was innocent and in danger she would have told us by now. His safety would be more important than Malcolm giving him a slap on the wrist. She'd be frantically looking for him. She's protecting him. Is it her husband? Or maybe her son?"

Reeve nods. "All right. Let me pull up Robert's file. There will be a picture and we can use that to trace him on the CCTV."

He clicks the mouse twice and frowns.

Oh, what now?

"What?" I look from him to the screen twice. "What am I not seeing? You're going to need to spell it out for me."

"What you're not seeing, because it's not there, is his staff photo. It should be right here."

"Let me guess. Someone deleted it." I roll my eyes. "I wonder who . . ."

"We get one step forward, then knocked two back. There's no way of telling if there ever was a picture for him. It might not have been taken yet, but the deleted thing is more likely considering everything going on." He taps his temples. "Think, think, think."

"Check the trash."

"I will, but these would be in the program. Nothing saves onto the desktop."

Reeve looks, but the trash is empty.

Groaning, I ask, "Okay, what do we actually have?"

"There's some information about him still. No picture or address, but not everything is gone."

"Just the thing that can identify him. We don't even have any service to look him up online. I could find him in half a second if the Wi-Fi was working."

He smiles as he works. "I bet you could. His emergency contact is listed. He's an operator for the Flame coaster but can be stationed anywhere if needed. Let me check. . . ."

"Check what? Reeve? Hello!"

"Uh, this. Look, the last time he punched in and out was

Tuesday. We've had ride operator practice all week. I've been with the staff, but I've never met Robert."

"You were?"

"What? Oh, don't give me that face, Paisley. I know how to check them. I don't do the repairs myself . . . unless it's turning it off and on again."

"Sorry," I say.

"It's fine. And for the record, I would know how to fix them. I thought back to when I wanted to be an engineer, when I was inside, but I don't think that'll happen."

"You can still take a class."

He clenches his jaw. "No."

There's more to that. Has he been told he's unlikely to get a job as an engineer because of his record? That kind of sucks.

I want to tell him that, but the hurt and anger flashing across his face tell me to shut my mouth. There's no need to make him feel worse about his situation.

"He might have stayed on the island beyond Tuesday but not punched in. No one would expect him to be here, then. All he had to do is stay hidden."

"Would you skip punching in if it was the only way to get paid?" Reeve asks.

I give him a look that tells him to catch up. "Maybe if you need an alibi. Does Camilla punch in?"

He laughs. "She's not a ride operative, cook, server, driver, or in maintenance."

Right. Only the lowly minions punch in.

"Got it. So, he either has nothing to do with this, their surnames are a coincidence, and Camilla is worrying about him for another reason. Or he didn't punch in because he didn't want to leave a trace."

Reeve pulls his own picture up on another screen and then opens the saved CCTV folders. "Ready to go on a murderer hunt?"

"Usually, yes. It's my favorite thing to do—don't tell my mom that—but it's less fun when you're doing it while being trapped with one."

"Your favorite thing? Damn, girl, you need another hobby."

"You sound like my parents. Should we go to Malcolm and Camilla with this?" Even as I say the words, I know we shouldn't. Something about them makes me hesitate to trust them.

"What are the chances they'll answer honestly?" he asks.

"Not great. But if there's another, more innocent reason for her tears, we could be wasting time here, Reeve."

"Let's just see if there's someone I don't recognize on the footage. If there's no sign of him, we'll go ask."

"All right. Besides, they could just lie." We need more before we go to them if we want them to be honest and prove that we know something is up.

Evidence might be the only way we'll get proof.

Reeve and I fall silent as we stare at screens. I'm relying heavily on him pointing out male strangers. I see him, Gibson, and Kenna a few times. Not much of Malcolm or Camilla. There's no one else I'd recognize anyway.

"There!" he says, pointing to someone near the ice cream cart.

I shudder at the sight of him near where Will was found. Was the creep scoping the best place to store a body?

"Could that be him?"

"I dunno," he says with a shrug. "Could be. He's the only person I don't know on this footage so far. I wouldn't be able to point them all out, but this guy I haven't seen before."

"You're sure?"

Reeve leans in to the screen and squints. "I think so. It's hard to make out his features, though. Plus, there are people I haven't met. Look at the time stamp. This was about ten minutes before you all arrived."

"You just walked straight past him! There you go!"

Reeve shakes his head. "I can't believe I didn't notice him."

There are a few other people around and Reeve was on his phone—throwback to when those worked here—so it's not surprising that he walked straight past.

"Where does he go?"

"I can't see, but he's heading in the direction of the hotel."

"Shouldn't he be going to the boat? We must arrive in minutes."

"Yeah," Reeve says. "He should be. He should follow me, but he's not."

"Wait, I see him."

He frowns and leans closer to the screen again. He's going to bump his forehead soon if he keeps doing that. "He turned back."

"Yeah."

The potential Robert went back toward the boat. The rest of the staff is clearly seen heading that way at the same time we enter the park.

It's impossible to see whether he went to the jetty because the footage cuts.

"Oh, come on!" I shout. "Does he leave the island?"

"Everyone was there at that point," Reeve says. "If he suddenly turned around then and walked back, surely we'd have noticed."

Would we, though? He wasn't on Reeve's radar. Or mine.

There's nothing spectacular about this guy's appearance. He's average. Great for blending in and going unnoticed.

When all this gets out, people will say "he never looked the type." I shudder.

"Gibson would know, right?" I ask. "He would've been on the boat with him for the twenty minutes it takes to cross to the mainland."

"Think we should let anyone else in on this yet?" he asks.

My very first question, considering they were close friends before working here, is, Why doesn't Reeve trust Gibson with this?

"Do we have a choice?" I ask. "We can't sit on this. We have to see if Gibson can confirm if that's Robert and then confront Camilla and Malcolm."

"Okay, but before that we could at least see if anyone else stays on the island. This is just the first guy."

I want to tug on my hair but it's already a miracle that stress hasn't made it fall out *yet.*

"All right," I reply. Though this sounds a bit like stalling. If we know who this person is, then maybe we can figure out what they want and where they are.

We might be able to stop them before they hurt anyone else. By some miracle, we might even find Kenna alive.

"Wait, Reeve. What do you know about Kenna?"

He does a double take. "What? No way, she's the sweetest. A real maternal type, and not just to her daughter, Gabrielle. She makes sure you have a jacket when it's cold and feeds you if she thinks you're looking thin. I've only known her for a month, but this isn't her."

"Yeah, I only saw her twice and I kind of got that too. I just wanted to make sure."

A killer doesn't seem like a killer until it's too late, though.

Reeve and I spend the next thirty minutes going back another day in the footage to see if we can find anyone else. I'm not much help, since I only know the people on the island now, and he doesn't see any other men he doesn't know who could be Robert.

By the time he's zoomed through the whole day, I'm going nuts.

"All right," he says, finally conceding. "Let's go back up."

I'm on my feet before he can finish talking.

Finally. That was a total waste of time. We should've gone up the second we saw that first guy. Almost everyone else Reeve didn't know was a woman, and there was one guy who we were able to trace using staff documents.

Reeve and I walk the corridor. I almost want to go back into that room and hide. Everything outside is unpredictable.

The killer is on the island somewhere, and there's a big mystery around Robert. It would be easier to lock ourselves away until help arrived.

"We need to eat something better than chips at some point," Reeve says, opening the door to the lobby. He holds it for me to go ahead.

The lobby is quiet when we step back inside. Ava and James are cuddled up asleep on a sofa, Harper is still reading her book. Camilla is now staring out the window—though she can probably only see her haunted expression at this point.

Can she see Robert in her reflection?

I open my mouth to ask if anyone knows where Gibson and Liam are. Malcolm too, since he's not here anymore. But before I can get a word out, the lights cut, and we're thrown into darkness.

I freeze on the spot. The rain is battering down hard on the windows. It's the only thing that I can hear for a few seconds. That, and my pulse whooshing in my ears.

It's faint, but I just about make out someone's gasp. I turn toward the sound, but who knows if I'm facing it.

My phone is dead, so I can't use it to see.

Harper's voice comes out in a terrified whisper. "What's going on?"

"Why'd the lights go out?" Ava shouts. "Hello!"

"Stay calm. I think it's just a power cut," Reeve says. "Does anyone have their cell on them?"

"I'm out of battery," Ava cries out. "I need a charger! I don't like this. Why is the generator not working yet?"

"I'm out too," I announce.

"Can you go put the power back on, man?" James asks. "My phone is here somewhere, but I can't find it."

"I'm trying to find my way. Everyone just stay where you are," Reeve says over us.

"We can't see to move!" Ava screeches. "Seriously, what's going on?"

"Calm down, Ava," Harper snaps.

I hear movement from somewhere in the room but it's hard to tell where.

"Camilla, do you have your phone?" Reeve asks.

"Yes."

"Can you use it, then? We need the flashlight."

If I wasn't so scared, I would laugh at Reeve's tone.

"It's on the table. I was using it to work."

I pinch the bridge of my nose. "Reeve, where are you going?"

"Breaker box."

I turn my head toward his voice. He sounds much farther away from me than he was a second ago.

"Where?" I ask.

"I think I'm getting near the entrance."

"Oh, yeah, leave us in here again," Ava sneers. "Will's dead and now we can't see. That's great."

The murder hasn't altered her attitude.

"At least he's doing something," I snap. "All you do is just complain."

"Now is *not* the time!" Camilla shouts through the darkness.

"Where's Gibson, Liam, and Malcolm?" Reeve askes the

question from even farther away. I wish he'd taken me with him. I don't like standing here alone.

Camilla clears her throat. "They went to try the radio. The one we use for the helicopters and air control. Not the handhelds. I can't find my phone; it was on the table."

That's a good idea. Our phones don't work, but maybe they can get the radios working.

"Why didn't they try that earlier?" I ask.

"Malcolm did, of course. Gibson and Liam said they'll take a look, as it was . . ."

I laugh but there's nothing funny. "It was tampered with like the phones and boat?"

Someone really wants us isolated here.

"Okay. Why hasn't the generator kicked in yet?" I ask.

Reeve is the one to reply. "The killer doesn't want it to. It should've come on by now."

"Oh god, we're all going to die," Ava says, a loud sob bouncing off the glass.

"Ava, for goodness' sake!" Harper shouts. "You're—"

A thud steals my breath and Harper's words.

I spin to where I think the noise came from. What the hell was that?

That sounded like a body hitting the floor.

"Reeve?" I say, my voice trembling with fear.

I'm met with silence.

Shit.

"Reeve, where are you? Answer me!" I sound as panicked as Ava and that's because I am.

I'm not sure who muttered "He's next," but it makes my heart constrict in terror.

"Reeve!" I shout louder. I spin around, still blinded by darkness, and raise my arms in front of me. "James and Camilla, find your phone! We need to help him."

"I'm trying," Camilla replies. She makes a crash as she knocks things off the table and swears under her breath.

"Who's still here? Call out your name," I say.

One by one, Ava, James, Harper, and Camilla let me know they're still in the room.

Nothing from Reeve.

"I told you we're all going to die here," Ava says.

"Why would you go there again?" Harper snaps back. "Idiot."

"I'm just stating the obvious! We're alone and no one is looking for us!"

"That doesn't mean we're going to die!"

"Girls, enough," Camilla orders, but it's useless. They continue arguing as if they didn't hear her.

There's another, louder, thud. No, two. Two in a row. Footsteps?

It's hard to hear over the bickering.

I stumble forward frantically, my hands out in front of me. "Shut up!" I shout. "I just heard something. Reeve?"

"Oh god, here he comes," Ava mutters. It sounds like she's crying now. She is not the person you want around in a time of crisis.

"Listen," I say, straining to hear anything other than our heavy breaths.

"Reeve?" I whisper.

From somewhere in the room, someone groans. It's almost a gargle, a desperate attempt to gulp down some oxygen.

My stomach ties another knot.

"Reeve!"

Then Ava screams. The sound could shatter glass. "It came from James! It's James! It's James!"

There's a scrambling and another crash, this time like something falling onto wood. It's so dark I can't see a thing.

I keep my arms in front of me and walk in the direction where she was sitting, but I can't be a hundred percent sure I'm going the right way. I've spun around since the lights went out.

"Ava, what's going on? Talk to me."

"He was beside me!" she screams.

"Ava!"

"Ava! Where are you now?"

The killer's in here with us.

"Camilla, your phone!" I shout. "Find it. We need to see her."

"Oh god, oh god, oh god," Ava chants. Her voice is muffled like she's speaking into something. Her hands, maybe.

"Ava, keep talking so I can find you."

I shuffle another step, desperately trying to find her and hoping I don't walk into a murderer.

A second later the room is filled with light again. I blink twice as I adjust to the sudden brightness. I lower my eyes, and the first thing I see is Ava huddled on the floor with her face in her hands.

The second is James slumped in his seat with a knife through his chest.

Ava looks up and her scream, this time, lasts for about thirty seconds.

Harper leaps to her feet and backs up. "Ah, Jesus!"

"No one touch him!" I shout, my heart racing, thumping against my rib cage.

"W-wasn't planning to," Harper replies robotically. "He's *dead*. Oh my god!"

Camilla shuffles along the window, pressing herself against the glass as if it will melt and let her escape through it. Her eyes are so wide I can see way more of the whites than I should.

I gag and cover my mouth.

Calm down.

Okay. I need to think.

*Clear your head, Paisley.*

I rub my temples. Come on. I'm sure Reeve went in the opposite direction. It sounded like he was on my right when he spoke, and they were sitting to my left. So odds are he's fine and just left to turn the power on.

Which means he should be back any second.

The killer was preoccupied with James, so Reeve couldn't have been taken.

"I'm going to check out the room," I say. "Everyone stay calm."

Ava slides along the floor, putting more distance between herself and James.

Harper crouches beside her and turns her head. "Don't look. Focus on me."

I walk around the back of the sofa where James is sitting and stuff my quivering hands in my pockets. There's nothing. Not even right in front where the killer must have come from. The knife is the right way up; if he'd been behind him, the knife would be upside down.

I'm not sure I would be able to tell from the wound and I don't want to look.

No tables or chairs were knocked. How did the killer manage to get into the middle of the lounge in total darkness without bashing into anything?

I couldn't even see my hand in front of my face.

He must have those night vision glasses to help him see in the dark, the absolute psycho.

That thought is so unnerving that my stomach almost rejects the chips and salsa I ate earlier.

I ditch the pockets and press my fist to my mouth so I don't vomit. I always thought I would be calmer in situations like this, but I never really thought I would have to deal with one.

Moving forward, I continue my search, walking around the lounge. No footprints. This person has been in the building a while, or they would have brought in water from the storm outside. There would be drops on the floor and wet prints.

"Paisley, what are you doing?" Harper asks.

She's the first one to speak in what must be five minutes.

"Looking for evidence."

Ava sniffs loudly. "What evidence? You're not a real detective. You're not the cops. And this isn't a game!"

"I don't think this is a game," I snap. She shuts up when I explain what I've found so far. Which isn't a lot, but we know the killer is hiding out somewhere in the hotel.

"We need to find Malcolm, Liam, Gibson, and Reeve," Camilla says. Her voice is a shaky whisper. Her palms are splayed on the glass behind her and she's still staring wide at James.

"Camilla," I say. "Hey, don't do that. It won't help. But you are right, we do need to find the others. Where's the radio?"

"Control room."

"Okay. I think we should all go together. No more splitting up."

Not that it seems to matter. James was killed when there were four other people in the room.

"Hopefully Reeve is with them," I say.

Why wouldn't he have come straight back when the lights turned on?

"Or Reeve's the killer," Harper says. "Don't you think it's weird that the lights went out, he disappeared, and James was murdered?"

Another knot. "No. He was with me until the lights went out. How would he have turned them off?"

She shrugs. "Don't let him fool you just because you think he's hot."

"I'm not letting anyone fool me. If you think it's him, back it up and we'll listen to your theory. How could he have done it, Harper?"

As far as I'm aware, there's no remote for the lights. We have an app at home, but I haven't seen Reeve with his phone. If he still has battery.

She shrugs. "I have no clue. It was just a thought."

"We all need to stop fighting. This isn't getting us anywhere,"

Camilla says. She straightens her back and walks away from the window.

Well, look who's back and ready to take charge.

It's a little late.

Harper gets to her feet and pulls Ava's hands. "Up you get, Ava. We're all staying together from now on."

The four of us walk down the stairs to the basement. This has to be my least favorite place to go, but here we are.

"I do *not* like this," Ava says.

I take a deep breath. This is totally a place to get yourself murdered. No one needs to come down here alone.

"Guys, you still down here?" I call out, almost at the bottom of the stairs.

Why am I the one to go first?

# 14

Harper moves down and stops on the same step as me. We're three from the bottom. "Paisley," Harper whispers. "Why haven't they answered?"

Good question. Here's another: why didn't Reeve and I hear them walk past the security room when we were down here?

"Maybe they haven't heard us calling," I reply, trying to make us both feel a little less scared. Though it's pretty clear they're not here . . . or they're dead.

If they've been murdered too, I swear I will leap over the edge of the cliff and swim off this island.

Ava and Camilla are silent behind me, but I hear their gentle footsteps. They're afraid to make a noise. I let go of the rail on the wall as we reach the bottom of the staircase.

"Ready?" I ask Harper.

"Absolutely not, but let's go."

That's *exactly* how I feel.

Breathing deeply, as if I can expel every ounce of anxiety with one breath, I step around the corner and prepare myself for the worst.

"Nothing," I say, taking a sweep of the room.

Ava walks around the back of the large boiler. "Clear. That's what you're supposed to say, right?"

"If you're a cop, sure," Harper replies.

I crouch in front of the cut wires. They're in the exact same condition as they were when Reeve and I found them. "Hmm."

"What is it?" Harper asks.

"Probably nothing. Gibson and Reeve said they were going to try to repair these."

She shrugs and kneels beside me. "They didn't have enough new wire, though, did they?"

No, but they had some. Where is it? And why not try to remove the snipped ends?

If that's even possible.

It can't be if they didn't even attempt to do it.

"There's no one down here," I say.

Harper crosses her heart. "Thank the lord."

"So where did they go? Camilla, where can you get to from here? Besides back up to the lobby?"

She steps around the boiler where she was hiding behind Ava. "The door in the corner leads out to the back of the hotel and into the park."

"Excellent. They could be anywhere by now."

But why?

"They might have gone out and we just didn't see them. They could be looking for wire outside the hotel," Camilla says, clearing her throat. "The door to the staff quarters is closer to the main entrance and we were almost at the end of the lobby."

"Maybe," I reply. It's possible.

"I bet they're all in on it," Ava replies. "It'll be the four guys against us four girls. We're as good as dead. We should grab weapons and take them out before they get us. There must be guns here somewhere."

I turn to her and glare. "Can you be any more ridiculous? How about, unless you have something constructive or positive to say, you shut up." I let out a breath. "And we could take them without weapons."

Ava rolls her eyes and turns her back to the rest of us. I feel a little bad about snapping at her. Without James, she's completely lost.

"Can we focus? What're we going to do now?" Harper asks.

"I don't know, but we need to get back upstairs before we make a plan," I say. "The lights could go out again and we do *not* want to be down here if that happens."

A shudder rolls down my spine, and Harper's eyes widen.

The darkness was bad enough in the lobby.

Ava throws her arms up. "You have got to be kidding me. We should barricade ourselves in here. I don't want to go back up there with . . . James. There was so much blood."

"I would usually agree with the barricading thing, but I like the idea of the light going out down here even less. Way less.

James was killed in the dark." Harper said all that in about two seconds. Her eyes dart between me, Ava, and the door.

"Staying is too risky, Ava. There's not a lot to block a door with and there are two of them down here," I say.

"Fine. Whatever."

I'll take that as her being with us.

"Camilla, tell me you know somewhere that's actually safe. Preferably somewhere that we can secure. Reeve said that some of the buildings outside have their own electrical circuits. Would one of those be safer?"

"Uh, maybe," she replies. "I think it would be safer than the hotel. Fewer entrances. Just one, actually. We would be able to control who came in."

"Where is this place?"

"The first-aid huts would be better. Bigger. There are three spread out over the park with roughly the same distance between them. The hope was to never have to use them." She laughs. "The worst we thought would happen would be the odd person falling over or someone getting sick."

"Where is the closest one?"

"Follow me," she says, walking to the door in the corner of the room. Looking back over her shoulder, she takes a breath and opens the door.

I hear it before I see it. Rain pelts the ground like bullets.

Camilla pokes her head through a small gap. "It's bad out there. I can barely see."

"We have no choice," I reply.

Harper grabs my hand. "Everyone hold on so we don't get separated."

Camilla goes first, me second, then Harper and Ava.

It takes all of five seconds before I'm soaked right through to the bone. Water hits my eyes, but I can't see anyway so it doesn't really matter.

Rain flashes in front of me, blurring everything past a few feet.

I'm not sure of the time but it appears as if the sun is setting. It's dark, even for heavy rainfall. Trees lean sideways in the wind, leaves and small branches fly past us.

"What can you see?" Harper shouts from the back.

I turn my head, or I know she'll never hear. "Not much!"

Camilla leads us onward. "We're only minutes away," she shouts, tugging us faster toward our destination.

Ava squeals from the back. "Are we really doing this? It's suicide!"

I blink the water from my eyes as I try to use the silence to hear anyone coming. It'll be hard with the sound of the rain bouncing off every surface, but we need both senses working together to stay safe.

Whoever this is, they have a sight advantage.

Camilla leads us past the cart where Will's blood has been washed away by the water.

I'm just glad Will isn't still there. The image of him falling out of that cart will haunt me for the rest of my life.

We pass a roller coaster, and I can only just see the bottom of the loops.

As we're hurrying through the park, I hear a bang like metal striking metal over the sound of the pouring rain. I jump and squeeze Harper's and Camilla's hands.

"Did you hear that?" I shout.

"Don't stop," Camilla calls over her shoulder.

"I heard something!"

Ava pushes us forward. "Go!"

Camilla walks faster, tugging us along.

My eyes are everywhere, my heart leaping at the possibility of being watched. I heard a noise but no one else seems to have noticed or they just don't care.

Through the thick rain, I look for any sign of another person. Robert. Thanks to the missing photo, I don't know what he looks like, but if someone shows up who we don't know, I think it's a pretty safe bet that it's him.

I'm not sure I actually want to find this person after what he did to Will and James, though.

Why wouldn't death be his plan for the rest of us?

I can barely see anything through the storm, but thankfully, I can just about make out a little hut. It's not something I really noticed here before. I couldn't ride it, so it wasn't important.

"We're here!" Camilla shouts. She punches in a code on the pad and, with shaking hands, unlocks the door.

We bundle inside like a dam bursting and Camilla flicks on a light.

The room is quite small. There are a bench running along the end of the wall, a doctor's bed in the middle of the room, and two chairs on either side of a small table. A cabinet in the corner is decorated with first-aid stickers and a map of the park.

"I heard a noise out there," I say.

"The wind and rain were fierce. It could've been one of the gates slamming," Camilla says as she presses a button on the thermostat. "It should warm up fast."

I thought wind was to blame when I heard a noise while I snuck out last night.

"Don't stress, Paisley. We're safe in here now," Harper says.

Ava sits down on the bench and wrings her hair out. Her teeth chatter as she says, "I'm s-so cold."

I'm dripping and my jeans are stuck to my legs in the most awful way. It makes me want to rip them straight off my body. Wet jeans are the absolute worst.

"Here are some towels," Camilla says, punching in a code to unlock the cabinet.

Rows of shelves are stacked high with medical equipment.

She hands each one of us a small towel wrapped in plastic.

"Thanks," I say, ripping the bag open and rubbing the soft plush cotton over my face and arms.

Camilla picks up a radio on the top shelf and tunes in to the channel Reeve and Gibson use. "This is Camilla. Come in. Can you hear me? Hello?"

She lets go of the button and gives it a few seconds before trying again. "Come in. This is Camilla. I have Paisley, Ava, and Harper with me."

Silence stretches out as far as the distance between us and the mainland.

*Please pick up.*

No one is answering.

A wave of nausea makes me dizzy.

No one is there.

If they're dead, what chance do we have?

We might really be alone now.

The four of us and the killer.

# 15

I chew my long nails while pacing around the small, clinical room. I'd managed to kick that habit last year and here I am, ruining all my hard work.

The towel is wrapped around my shoulders, and I'm hoping that the warm air will dry my hair and clothes soon.

"That's not helpful, Paisley," Ava says, watching me go back and forth.

I raise my brows. Out of everyone on this island, she's the one judging. "You're talking to me about what's helpful and what's not?"

"Don't start, you two!" Harper says.

"Shhh!" Camilla hushes the three of us. "Hello? This is Camilla, is anyone there? Malcolm? Reeve?"

There's static on the radio as we listen for a reply.

Around the cracking, someone groans.

"Do you hear that?" I ask.

Harper walks over to me and Camilla. "I *definitely* heard that."

We all look at the radio as if we're FaceTiming.

"Hello?" Camilla says again. "Come in."

The voice groans again, saying something muffled, like "help."

"Reeve." Camilla looks up. "I'm sure that's Reeve's voice."

I'm sure that's his voice too.

"He's in trouble. We have to get to him before the killer does."

Harper grabs my wrist as I go for the door. "He might be the killer luring us out."

"If he was the killer, he would just come in. He has codes to every door and gate."

"He doesn't know where we are, Paisley."

"The killer can see in the dark. Do you think he wouldn't have seen us run a quarter of the way across the park?"

She shudders. "I don't want to think about him watching us."

"Then don't think about it. But I need to go before Reeve is murdered."

I couldn't help Will or James. We haven't properly searched for Kenna. I'm not making those same mistakes with Reeve. We didn't know about them, but I can't hear someone call for help and ignore them.

"Take this," Camilla says, handing me a hammer.

I grab the red handle and pray that I never need to use it. "Where did this come from?"

"There's a very basic toolbox in the cabinet, no flashlight. I don't have anything to help you see out there, but if you take your towel, you can hold it up over your head. Paisley, *please* be careful."

I'd promise Camilla that I'll be back, but based on the movies I've watched, that's always a mistake.

"I'll shout when I get back. Make sure you lock the door behind me."

"Should I come?" Harper asks.

"No. If I don't come back . . . You should be here for these two."

Harper squares her shoulders, understanding that I'm telling her I need her to look after Ava and Camilla if I don't come back. They're the two who are most likely to do something stupid.

I grip the handle and notice I'm shaking. It's not a surprise.

I swallow the urge to gag and try not to think about my parents.

Without looking back, I open the door and step out into the rain.

The door slams behind me as they waste no time in locking me out. That'll be Harper being smart.

Rain hits my shoulders, freezing me down to the bone.

I pull the towel around my shoulders and over my head, holding the front out over my eyes. It flies behind me, whipping me on my back with a constant rhythm.

With the hammer in my other hand, I move forward.

Visibility is still awful as rain pours from the sky like a waterfall. It hits the towel over my head with constant little thuds. My feet squelch in cold puddles.

"Reeve!" I scream. The killer can probably see me anyway; I might as well find him as fast as I can.

"Reeve!"

I move forward, turning in full circles to see if anyone is coming toward me. With visibility nonexistent past three yards in front of me, I wouldn't know if it was Reeve or the killer until the very last minute.

Don't think about that.

Gripping the hammer tight, I hold it up and shuffle forward, ignoring my heart trying to punch through my chest.

"Reeve! Where are you? Reeve!"

My voice is whisked away with a strong gust of wind and rain.

I stumble ahead again, blocking the rain from hitting my eyes. It's too dark to see anyway.

"Reeve?" I shout.

Where did he go?

A minute of wondering and I come to the Waltzer. It's only visible now that I'm close. I step up on the platform and look out over the park. I can see a few meters in front of me. Beyond that is pitch black.

Swinging around at a thud behind me, I begin to tremble. Why would Reeve come from behind the cars?

I crouch behind one of the cars and peek around the side. The ride is huge, consisting of twelve cars. He could be anywhere here. There are plenty of places to hide.

Maybe it was just a noise.

I'm not brave or confident enough to stand up and walk as if

I believe no one is there. I know full well the things that go bump here can kill.

I stand a little taller and look over the top of the Waltzer to get a better view. Directly opposite me, at the other side of the ride, is a tall figure, facing away from me. Rain pelts down, bouncing off his body, framing him . . . and his knife.

Robert.

Gasping, I drop back down and peer around the corner.

He walks my way slowly, but I don't think he's seen me. He's probably coming this way because he heard me screaming for Reeve, who I still need to find.

I crawl on the floor, pushing my body as tight as I can underneath the Waltzer.

Water runs down my back. I push my wet hair out of my face and crane my neck to see where he's going next.

His steps are heavy on the ride floor as he walks directly toward me. It won't be long until he's standing over me.

With my stomach churning up, I shuffle backward on my hands and knees. I move around the Waltzer, and right when he's on the other side of my car, I slip and knock into the side of it.

The car twists and his footsteps halt.

My heart stops.

He knows someone is here.

There must be about six steps between us and I'm on the floor.

I leap to my feet and bolt.

He's right behind me, but I don't turn around. I jump off the ride floor and run deeper into the park, leading him away from the hut where the others are safely locked away.

I purposefully stay along the back end of the park where the smaller fairground-style rides are. There are more places I can hide, and nothing is fenced off.

There's a carousel ahead with dozens of beautiful ornate horses that will shield me.

My side pinches in pain but I push harder and jump up onto the ride. Running to the middle, I duck behind a horse that's stopped down low and I peer out.

Rain cascades from the sky in a sheet of water that makes it impossible to see too far in front of your face.

He saw me and he knows which way I ran. So where is he now?

I crawl forward, keeping my eyes on the direction I came from. The direction that he would've been following. He knows I am alone, so I really believe he's coming for me now. It's the perfect time.

I shuffle again and then my heart drops.

What if it *is* Reeve and he was drawing me out by pretending to be injured?

*No. Trust your instincts, Paisley.*

I weave between two horses, keeping my eyes on the edge of the ride in case Robert shows his cowardly, concealed face again.

Rain pelts down onto the roof of the ride. At least under here

I'm sheltered from the elements. It means I can see a little better without water hitting my eyes, but visibility beyond the ride is nonexistent.

I will only see him when the rain parts and he steps up.

Slowing my heavy breaths, I crawl forward without a plan. I have to find Reeve and get back to the others . . . but how?

Robert could be lying in wait. Surely his stupid night vision glasses won't allow him to see through rain. There weren't any on his head when I saw him, he was only armed with a knife. There's a chance he doesn't have the glasses with him. The rain isn't supposed to stop until morning.

I shiver as I consider my best move. Staying here isn't an option. Robert knows the direction I ran in, so it's only a matter of time before he looks here. Reeve is hurt and everyone else is relying on me to bring him back.

I can't let them down and I can't abandon Reeve.

With renewed courage, I move forward and crawl under a horse near the edge of the ride.

But I don't get far.

A strong hand clamps down on my ankle and yanks me backward.

I slip and land flat on my face.

A scream tears from my throat as I turn over and kick my legs as hard as I can at the arm of my assailant.

A ski mask. Oh god. This freak is in a ski mask!

That makes it worse somehow. The killer's identity is well hidden.

He blocks my kicks with his forearm and pulls harder. I slide toward him again and know that it's now or never. I either fight like hell or he's going shove his knife into my chest.

With my free foot, I take aim at his kneecap and kick with such force that he stumbles backward and lets go.

In a heartbeat, I roll onto my stomach and launch myself up. I jump off the ride and into the rain without a clue where I'm going.

"Reeve!" I scream.

Robert knows where I am. There's no point in trying to be subtle.

"Reeve! He's here!"

My lungs ache as I gulp oxygen and almost choke on the rain pelting my face.

"Reeve!"

"Paisley?"

I gasp at the sound of his voice and switch direction, hoping it's the right one. His voice was quiet and sounded pained.

"Reeve! Where are you?"

I turn around, looking for Reeve and Robert. But I don't stop because that's suicide.

"Reeve! Answer me!"

"Run!" he shouts, closer now.

I spin toward where the restaurant is. At least, I think I have the general direction right. The ice cream cart has just come into view and is to my left.

"Paisley, he's here somewhere. I think. Run!"

My insides seize. He's definitely here somewhere.

"Where are you?" I shout. "Tell me! Reeve!"

"Run," he rasps. "Just go!"

We're both shouting but he can't be too far away if we can hear each other over the storm. He has to be close.

So does Robert.

"Are you hurt? You sound hurt!" I shout, walking blindly toward his voice.

I'm vaguely aware that I'm shivering, but I'm not cold.

He had me. For a few seconds, Robert had me.

Reeve coughs a reply that I can't understand.

No.

"Reeve!"

Something bad has happened to him. The killer might have gotten him.

Why not kill him too?

I'm quick on my feet, knowing that, one, I need to get to him fast, and two, that a moving target is harder to hit. This asshole already has the advantage of sight.

I stumble around in the dark, my nerves frayed as I try to ignore the fact that the killer might be watching me.

"Just *run,*" Reeve repeats. He sounds out of breath and there's an edge to his voice. Terror. He's petrified and obviously in a lot of pain.

I *have* to find him.

"Reeve? Where are you? Please! Follow my voice." I swipe water from my eyes, but it's replaced a second later.

The next voice I hear isn't the one I'm expecting, and I freeze.

"Paisley? Hey, Pais? Is that you?"

I step forward and a tall frame comes into view. Water runs down his face and makes his hair stick to his forehead.

I sob a sigh of relief. "Liam. Thank god. Where did you come from?"

He smiles and his shoulders slump in relief as he stops inches in front of me. He looks around and then steps closer. "You're okay. You're really okay. I was *so* worried."

"Yeah, fine, but Reeve isn't. We need to find him."

"I know. I've been following him, trying to catch up. He sounds weird."

"Look, Robert is here, so we have to move."

I don't have time to explain what happened, but Liam is suddenly on high alert. He tugs me closer to him and scans the area that we're able to see.

It's only when I open my mouth to protest, tell him that he needs to let go so we can find Reeve, that I hear the others.

Gibson and Malcolm are shouting my name repeatedly, overlapping each other.

I gasp and try to figure out which direction they all are coming from.

They must have heard me shouting for Reeve. But if they want to find me now, they need to shut up so I can reply.

Liam and I turn to follow their voices. I'm walking almost blind when I bump into a body.

I almost lose my balance as my lungs empty. Liam steadies me, still having hold of my arm in a protective manner that warms me from the inside out. Even at a time like this.

It only lasts a second because Reeve's face comes into focus.

My breath catches. He's bleeding.

I step out of Liam's arms. "Oh my god, Reeve! What happened to you?"

Blood is seeping from a head wound. I reach out and place my hand over it, stemming the flow. Blood and water wash down the side of his head.

"Dammit, man," Liam says.

Reeve winces and replies with a shaky voice, "I—I was hit. I woke and . . ."

"It's okay. You're going to be fine. We're hiding in a first-aid hut near here," I tell him. "Liam, we need to get him inside so we can see how bad this is."

We have to get out of the open. Robert could stumble upon us at any second.

"Paisley? Reeve?" It's Gibson. He slaps Liam on the back. "Glad you're here too."

Malcolm is behind him, staring through us all. His hair is plastered to his face and water bounces off his long leather coat.

"Shelter!" I shout. "Come on, we need to get out of here."

They follow me and together we drag a rather lethargic Reeve along with us. Liam and Gibson practically carry him. Gibson's saying things to Reeve, telling him, begging him, to hold on. Ordering him to be okay.

We push forward through the heavy rain, and I lead them to the others.

It's such a relief to find the door to the hut. I pound on it with my fist. "Open up! It's Paisley. I have Reeve, Liam, Malcolm, and Gibson with me. Hurry!"

Harper has the door open the next second. Her jaw goes slack when she sees a bloody Reeve between Gibson and Liam. "God! What happened to you?"

Reeve groans as they move him to the bench. Ava's face is more grossed out than concerned, but she does move so Reeve can sit down.

I crouch in front of him when Liam steps away. "Let me see."

"I'm fine," he replies, but his dark eyes flutter, showing that he's very much not fine.

"You're not, Reeve. Sit still and let me look."

"Jeez, dude," Gibson says, reaching for a first-aid box in the cabinet. "You look terrible."

Reeve laughs and winces. "Thanks, man."

"Does anyone have any water?" I ask. You can't drink from the sink in here.

No one does and it's not like we were prepared for this. Reeve will have to take tablets without it. I would gag too much.

I hand him two pills, which he swallows without question. Then I clean his wound, trying not to let my trembling hands impede my job, and place a bandage over it.

"Dammit, girl," Reeve mutters, half wincing and half laughing.

"I'm sorry," I reply, wringing my hands to try to stop them from shaking.

"Do me a favor: stick to solving crimes, not saving lives."

I roll my eyes. "Maybe you just have a very low pain threshold."

"Ouch. You're freezing."

"We're all freezing."

"Yeah, but you're shaking."

That's more to do with the fact that I almost died. "Robert was out there. I'm okay."

"You saw him?"

Oh, I really saw him. "Yeah. I couldn't see his face. He's still in the mask. Do you feel dizzy?" I ask, stressing over a concussion or a bleed on the brain.

I've had first-aid training at school, but I have no idea about anything internal. His eyes are now focused and he's not slurring his words.

"No dizziness, I promise. I'm fine, Paisley. Don't fuss." He smirks, and he looks so cute even if he's disorientated.

"You were hit over the head, and you don't look good."

It's a lie. He does look good.

"You and Gibson are really keeping me humble tonight."

Gibson slaps him on the shoulder. "Glad you're all right. We never should have split up."

I wholeheartedly agree.

While Gibson and Reeve catch up, I bundle the medical waste and throw it in the trash. Then I clean my hands in the little sink by the cabinet.

"Where were you?" Camilla asks them all. "None of you came back."

So, it's answers time. Now that we're all back together, we need to have this conversation. I also have a lot of questions. One big one for Camilla.

Who is Robert?

Liam leans against the wall and slides down to the floor. "We went to the control room to try to get the Wi-Fi on. Gibson heard noise coming from outside. We weren't sure what it was but we thought it was one of you, so we went out."

We were in the hotel the whole time and they haven't mentioned the lights going out.

Malcolm, Gibson, and Liam split up before the lights went out. Before Reeve was attacked and James was murdered.

# 16

I take a breath to settle my nerves, but it has no effect at all. "We went looking for you down there. It was empty."

Liam frowns. "So it wasn't you who I heard outside?"

"It couldn't have been. We only went outside once we realized you were gone. Robert was out there, though. He chased me but I got away, obviously. It was probably him trying to draw you out."

He leans his head back against the wall. "I'm sorry, Pais. We ran outside because I thought it was you all. It was *him.* I could've gotten everyone killed."

"You didn't know, dude. We all made the decision to go," Gibson says, clapping him on the shoulder.

They were really running after the killer.

I take a seat next to Reeve to keep an eye on him, but I address Liam and Gibson. "Did you see anyone or anything?"

Liam shakes his head. "Malcolm, Gibson, and I split up and

regrouped by the big coaster. We realized that something was wrong when the shouting stopped suddenly at the same time we heard you screaming Reeve's name."

"Was it Reeve you heard shouting?" I ask. "We heard him on the radio and that's when I came outside. Robert was waiting."

Gibson frowns as he thinks about if it was his friend he heard. Wouldn't you know that instantly? We did, but I suppose we weren't in the storm. "It was too hard to make that out. I was too far away to make sense of the voice."

"So, you were all running around separately?" Harper asks as if that's the dumbest thing she's ever heard.

Liam scowls at her. "We were worried one of you was being murdered. We split up to find you faster. Paisley almost died!"

"Knock it off. We're not arguing over this, and we don't need to justify anything to you," Gibson says. "Now that we're all back together, we need . . . Wait, where's James?"

Ava sobs at the sound of his name and curls into a ball in the corner of the room. She puts her head against her knees. Harper is on her in a second, wrapping her arm around her shoulders to comfort her. She's a good friend, but I can tell she's getting annoyed with the dramatics.

Harper doesn't seem to have much time for emotion. She, like me, just wants to figure this out.

There will be plenty of time to process later. Good thing I have money now because therapy is going to be expensive.

"Um. James . . ." I can't say the words, and I can't believe it was only an hour ago that he was murdered. It feels like days already.

"What?" Malcolm clutches a fistful of his gold sweater over his heart. "No. Please don't say . . ."

"He's dead." I tell them what happened back in the lobby, about the electricity cutting out and us finding James dead when it came back on. I leave nothing out.

Which leads to a follow-up question.

Where was Reeve when the lights went out?

Malcolm is the one who asks, and I'm so glad that he did because I don't want to sound like I'm accusing him. Reeve has done nothing but be open and honest with me and try to protect me.

"It's a valid question, Reeve," Malcolm says, following a glare at his accusation. "Where did you go?"

Reeve disappeared without a word and then James had a knife in his chest.

Reeve points to the white bandage taped to his head. "I was *jumped.*" There's a slight red tint to the center of the bandage already.

"When and how?" Malcolm asks. He sounds like he's already decided Reeve is the killer.

Reeve leans forward, his elbows on his legs. "The lights went out. I felt this presence beside me, so I called Paisley's name. I thought it was weird because she was on the other side of me when we came back into the lobby. I knew I had to try to get the power back on, but the next thing I knew, I'm waking up in the kitchen with a pounding headache. The hotel was empty, so I came outside looking for . . . anyone."

All right. That kind of makes sense, but there's something that bothers me. "That must have been the first thud I heard, someone hitting you. But you didn't make a sound."

To that he shrugs one shoulder. "I was out the second he hit me. I remember pain and nothing. Not even hitting the floor. He must've caught me. I don't know."

"He?" I ask.

"Oh, I dunno, Pais," he replies, exasperated. "I assumed because this asshole had to have dragged or carried me to the kitchen, but it could've been anyone with the strength to do that."

"Why would he murder Will and James but only hit you?" Harper asks Reeve. "It doesn't make sense."

"He's not an influencer," I say. The killer was coming for me.

Ava gasps. "You think this person is out for us?"

"I'm not sure. That's just one difference between Reeve and Will and James."

"Well, whatever. It doesn't matter now. I thought we needed to find this cell jammer," Harper says. "Have we forgotten about that?" She looks over at me. "That was a theory, right?"

Of course we haven't forgotten.

Ava snorts. "That could be anywhere, and I don't exactly want to go back outside."

Reeve replies, "No, Harper's right. We know that to cover the range that this jammer's reaching, it can't be a handheld device. Not something you could hide in a plant pot. If we find that . . ."

Gibson points to his friend. "See. He's good with this stuff and he thinks it's our best chance. Even with a brain injury."

"I don't have a brain injury!"

Camilla holds her hand up. "But there's someone out there who is . . . well, you know what they're doing."

It's both an obvious and a good point.

"We have to weigh our options. We can either try to find the jammer and turn it off so we can call for help, or we find somewhere in the hotel to hide out until someone realizes we're not coming back," I say.

On *Monday.*

Malcolm's red face doesn't like either of those options. "There are other boats we could use."

Gibson's shaking his head before Malcolm's even finished speaking. "In this weather? We'd capsize in minutes, hopefully before the boat hits the rocks and kills us. We can fight a person. We can't fight an ocean."

"You think we should fight?" Harper asks. "I do Krav Maga."

"Respect the sea," Reeve mutters to himself, as if he's heard speeches like that from Gibson hundreds of times.

"I'm not drowning in this hell." Ava's words are muffled with sobs. "I just want to go home. I don't want to die."

Malcolm clenches his jaw. She's getting on his nerves too.

"We'll be okay, Ava," I say. "I think our best plan is to wait until daylight so we can find this jammer."

"There's something else we need to discuss," Reeve says. Right before his head lolls to the side, he murmurs, "Robert."

His chin touches his shoulder, and I immediately think he's dead.

What the hell!

"Reeve!" I gasp, leaning over to lift his head.

There's a flurry of activity as everyone crowds him, trying to figure out what's wrong and how we can help.

He groans and lifts his hand to his head, only out for a second. "I'm okay."

"Hey, talk to me, dude," Gibson says, his eyes wide and afraid. "Stay awake. You can't sleep. Wow, you really don't look great."

Reeve chuckles but it sounds a bit like he's underwater. "That'll be because I don't feel good."

"Gibson's right. It's important that you stay awake. Okay?" I tell him.

"You think I'm going to die."

It's an accusation.

I place my hand on his arm in an attempt to comfort him, even though I'm the one who needs the reassurance. "No, I don't. You're going to be okay. We just need to keep you awake."

"He needs water," Gibson says.

Malcolm stands. "I will go and get water."

He sounds far too calm. No hesitation, no sign of being scared that the killer will get him. He's either much braver than I thought or stupid.

"You can't!" Camilla leaps up and grabs his hand. "It's not safe for you. This is your island, so killing you is probably what this person wants. *I'll* go."

She wants to go?

"This is my island, and he is my employee." In a lower tone that we can still all totally hear, he adds, "*We're* the adults and we have to protect them."

Liam mutters, "Protect his reputation, more like."

Ava and Harper nod in agreement.

Liam's only saying what everyone else thinks.

Malcolm hasn't been particularly helpful so far and he's let us lead on figuring this thing out. Now he wants to play the hero. He wants to be able to tell the press that he risked his life to save Reeve.

Damage control for having a murderer on his fancy island.

"All right. We'll go together. There's safety in numbers," Camilla replies.

I half expect him to say no. He should. Camilla is also his employee, but he agrees, and they walk up to the door.

Reeve and I exchange a glance. The slight lift of his brow tells me that he's thinking the same thing. Camilla is just a little too anxious to leave this room. After being an advocate of staying in it.

"Don't open this door to anyone else."

It's quite possibly the dumbest thing Malcolm has ever said.

Liam opens his mouth, but I nudge him before he can speak. He smirks.

"Gibson, keep an eye on them" are his final words as he and Camilla disappear into the torrential rain and pitch-black night.

Gibson is the one to lock the door once they've left.

Now it's just the six of us alone.

Reeve puts his head in his hands, careful not to touch the wound on his head.

"How long do you think they'll be?" Harper asks.

"It's not far, but the weather will slow them down," Gibson replies.

That and the knife-wielding murderer.

"It's weird how easily they both decided to go," I say.

"They're weird," Gibson replies.

Ava shrugs Harper's arm off her shoulder and gets to her feet. "And if they don't come back?"

"You're not helpful, Ava," Gibson snaps.

"I have a right to complain! My friend is dead."

His laughter sounds harsher than it needs to be. "You mean the guy you've known for two days? Grow up."

"How dare you! He's *dead,* Gibson!"

"I know, Ava. We can either sit down and moan about it or we can work on getting out of here."

"We go out there and some psycho kills us!" she screams.

"All right! Stop!" I shout, stepping between them. "This isn't getting us anywhere."

Ava folds her arms over her chest. "You're too calm."

"I'm sorry, would you prefer me to freak out? Because that would be *so* helpful. We have to keep our heads or things are going to get much worse."

Gibson turns around, shaking his head. He's mad at her, but we need to bring this back.

I can tell the others are wondering how much worse it could possibly get. We're already being hunted.

"Let's not argue with each other. It's not going to help."

"I've got a banging headache," Reeve says. "Can we please get back on track?"

"That track being Robert?" Gibson asks. "You said that name before you fainted."

"I didn't faint. I was conscious the whole time."

"Who is Robert?" Gibson asks again.

"We think he's Camilla's son," I say.

Harper says, "Huh."

Liam sits up straighter. "Her *son.* What the hell does he have to do with this?"

"Before Reeve and I went to check the CCTV, I overheard Camilla and Malcolm whispering. She looked scared and said his name a couple times. Malcolm was trying to reassure her."

"That's a bit of a reach," Liam says.

"Did I say I was done?"

"Fine. Go on," Liam says, raising his palms.

"We found Robert in the staff files. His last name is the same as Camilla's and his staff photo had been deleted . . . or was never there in the first place."

"What the hell? Did you check the trash?" Gibson asks.

"Dammit, why didn't we think of that . . . ," Reeve mutters with as much sarcasm as a person can muster.

Gibson rolls his eyes. "All right, you did. What else did you find out?"

"He punched out earlier in the week and hasn't punched in since."

"Doesn't mean he didn't come back," Liam says. "Dude could be running around the island with his weapons."

Reeve points at him. "That's what we were thinking. It doesn't help that we don't know what he looks like, to find him on CCTV. Gibson, do you know a Robert?"

"Not a clue. I don't pay much attention to the male staff."

Gross.

"He was wearing a black ski mask, anyway," I tell them.

Liam's lips curl. "What the hell?"

"Great, so we're not going to know who he is anyway," Gibson replies.

"Hold on," Ava says. "We're stuck on an island with Camilla's murderous son?"

"I think you're supposed to say *allegedly* if you're unsure. Paisley?" Gibson says. He's making jokes and trying to keep this light, but his eyes flash with fear.

"That's what we *think* is going on here," I clarify. "We could be wrong, and to be fair, it doesn't matter who this person is. We've got to figure out how to get help."

Reeve lets out a breath I didn't know he was holding. He expected me to mention the CONVICTIONS folder that had details of his time in juvenile prison.

Maybe I should. They deserve all the information too. But the way Camilla is acting makes me believe that Robert is behind this and not Reeve. Besides, it would be difficult to cause your own head injury and fake the drowsiness.

"Why didn't you confront her when she was here?" Liam asks. "Now she's gone and who knows if they'll come back."

"I'm sorry, that wasn't my priority when we were scared to death and Reeve needed help. My mind was a little frazzled.

We also don't know if she's in on it, but if she is, she might be armed. Well, she would probably be armed. Did you see how fast she wanted to get out of here after Reeve said Robert's name? I thought it was strange when they volunteered to go so fast."

"I don't want that woman anywhere near me. We don't let them back in," Ava says.

"Do you think Malcolm is in on it?" Liam asks. "You said he was reassuring her and he left too, but this is his island. He'd only be screwing himself out of money, and I don't think he'd want that."

"Yeah, I agree. Not only is it bad press but it's also jail time. He did seem to know Robert or at the very least know *of* him, so I don't understand why he would keep quiet."

"When was this, exactly?"

"Right before I went to the security room with Reeve, and you went searching for wire with Gibson."

That must have been a few hours ago. I check my watch and see that the stupid thing is already dead—the battery only lasts half a day now. I wish I'd bought a replacement before coming here.

I stifle a yawn.

"Hey, what are we doing about Robert?" Gibson asks.

"I think it's safe to say that the only people we can trust are in this room," Reeve says. "Therefore, we stick together. Camilla and Malcolm are mixed up in this somehow."

"We don't think Malcolm is, though," Harper cuts in.

Reeve shakes his head. "But he knows that Camilla is worried about Robert, and he didn't say anything to us. That's suspicious as hell."

"Yeah, why wouldn't he mention it?" Liam asks. "That's the part that doesn't make sense. Unless he doesn't think Robert is involved. Maybe Camilla is worried about not being able to contact him or something innocent like that."

"I don't know," Reeve admits. "But do you want to take the chance and let him back in here?"

Liam pushes his tongue into his cheek. "No."

"All right, then. So we all agree we're not letting Malcolm and Camilla anywhere near us?" Gibson asks, standing up and looking at us all individually for confirmation.

No one disagrees with him.

"They should be back by now. It wouldn't take that long even if they've been slowed down by the wind," Reeve says. "That means we're definitely on our own and we need to move."

"Hell no!" Ava shouts.

"They know we're here. There are other places we can go for safety, where we're not sitting ducks."

I've felt like that since we found the boat missing and lost cell service, but I don't argue with Reeve. This whole island is our duck pond. This guy has proven he can get into anywhere.

"Where do you want to go? We have no control at the hotel, not after the light show you guys got earlier," Gibson says. "There's the main restaurant in the park, the Black Tulip. The sun will be up soon, and you can't see in well from the outside."

"Sunrise? What time is it?" I ask.

"Five-ten a.m.," he replies.

We've been running around the island for hours. A lot of the night was spent waiting in the lobby too, I suppose.

"The Black Tulip's also pretty central and has windows from every angle."

We haven't been there yet. Kenna served our meals in the hotel restaurant.

"Plus, we'll be able to get something to eat and drink," Liam says. "I know now is probably not the time, but I'm starving and thirsty. We all need the energy."

"He's right," Reeve says, pushing up to his feet. He's surprisingly steady. "We're not getting through this without anything in our stomachs. Sunrise is in an hour and thirty, and by the sounds of it, the rain has slowed a bit. We'll have as good a view as this sick asshole."

The killer won't be able to sneak up on us. We'll have a better chance moving around the island and making sure we aren't followed.

"I just want to say on the record that I think leaving this building is a *terrible* idea." Ava folds her arms but she's on her feet, ready to follow us. Is she just disagreeing for the sake of it?

I grab a few bandages and stuff them into my pocket.

"I'll re-dress your wound when we reach the restaurant," I tell Reeve.

"It doesn't hurt."

"Yeah, I'd believe that if you didn't wince every time you speak. Grab the pill bottle—you can have some more in a little while."

We're lucky he doesn't need stitches.

Gibson picks up my hammer and turns to us. "Liam, grab that wrench and stay at the back. Everyone else, grab what you can to defend yourself and stay between me and Liam."

"I'm not dead yet," Reeve says, sounding frustrated to be treated like he's not strong enough to defend us.

"Bad joke, bro."

I open the door and Gibson steps half out first. He looks around and says, "Clear. Let's roll."

The sky is starting to lighten, and the clouds are clearing. Heavy rain has eased slightly, but it's still bouncing off the ground.

With my heart in my throat, I follow him into the open and hope we're not being hunted.

# 17

We scurry through the park. Without discussion we all pick a direction to watch. I take our right. Harper our left. Liam keeps looking back. Gibson ahead. Reeve kind of everywhere. Ava . . . at the ground.

Gibson leads us to a park map, and we crouch behind that.

Has he seen something or is this just a rest stop?

"Shhh," Gibson says, as if anyone was thinking about breaking into song. "We're almost there. We'll go in through the back. I have the code for the gate and a key for the door."

"Go," Reeve says, pressing on the wound on his head.

He turns and we're running again. The rain fizzles out and a last gust of wind blows the final cloud out of the way. The sun is slowing, making its way up the horizon as if it's racing to help us out.

The storm is over.

But not for us.

I feel like we're coming into the eye of the hurricane. It always gets worse before it gets better, right?

Robert is unlikely to stop unless we make him. How many more people could be killed before that happens?

Gibson stops dead in front of the gate. I look over my shoulder to see if anyone else is around as he punches in a code.

No black hoodies. No masks. We're safe for now.

We file through the gate and Liam shuts it behind us.

I'm restless until he unlocks the door and we're inside. Once we're out of view from the park, I breathe easier. Not by much, but I'll take it.

Gibson and Liam take a quick sweep of the staff room, bathrooms, kitchen, and dining area. We're alone.

I look longingly at the pantry and coffeepot.

"We're alone here," Gibson says, pushing his way through the revolving door. "We should stay in the kitchen where we can't be seen."

"Then we won't be able to see," I say as we all follow him. "Wasn't the whole point of coming here so we can watch outside without anyone seeing us?"

"It's not light enough yet. Once the sun hits the building, you can't see in at all," he replies. "There's a hatch from the kitchen that we'll be able to look through, but we can't risk him knowing where we are. Let's eat and drink before we play hide-and-seek."

Liam holds up a loaf of bread. "Sandwiches?"

I can't believe we're talking about food right now, but I'm *so* hungry I could eat that bread plain. The entire loaf. By myself.

"I've got sliced ham, cheese, and chicken here," Reeve says as he raids the large refrigerator. "Pickles and sauces are in the pantry."

"You know where everything is," I say, trying to hide the sound of my stomach rumbling. I've not eaten since lunch yesterday. Besides a few chips. It's just one missed meal, really, but it feels like five.

I grab Cokes from the fridge and pass them around while Liam and Gibson make some food. Although I know it's now morning, it feels like it could be any time of the day. It doesn't even feel odd that we're having lunch for breakfast.

Reeve sits on a counter and drains a bottle of water.

We stand around the stainless-steel island to eat a feast of sandwiches and more sandwiches. They must've used two loaves. Reeve looks less drained once he's eaten and had a Coke. The sugar is good for us. It's woken me up a bit.

Reeve catches me smiling his way. No, no, no. I turn my head and contemplate volunteering to be bait for Robert. My cheeks are on fire. He definitely caught me staring at him. This is just great.

I'm such an idiot.

I finish my sandwich while keeping my gaze on my plate. Looking up is a risk—Reeve must think by now that I have a crush on him. I'm probably not the only person in this room who does, so I shouldn't feel embarrassed.

Harper and I clear up the plates once everyone is finished. We slide them into the dishwasher and Gibson throws away the trash. We might be running for our lives, but we still have manners.

Reeve and Liam watch outside through the hatch.

The only person who hasn't done anything to help is Ava. No shock there. I'd be annoyed at the princess thing, but she's completely shaken up, especially since James was killed.

"What now?" Ava asks, leaning against the counter.

I close the dishwasher. "We wait until it's lighter out and then we search for the cell jammer. Once we disable that, we can call for help."

"Why don't we just stay here until Monday?"

"Because that's *tomorrow.* We're not due back until midday tomorrow, so that means no one would even come for us for another thirty hours. You really want to risk that long with a killer?"

She presses her lips together and scowls as if we're doing all this just to irritate her.

"Ava, if you don't want to, you don't have to leave this kitchen until we've called for help and the cops arrive," Harper says.

"Yeah, no one is expecting you to do anything. The rest of us can do this and you can be on the radio, watching out the window. You'll be able to see more."

Her back straightens. "I could be the lookout."

Her eyes catch fire as she realizes this is how she's able to help. Before now I didn't think she even wanted to do anything.

"We'd have an advantage. Finally," I say.

"Advantage to what?" Reeve asks.

I tell him, Gibson, and Liam about our latest plan and they're all in agreement. Ava will be the lookout while we scour the island.

Liam shoves some chips in his mouth as we look at a map of

the park. He's not done eating. Gibson and Reeve split the map in half. Reeve will take Harper and Liam, and I will go with Gibson.

We'll meet back here once we've found the jammer and destroyed it.

"Well." Gibson claps his hands. "Before I try to destroy jammers from murderers, I always have coffee. Who wants?" he says, keeping it light again.

"I'd tell you that was in bad taste, but I actually do need coffee," I reply.

"I make the best coffee," Ava says. "Let me."

Gibson and Reeve share a look of shock that makes me laugh. They didn't expect Ava to lift a finger either. She seems to be trying now.

"She's suddenly grown a conscience," Liam mutters, offering me a chip.

"No thanks."

"I'm going to look for another radio so we've all got one," Reeve says. "Help me out, Gibson. The staff room is the most likely place, but there's a storeroom too."

Right. Our plan only works if we find a way for Ava to be able to contact us. We currently only have two radios.

I sit up on the counter in the far corner. Ava is making coffee and Harper is getting mugs for her.

"Do you believe Reeve's story?" Liam asks, leaping up onto the counter beside me. He's waited until Reeve left the room to come talk to me.

My stomach uncoils, and I realize I've been waiting for someone to ask that. I can't help replaying it over and over again. There was only one thud before Reeve stopped talking to us. Wouldn't there have been two? One when he was hit and the other when he fell to the floor.

Why was he the only one who was attacked and survived? If the killer just wanted the influencers to die, why hit Reeve at all?

He was also arrested and sentenced to time behind bars for violence.

But there is nothing violent about him now. We've been pushed to the limit, and he's been nothing but proactive and protective.

The old Reeve and the new one seem like two completely different people.

"Do you believe him?" Liam presses.

"I want to."

We've become friends, I'd like to think, so I don't want to believe he would hurt us.

"He wasn't here when James was killed." He looks up and I'm not sure who he's checking for because Reeve is still gone. "And so was Gibson."

"So were you."

"All right. Gibson and I were outside, though. Running around on a wild-goose chase looking for what we thought was one of you."

"It's just . . . messy. He would've had to get his psycho nighttime glasses from wherever they were hidden in the dark, murder James, and get out."

"Would he have had time, Paisley?"

"Well . . . Yeah, he would've in theory. It would've been tight and no room for error. I'd say unlikely but not impossible. What side of the park did Gibson go off to when you split up?"

He frowns as he tries to remember. "Um, toward the Helter Skelter." It's not a convincing tone. "That's not millions of miles away from the hotel."

"Right."

"You didn't see if he swooped back toward the hotel?"

"Nah. The rain was coming down hard and the wind was crazy. I would've gone that way if he'd told me to take that side of the island."

"He was the one to tell you where to go?"

If he did, he would've had control of where two of the other men were. Neutralize the main threat first is rule one in homicide.

"No . . . Malcolm was."

There goes that theory.

"Do you think Gibson and Reeve could be working together?" I ask.

"Maybe. What do you know about them? You've been friendly with Reeve."

"They knew each other before working here. Gibson was headhunted for the boat gig, and he got Reeve the job." I sit straighter. "Do you think he got Reeve the job so they could do this?"

"Kill us? I doubt they even knew who we were then," Liam says.

"No, but this doesn't necessarily need to be about us. It's Malcolm. This is his island, and this weekend is about us endorsing the park. You know how many millions Malcolm has sunk into this place? I don't know if he'd go broke if it failed, but it couldn't be good. Yesterday Reeve slipped up when he was talking about Kenna. He used the past tense."

"Did they know Malcolm before here? If this is linked to him, there has to be something making them *that* angry," he says.

His eyes are cautious now. I've taken a leap with a theory, and it's flimsy at best. I have to make sure I don't get ahead of myself.

"Great question, Liam. I have no clue. If we had cell service, we could check it out. We're going to have to go old-school to figure that out."

"Shouldn't we warn people?"

"How do we do that without alerting Reeve and Gibson?" I ask. Ava's already accused just about everyone. How could we get her to stay calm and have a conversation without flat-out telling them we think they're guilty? The last thing we need is to alienate each other. One big group is better than a bunch of smaller ones.

His shoulders sag. "Right. We're just going to have to make sure no one is alone with them."

Jeez, I've been alone with them both. Why didn't they just kill me when we were outside? No one would have seen.

Why would Reeve risk going back to jail? He said that Malcolm was the only one to give him a chance, so it's not like he has a lot of other employment options. Why do this? Something isn't adding up.

"I'm scared, Liam."

"Yeah. So am I. But we can do this. You've been so calm, Paisley. Please don't freak out on me now."

My mom would be going insane right now. She was the first one to tell me to go on this trip. She hoped that meeting beauty, book, game, and movie bloggers would make me ditch the crime and killers.

If I don't get off this island alive, she will never forgive herself.

Thoughts of home and my family refocus me. I have to get through this so next week I can sit on my sofa with my family and eat pizza on family night. Every Thursday is the same. Board games, cards, or movies and three large pizzas.

I can't believe I ever thought that was boring. I would give anything to be curled under a blanket between my parents again.

"Paisley."

"Yeah. I'm fine. This has been said before, but we need a plan."

"Any ideas?"

"Why am I always the ideas person?"

"You spend your life in this world."

"It's hardly the same."

"Psychos are psychos."

"Right." I turn to him. "Hold on. That's right. So, what does this psycho want to achieve? I think it's safe to assume that whoever's doing this is working as a team. Right now, we have Gibson and Reeve, but we shouldn't get too hung up on that because it doesn't fit. And Camilla and Robert, who are much stronger suspects due to her reaction and the fact that Robert is hidden in the staff files."

"Well, the reason this is happening is to ruin Malcolm, right? You said it's probably all about him."

"Yeah, but *why?* You don't do this just because you're jealous that he has an amusement park on an island. This is personal. We should find out if he has any enemies."

"How?"

"By talking to him. He's borderline narcissistic. We start talking about him, particularly about people doubting or hating him, and he'll talk. That's if we can find him."

That's if he's still alive.

Liam clicks his tongue. "You should do that."

"Why me?"

"I'll be there, but I don't want to say the wrong thing. You know this stuff. Give me a gun and put me in the middle of a fight, and I'm up."

I don't know what video game he's talking about, but I do get his point.

This is supposed to be my area of expertise.

Though I think we're forgetting that I'm a seventeen-year-old high school student who vlogs about murder in her spare time.

From the corner of my eye, I see a flash of black outside through the hatch.

At the same time, Gibson bursts through the door. "There's someone outside!"

I jolt, doing a double take, and leap down from the counter.

He's gone now, but I definitely saw him too.

Reeve is right behind Gibson, holding a radio and a bemused look. "Where?"

They're both gone a second later and we race after them, from the kitchen to the dining area.

"He was walking toward the hotel," Gibson says.

I see him again just as he's about to disappear around the corner. Robert.

I tilt my head. In daylight, he seems different. Less scary. Probably because he walked past so he can't know where we currently are.

Both times, he's a flash of black and then gone. Like getting a glimpse of a ghost. This person is *very* real, though.

My stomach sinks to my toes.

"He doesn't know we're here," I say. "Or she."

We can't get wrapped up thinking this could only be a man. I need to remind myself of that.

Gibson's jaw drops, and he points to the empty space the killer just left. "You think that could've been a woman?"

I shrug. "There was nothing identifying whoever it was. It was only a second, but they were average height and dressed in dark colors."

"I'm guessing dude," Liam says.

"Women count for sixteen percent of serial killers. There's nothing right now to suggest that the person out there isn't part of that statistic. We should keep an open mind. Besides, it's probably a team."

"This dude-slash-chick is gone now, so let's get out of here and find that jammer," Reeve says, handing a radio to Ava. "It's on the right channel. Sound is on low, but only contact us if we're about to be stabbed, okay?"

Ava's eyes bulge, but she takes the radio.

Liam hangs back a few steps as we head to the door. "No need to tell Reeve and Gibson that we suspected them now."

Knowing Reeve isn't the killer is a massive relief. I don't want to think about why, since I've only known him for two days.

I nudge his side. "I was thinking the same. Be careful out there."

"You too. Stay close to Gibson."

"I really, really intend to."

Liam flashes me a smile as we leave the restaurant and walk out of the gate.

Gibson clips his radio to his jeans and gives me a nod.

This is it. Time to catch a killer.

# 18

The sun rises higher in the sky. It slowly brightens the park and the warmth touches my arms. Gibson and I walk in the opposite direction from where the killer was going. We stick close to rides, maps, carts, anything that we can hide behind.

Our eyes are everywhere, but I think we're alone for now.

"Hey, Gibson." I say. "Do you think you'd recognize Robert if you saw him?"

He takes a few seconds to think about it, probably trying to put a face to the name in his mind. "Maybe. I've worked the rides a bit in preparation for this week and to cover vacation and sickness, but I'm mostly here for the boat."

"But doesn't that mean you see *everyone*."

He shrugs. "Like I said before, I'm not really focused on the guys. And once I'm on the boat I'm focused on the sea. You don't respect the sea, you drown. The ocean can change in an instant if you're not vigilant."

"Sounds like there's a story there," I say, looking over my shoulder, totally paranoid.

He laughs. "You don't miss a thing, Paisley, do you? There's a story, and it's not a nice one. I've always sailed, my dad and grandpa had boats. When I was fifteen, I was with friends. One guy, Damian, decided to take his boat out. He was reckless, had been as long as I'd known him. We told him not to go because the conditions were unstable. There were reports of a storm, but we weren't sure if it would just miss us. He went anyway when we all went home. The storm hit, and he capsized and drowned."

"I'm sorry. That's awful. Was Reeve with you? He doesn't sail, does he?"

"He was there, but he's never been interested in sailing."

I look around, high and low as we walk. "He told me about what happened. The night of the fight."

"What?" Gibson grabs my wrist. "He told you that?"

"Uh, yeah."

Letting me go, he says, "He doesn't tell anyone who doesn't need to know. What happened?"

"I saw the folder in the staff files when we were looking for Robert. It was a folder that had his conviction in it."

Gibson grinds his teeth. "That whole thing was total bullshit. He was just trying to stop this asshole from punching me again."

"Did you want to press charges against him? Reeve said the other guy threw the first punch."

Gibson frowns and his reply comes just a second too late.

"The cops weren't interested in our side. Not when the punk's dad was loaded."

Which part is he lying about? The first punch or pressing charges?

"Reeve's worked hard to get his life on track since he got out. He's a good guy, Paisley. He wouldn't hurt anyone who wasn't trying to hurt him or someone he cares about."

"Yeah, that's what made it so hard to think he was behind this."

"Wait. You suspected him?"

Me and my big mouth. "It crossed my mind when I saw his conviction, before he explained." It's a white lie. I don't want us to turn on each other.

Gibson gives that a second's thought and then seems to understand that it's pretty reasonable. "I trust him with my life," he tells me, and I believe him wholeheartedly.

He would if Reeve has stepped in to stop some guy beating him up . . . and ended up doing time for it. Gibson must feel like he owes a lot to Reeve.

He got him the job, after all.

"You see anything yet?" he asks.

"Nope. It's supposed to be obvious too. How come we never saw it? I have hours of footage from the island. I took selfies with just about everything. I never saw the jammer."

"We weren't looking. It'll be a black box, easily mistaken for a speaker," he says.

I glance around the park and gasp. Grabbing Gibson's arm, I tug him closer and point with my other hand. "There!"

A figure is in the distance, walking away from us.

"Shit!" Gibson bundles me behind a block of toilets. "I think it's a guy. Look at the shoulders."

I crouch down and peer around the corner. Yup, broad shoulders. Those can't be hidden. Gibson follows my lead from above me. It's awkward—my neck is bent at a weird angle and I'm kind of being crushed a little, but I can't complain about that.

"What the . . . ," he mutters. "He's not leaving."

The killer walks in circles around a food cart and picnic tables. We watch him do that three times.

"Why is he hanging around here rather than off killing people?" he whispers.

"Because there's something or someone here that he needs." I scan the area close to him and finally see it. "Gibson, look over by that tree, just poking out from the trash can beside it. . . ."

I smile up at him and feel a glimmer of hope for the first time since I found Will's body. I'm even drying off.

"The jammer. Hell yeah," he whispers in reply. "Nice one, Paisley."

"That's why he's hanging out here. He's guarding it."

"He wants to stop us from getting to it. So, he knows our plan. Not that it would've been too hard to guess."

"No, it was obvious that we needed to get cell service back. We have to get over there, Gibson."

"How? The maniac is on guard."

I retie my hair into a tight ponytail, getting all of the frizzy loose strands out of my way. "He's on guard because he knows that's what we're out here looking for. If one of our groups finds it, then this is over, and he can't be in more than one place at a time. Though . . . I thought this was a team. Where's his evil little partner?"

"Camilla is probably off making a hot cocoa for her mini freak. Maybe one is hunting and the other defending."

The thought sends an ice-cold chill down my spine.

Could Camilla really be a killer too? It was easier to think of her as a silent partner. Hiding in the shadows, cheering her son as he . . . does whatever he's doing. But to think of her getting her hands dirty turns my stomach.

Could that be what was different about the person I saw from the restaurant? I thought it was just because it was light and we were safe. But now that I think about it, maybe it's because it was another person.

I didn't see them long enough to figure out if there was a height or size difference.

"If I was doing this, I'd have one playing offense and the other defense."

"Are you confessing, Paisley?"

"Of course I'm not! Let's focus on our next move. How do we get past him and break that jammer?"

Gibson jerks his head my direction. "I could make a run for it. Distract him while you go take care of the jammer."

"No way, he might kill you! The dude has a *knife* and my hammer is in the restaurant."

Stupid mistake leaving that behind.

"Well, he's not moving without a distraction."

"Agreed. But does that have to be one of us?" I ask.

"No, it has to be me. There's no way I'm letting you do it."

"Not *letting* me?"

I feel his eyes roll. "You can smash the patriarchy later, Paisley. I'm going to do a bad job of hiding while I run past him. When he starts to chase me, you go for the jammer. Make sure it can't be used again."

"Gibson!" I grab his wrist.

"We have to. Break it and find someplace to hide until the coast is clear. Then make your way back to the hotel, charge your phone, and call for help. Do not trust Malcolm or Camilla if you see them. I'll meet you there when I can."

"I—I . . . Yeah, okay."

Our whole conversation is in frantic whispers while we watch the profile of a madman. I'm not at all sure about this but we have to try. There's a lot at risk.

"Are you ready, Pais—"

I nudge him to shut him up as someone else has appeared. "Look! What the . . . Oh god."

Camilla. What the hell is she doing?

She's walking *toward* him with her palms raised in surrender.

Gibson gasps. "Shit. It really is her and her son."

"Robert," I whisper. We're about to witness this killing team interact. There's always a dominant and a submissive. It's fascinating in a way that terrifies me to my very core.

"Why would she be holding her hands up?"

"Who cares."

"I do," I reply, and take a step forward.

I don't get any farther than that because Gibson scoops me up like I weigh nothing. "No way!"

I'm placed back on my feet, and we crouch.

"We can't hear them from here. Don't you want to know?" I ask.

"Are you crazy? It's too risky. We don't know what's going to happen yet. Just wait and lip-read. You seem to be good at that."

Lip-reading isn't hard when it's only one word. I'm not sure I can do a whole conversation.

I grip Gibson's arm tight as Camilla gets closer. He doesn't complain, but it wouldn't surprise me if I'm cutting off his circulation.

My eyes bulge as the man watches her approach. He's so still he doesn't look real.

"Gibson, is she . . . Yeah, she is. They're talking."

"God, she's in on it, Paisley. This is proof."

"Yeah," I whisper, my heart in my stomach. A mother-and-son killing team.

Why?

How could she? She was supposed to be one of us. It was one thing when her involvement was just a theory, but now that it's real, the deception hits me like a truck.

"No one knows what Robert looks like."

"Maybe he'll take the mask off to talk to her," I reply.

Gibson is about to respond when Robert jabs the knife into Camilla's gut. I let out a scream that is masked by her own. Gibson's hand clamps over my mouth. He smells like mud and sweat.

"Shhh. Shhh!" he whispers into my ear, dropping his hand. "Shhh."

Camilla drops to her knees, staring up at the man with wide, horrified eyes.

A look of betrayal.

Her son did that.

He bends over her, and his arm moves with such rapid succession that I almost miss him doing it. He stabs her again and again.

I sob silently and squeeze my lips together so I don't vomit.

"Shhh," Gibson whispers like you would to a small child.

I cling to him and hope that he doesn't let go. If he does, I might fall apart.

Robert stands tall and watches as Camilla's blood drips off the blade and onto the ground.

Camilla falls again, curling onto her side. She cries out, but her voice is too jumbled for me to make out what she's saying.

I go to take a step, but Gibson pulls me back.

"What are you doing? We have to help her!" I say.

"She's dead." He looks at me like I've suddenly lost my mind. "Plus, didn't we just agree that she was in on this?"

"If she was working with him, why would he kill her, Gibson?"

"Look."

Camilla is talking from the ground. Spluttering. Her mouth opens wider than usual as she tries to shout, but we hear no noise.

"What's she saying?" he asks.

"It seems rhythmic. Like she's saying the same thing over and over. Two syllables, I think," I reply. "Robert."

"Makes sense. Her demon spawn. This is what happens when you don't tell your kids murder is wrong."

His comment is lighthearted and much needed right now because my stomach is churning.

I tug on his sleeve. "We have to get the others. I can't stay here."

He looks around and opens his mouth as if he's about to tell me he has a great plan. Then he closes it again.

"Gibson?"

"Right. The others were headed east, but it's been a while now so let's head south. They're doing a loop, so we should eventually run into them."

"Will we still be able to see *him*?" I ask.

"I hope not. But there's a chance he'll be able to see us."

I slump with dread. "But I don't want to lose him. If we don't know where he is . . ."

He grabs my hand and pulls me along. "Don't let go."

The sun beats down on us, stinging my burnt shoulders despite it being so early. It's a nice contrast to last night, when I was cool and wet. It's the type of day with fresh, clean sea air and bright sunlight that makes you want to chill outside. Today is going to be hot.

I should be at a pool with my friends, trying to get the attention of my bestie's gorgeous older brother.

I shouldn't be here. My dad was right. This was a stupid idea.

Gibson and I sprint around the corner of the Black Tulip. I have to swipe tears and blink rapidly to clear my watery vision.

A sharp pain in my side slows me down and Gibson has to pull me along so I can keep up. He doesn't complain about basically carrying me.

All I want to do is fall apart.

The look on Camilla's face. The devastation of knowing someone she loves has hurt her.

Gibson doesn't let go of my hand. I'm holding so tight it's probably impossible anyway. We move quickly, hiding behind fairground stalls, trees, shrubs, and ride booths.

"Paisley, come on," he says when I trip and stumble.

"Sorry." I'm hollow. "She's d-dead."

I saw a person murdered in front of me. Her blood was everywhere.

It's so much worse than finding Will and James dead.

I watched her take her last breath.

Gibson ignores me as we race toward the hotel side of the island. We're both out of breath, but we don't stop.

It feels so wrong to not know where the killer is. He could be following us.

I look over my shoulder and let Gibson lead me. I've pushed past the stitch in my side, determined not to be the weak link and get him killed.

"Down!" With a gasp, I turn and jump on him.

We crash to the ground, and I land on his back.

"Where?" is all he asks.

I shuffle off him and we duck behind a tree as the killer strolls west. I press myself into Gibson's side and he shrinks too. We try to make ourselves as small as possible.

I clamp my mouth shut to stop a cry from escaping.

Please, just let us get away.

I listen carefully. Waves gently crash against the island. My heartbeat's in overdrive. No footsteps.

"He didn't see us," I say, peering around the tree. "He's gone. Where did he go?"

Gibson sneaks a look. "I don't know. He disappeared fast. Down to the jetty, maybe."

"Why? There aren't any more boats to steal," I say.

He shrugs.

"Do you think we should go for the jammer?"

"Yeah, but we have to warn the others."

"I think they know there's a killer on the loose by now."

He laughs. "We sort of *know* where he is, though, and I don't want to go back that way yet. Come on."

Gripping my hand, he leaps up. I'm on my feet a heartbeat later and this time, I run beside him.

Behind us, I hear a scraping sound, like metal on metal.

# 19

"What's that?" I pant as we sprint past rides and posters with promises of epic times. I can hear him everywhere. He might as well be right beside us. In front of us. Behind us. The moment we lost sight of him, I lost my head.

Ignoring the sharp digging in my side is getting almost impossible again, but I can't stop. I've been pushing through, and I have to keep doing that.

Stopping is death.

"He's not behind us," Gibson says, pushing me toward the entrance of a building. "Hide in here."

He unlocks the haunted house, fumbling as he tries to do it as fast as possible. The second the door gives, we stumble inside and crouch below the window.

"Did he see us?" I ask, peering up over the sill and trying to catch my breath.

I was too slow back there and it put Gibson at risk. I resolve to do better so I'm not holding anyone back.

Gibson shakes his head. "I don't think so, but we can't be certain. We ran pretty quickly, so we would've made a noise."

"Okay. Well, it's a good sign that he didn't run after us. How long should we stay in here for?"

I turn around, and that's when I see three masked figures.

My heart skips a full beat.

"Gibson, hiding in here is a *terrible* idea."

"We'll be fine. He's not in here."

"He just killed his *mom,* and he's going to kill all of us too."

"Paisley, now is not the time for a breakdown. We— *Dammit!* Get up."

"What?"

Robert's masked head peeks over the top of the seats of a pendulum ride.

Gibson grabs my arm and yanks me roughly to my feet. "He's seen us. Run!"

I get another glimpse out of the window of the masked killer as I prepare to run. We make eye contact for a fraction of a second and I almost lose my breakfast.

I fly after Gibson. We turn right and we're in the room with all the goblins, and I feel like we've made another mistake. The room is almost completely filled with them, like being in the New York subway at rush hour.

We push past, weaving in and out of hideous *Lord of the Rings*–style goblins.

I bump into one that's the height of a seven-year-old and almost fall to the ground. My ankle rolls underneath me. There's a sharp pain as I stumble, but it's gone quickly. That or the adrenaline and terror are masking the injury.

Whatever it is, I'll take it.

Gibson is a good five strides in front now. He didn't notice me stumble.

The haunted house gets darker the deeper you go into it. Not all rooms have windows. Why is he taking us this way?

"Paisley!" he shouts, bursting through a door and hoping I'll follow.

I ignore everything that isn't a door or Gibson. Or at least, I try to.

Out of the corner of my eye, I see something taller and straighter than the goblins. Clad in back with a mask. The killer is in the room, between me and the door, so I can't follow Gibson.

We have to get out of here.

Panic grips my throat. I hang right and sweep the ripped curtain out of my way and get only a second to take in my surroundings.

I've only been in the haunted house once, and I've made a huge mistake.

This is the room that scared me the most.

I'm in the serial killer room. Malcolm's horrible idea for a theme park attraction.

I'm breathing too hard. I slow it down and try to make out the wax figures in relative darkness. *Don't let him near you!*

H. H. Holmes, Ted Bundy, Jeffrey Dahmer, Richard Ramirez, Harold Shipman, a character in a black cloak and top hat who I'm assuming is supposed to be Jack the Ripper, Peter Sutcliffe, and Fred and Rose West, to name a few. I've watched documentaries and read articles on all of them.

They're all brandishing the weapons they used to murder their victims.

In this house every room plays to the haunted theme—ghost and ghouls and fantasy—except this one.

Here the monsters were human.

Just like the man trying to find me.

I press my lips together and breathe evenly through my nose. I'm still making too much noise. Robert will hear me. The curtain is whipped to the side, and he joins me in the room.

Dammit. I crouch down beside Ted Bundy's legs, wishing I was anywhere else than in this serial killer hall of fame. Is Robert looking to join them? Get his own wax model up on the wall?

He steps deeper into the room.

A ski mask was a poor choice for a hot island, and that has to be about the dumbest thing I could focus on right now.

When I get out of here, I'll need to tell the cops everything. So I take in every detail. From the confident walk, to the subtle tilt of his head as he tries to hear where his victims are, to the clunky thud of his shoes.

They didn't sound that loud outside.

The door is on the wall opposite where I'm currently hiding. There are three serial killers between me and it.

Four if you count Robert creeping closer. It's dark enough that I could duck behind each one and hide.

He moves slowly as though he knows that I'm in here

somewhere. He's no longer running to catch his prey. He's steady, calculated, a lion right before it pounces.

I clench my jaw.

He's *not* going to win.

Hate and fear swirl in my stomach in equal measure. They give me the courage that I need. This asshole isn't killing me.

I'll fight for my life, and I'll win.

I wait until he's facing the other way and crawl from one sick murderer to the next. Now it's Rose West I'm hiding behind. My skin itches at the thought of the horror the real people behind this attraction have caused.

Robert spins around, scanning the area I just left.

*You're not getting me, jackass.*

Curling down smaller, I watch as he tries to find me. I'm here alone without a weapon. Gibson will know that I'm not with him anymore. He would either come to find me or keep running. I wouldn't blame him if he gets the hell out of here.

We should have known that Robert was coming after us. There's a clear view of the haunted house from the Black Tulip.

Ava missed it. What was more important than being lookout?

When Robert begins to walk back toward me, I slide silently around Rose West's legs.

I clench my hands into fists, so angry with this guy I could combust on the spot. I wish I could leap up and take him down. All my life I thought I would be the one helping people. When I was a kid, I wanted to be a doctor. When I started reporting and vlogging about crime, I thought I would be a detective.

Now I think I could become one of them.

I think I could kill.

It's a realization that I'm not at all comfortable with.

If I had a weapon, I would use it right now.

Thankfully, self-preservation kicks in and I push my hatred to the side. The next wax murderer who's going to hide me is Jeffrey Dahmer. A guy who dismembered his victims after he killed them.

Probably not a good omen.

I stand up, keeping right behind Dahmer, and peer over his shoulder.

Robert is creeping along the wall, his hand brushing slowly over each killer as he walks. Does he admire these people?

The air is so thick I could choke on it.

Does he feel it too?

I'm closer to the door now, and Robert is behind me. I itch to run, to get the hell out of here as quickly as I can, but it'd be smarter to leave without him knowing where I am.

So instead of running, I back up a step. Then another and another. Now I'm in the open, but I have no choice. There's a larger gap between Dahmer and the next creep.

Crouching lower, I shuffle silently to the side and drop behind Harold Shipman's doctor's chair.

The most prolific serial killer, with two hundred and eighteen known victims.

What was Malcolm thinking when he had this room made?

On the floor, I back up again, using my hands and feet to move toward the door behind me. I look over my shoulder and see it a second too late.

I've bumped into a dismembered leg leaning against the wall. It's fixed, so it doesn't fall, but it does make a thud as I hit it.

Robert spins around. My breath catches in my throat as he looks me dead in the eyes. I want to take a good look, to see if I recognize him, but the shock and fear of being caught takes over everything else.

Shoving myself to my feet, I run to the door and yank it open.

I scream so loud I'm probably heard by the entire island. Kenna is lying behind the door, in the room with all the ghosts. Her throat has been slit. A halo of blood lies under her head.

Robert closes in on me, weaving around killers as he makes his way toward me. Pressing my fist to my mouth to stop myself from throwing up, I jump over Kenna's dead body and run.

Ghosts made of fabric—some sheer, some more substantial—fill the room, hanging at different lengths on hooks. If the power was turned on in here, ghosts would be flying around the room from all angles.

Robert's heavy footsteps echo through the narrow room. I run up a set of stairs, knowing that I can get back down the other side of the building. There are four sets of stairs leading to the second floor in the house. If I remember correctly, I'm not too far from another one.

I slide into a small nook in the wall, and a gargoyle jumps out. Its long pointy nose gets tangled in my ponytail.

Somehow, I've managed to lose Robert. He would've seen me go up the stairs, so that tells me he doesn't want to follow me up here. At least, not now.

Bile hits the back of my throat as my mind replays the image of Kenna's dead body on a loop.

Footsteps along the hall thud toward me. Winching, I push myself deeper into the corner and turn my feet in to the wall.

"Paisley?"

That's Gibson.

The only problem is that his voice is coming in the opposite direction from the footsteps.

I want so badly to call out for him, but Robert is closing in on me.

I hold my breath.

Robert walks past. He looks between two doors on either side of the hallway. He either doesn't know these alcoves exist or he doesn't think a person can fit into one with whatever character pops out.

I barely fit.

When he opens one door and walks inside, I quietly suck in a breath of air and tiptoe back down the stairs, looking over my shoulder just in case. I reach the bottom when I hear Gibson call my name again.

He also alerts Robert. Overhead, his heavy footsteps are already on the stairs.

It's all or nothing at this point.

I swallow my fear.

"Gibson!" I shout, running back through the rooms I've just been in.

"Paisley! Outside!"

I turn on my heel, stumble into a wax figure again, and run toward the exit.

Ahead of me is the glow of the exit sign above the door. Tears run down my face as I sprint toward it. "Gibson!"

I reach for the door, and that's when I'm grabbed from behind. A large hand covers my mouth.

# 20

I scream into a thick leather glove and thrash my body from side to side in a desperate attempt to get him to release his grip.

Robert lifts me off the ground with ease, squeezing my chest so tight it's hard to breathe.

Panicked, I kick the heel of my Converse hard into his shins. He's prepared for violence and doesn't flinch as I repeatedly kick out. He has both of my hands pinned to my sides with one arm. He's so damn strong I don't stand a chance.

My heart stops when I realize that it's not working. I'm not hurting him.

I always thought adrenaline would kick in and I would be able to get away, but I can't move in his death grip.

He's too strong.

I scream until my throat is raw, but I don't make much sound against his hand. I wriggle my body in the hope that I'll make it too difficult for him to keep hold of me.

This is *not* how I'm dying.

Fi*ght,* I order myself.

I need to think, but the pain in my chest intensifies. If he squeezes me any harder, he'll crack a rib.

Then I remember that he's armed, and the knife must be on him somewhere. My arms are stuck by his thighs. So that he doesn't realize what I'm doing, I continue to wriggle in his grasp, but at the same time I use my arms to pat around his pockets.

His trousers are thick, and there's something odd about them that I just can't place.

*Hurry up!* My vision blurs, and just when I think I'm losing, I finally feel what I'm searching for. A handle.

A flicker of hope spurs me on.

Bending my back, I lift my shoulder, and he chuckles in my ear. The sound is menacing, devoid of emotion, and sick. But it's working. He thinks I'm fruitlessly trying to get away. He thinks he's winning.

If your escape isn't working, try something else. I'm doing just that.

"Gibson!" My scream is muffled, but there's a chance he will hear the noise.

I can't breathe.

Robert goes to walk forward, but he suddenly realizes what I'm doing and halts. Probably because he feels me draw the knife out of the holder.

I hear his gasp as I grip the knife and twist my arm to stab him in the leg. He lets go and leaps back as the blade comes into contact with the thick fabric of his cargo trousers.

The sound of a light tear in the material makes me shrink in terror. No! I didn't get him. Out of the corner of my eye, I see someone else, someone wearing dark clothing. It's just a flash of black and then gone as if I've imagined it . . . or seen a ghost.

I don't have time to figure it out because Robert puffs his chest out.

I've not frightened him with the knife. All I've done is piss him off.

I spin around and point the knife toward his cowardly face. "Back up, asshole!"

Now *I'm* the one who's armed. And I'm *more* pissed off.

His eyes crinkle as if he's smiling. This is fun to him, a game. Well, I'm going to give him one hell of a fight.

It's kill or be killed, and I don't plan on dying today. I give myself permission to do whatever is necessary to survive.

My heart beats a new rhythm, and in one swift movement, I launch myself forward, aiming the knife at his gut.

I hear his gasp through the small mouth hole cut from the black material. He leaps back, raising his hands into the air and arching his back like a cat. I miss.

For a millisecond I hesitate. I almost stabbed him then. There's no going back: either he dies, or we all do.

It's now or never.

I grip the knife harder, grit my teeth, and run forward.

But he's ready for me. He swings his fist at my head. With

a thud, I fall into the wall. Pain slices through my skull and the world turns into a black smudge.

I blink to focus. When I look up the next second, Robert is gone and the knife I'm holding is buried in a fake torso.

"Paisley! Paisley!"

Gibson runs toward me. He drops to his knees and holds my cheeks in his palms. "God. What the hell happened? Are you okay?"

"He was here. Kenna's dead. She's dead. Her throat . . . He had me and . . ."

He swears, then ducks his head. "I can't believe this."

"He sliced her throat, Gibson."

He swears again and then shakes his head. "Okay. All right. You're safe now. I've got you." He checks me all over, seeing if I'm injured. "You're okay. You're not hurt."

No, I'm not safe. Who's he trying to convince? None of us is safe here.

He strokes my cheek. "Hey. Breathe. What happened?"

"I have his knife. I tried to use it, but he was too fast. He punched me hard, and I fell. He's so strong, Gibson. If I hadn't grabbed his weapon, he would've killed me."

I press my hands to my sore ribs and feel an ache in my chest. There's no searing pain, so I don't think I've broken a rib.

Gibson spins, looking over his shoulder and into every corner and hiding spot in the serial killer room. Robert could easily be in here as it's so dark, but I don't think he is anymore.

"He's gone. He was probably shaken up that I was able to

escape from him and take his weapon. I don't think he expects any of us to be able to do that. It must have damaged his ego. He'll regroup."

"I'm so sorry I lost you. I turned around and you were just gone. I looked, but . . ."

"It's okay. He was in the room, between you and the door. There was no choice. I had to go the other way."

"You're okay now, but we have to get out of . . . What's that?"

I hear it too. A mechanical click. Then another.

The haunted house bursts to life. A creepy jingle blasts from the speakers and the serial killers begin to move. Low light flashes, some at the body parts covering the walls, some focused on weapons, and some illuminating the evil faces of killers.

"Hell no."

"Gibson," I say, gripping his shirt.

This house is about to let ghosts, goblins, and serial killers leap out at us in every room. One time it might be Robert and we won't see him coming.

We should not be in here.

Gibson's face falls and his sudden loss of confidence is petrifying.

I need him to believe that we're getting out of this.

"Go," he says. "Go." This time he grabs my hand tight and we run together.

We don't have time to look. The characters that are now alive move and scream and jump at us, but we don't slow.

The ghosts are a blur, white flashes zooming all around us. I don't remember them zooming around that fast yesterday.

Some of them have faces, but I don't look up.

I swallow the urge to scream.

Gibson shoves the door open, and we pour into the daylight. "We're okay," he says. "You said he punched you."

"I'm fine," I reply. "How many exits are there here? He could be coming from anywhere. We have to get to that jammer."

"Breathe." Still holding my hand, he backs up and tries to find the best way to go.

"Ava," I say. "Where is she? She didn't warn us!"

She would have . . . unless he got to her.

He knows exactly what I'm thinking and pulls his radio out of his pocket.

"Ava, it's Gibson, come in."

I chew on another nail as we wait for her reply.

"Ava?"

"He killed her," I say. "We need to get over there."

"Whoa, we don't know that. The jammer is the most important thing right now. The killer was just with us, so if Ava didn't warn us because she's dead, there's nothing we can do."

"We should still check!"

He starts running, taking me along with him. We're going in the opposite direction of the restaurant where Ava is. Hopefully still safe.

"We will, but for now we need to destroy the jammer."

"There!" I say, spotting Harper dashing into the hotel. I put the brakes on, and Gibson almost pulls me to the ground.

We're all due to meet there in ten minutes, but I guess they're early.

"Paisley, we know where the jammer is. We'd be crazy to not go for it."

"We also know where the killer is. I didn't see anyone with Harper. We can't leave her alone. I've escaped twice now. He'll make sure he doesn't miss again."

Gibson groans, relenting. "We'll meet up with the others and all go to the jammer now that we know where it is."

My feet hit the ground heavily as we run without trying to hide ourselves now. We've officially reached the hysterical part of the weekend. It's not a fun place to be.

"Harper!" I shout when Gibson and I enter the lobby.

She turns around, alone, and runs toward me. "Oh my god! Paisley, I'm so happy to see you."

Harper doesn't seem like the hugging type, but she squeezes me for a good five seconds. Her breathing is erratic as if she's ran a marathon. "You're alive. Gibson's alive."

"So are you. Are you alone?" I ask.

She stands back and nods, teary-eyed. Then she swallows. "I'm sorry. I was *so* scared. I just ran and ran. I . . . I . . ."

Gibson steps between us, his face drained of color. "Where's Reeve? Is he . . . ? Harper?"

"He's fine. I don't know. I think he's fine, at least. We got split up, but the last time I saw them, he was alive."

"Why did you split up?"

"We heard a noise coming from inside the haunted house. Reeve and Liam went inside."

Gibson and I exchange a look. They heard *us* in the haunted house.

"They went inside?"

Nodding, she wraps her arms around her stomach. "Yeah. I was supposed to be a lookout. If I saw the killer, I was supposed to throw rocks, so he thought we were near the coffee cart. But I couldn't see or hear them. Then I heard noises coming from around the back, then running and I got... scared. I thought the killer might be outside chasing them, so I ran too. The hotel was closer to me. From there I was going to go back to the restaurant. I'm sorry."

"You don't need to be sorry. Did you hear anything from Ava?"

She shakes her head. "No. Nothing at all."

"Dammit. I don't like that, Gibson. No one's heard from her. We need to go see."

Harper gasps. "You think she's dead?"

"She didn't warn us and she's not replying. I know the outcome won't change if she's already dead, but we have to go to her."

So many people have died already.

We need to find Malcolm too. He was last with Camilla. At some point she went out to find her son and left him behind.

The sun is overhead now. My watch is dead, but it must be somewhere around midday. We've still got a full day before anyone would realize we're missing. I can't imagine my parents would let another twenty-four hours go by without hearing from me and think everything is okay.

They will surely try to contact the island and then raise the alarm.

We run out of the hotel and toward the Black Tulip.

I let Gibson and Harper go in first because I can't discover another body. I've seen enough.

"Ava!" Harper calls, looking around the dining area.

Gibson goes into the kitchen.

I should help them and check out the bathrooms. Bile rises in my throat as I step deeper into the room.

My feet are heavy.

Leaving it up to Harper and Gibson would make me a coward again. I vowed to not let that happen.

So I take a breath and force myself to move around the restaurant.

Outside it's bright and quiet. As I'm glancing around, I see someone. Crouching down, I watch the dark figure, a dot on the horizon, walk past a roller coaster.

My fists curl beside my thighs.

When he's gone, I do a double take.

Wait.

Was he wearing a hoodie or a long coat?

"She's here!" Gibson shouts.

I spin around in the direction of Gibson's voice.

Is she dead or alive?

Harper moves over to me while I totally freeze up as if my muscles have turned to stone.

Gibson emerges from the kitchen, scowling, as he drags Ava along. She shuffles her feet, clings to the radio, and stares down at her pink Converse.

I release a breath. She's alive.

"She was hiding," Gibson spits. "While we were searching for the jammer, watching Camilla getting stabbed, finding Kenna's dead body, and being attacked, she was hiding in a cupboard!"

What?

He's thoroughly disgusted with her.

"I was *scared*!" she shouts.

"Camilla and Kenna are dead?" Harper asks.

I nod. "Robert stabbed Camilla. I just saw him outside, but he's over by the big roller coaster, so we're okay for a bit."

"At least we know where he is," Gibson replies.

"Yeah. Thing is, I could only really see the top half of him."

"Why's that a problem?"

"It was only a couple of seconds, but I don't recall seeing a hood."

Harper frowns. "So?"

"So I don't know if it's Robert in a hoodie or Malcolm in his long coat."

Groaning, Gibson shakes his head. "My brain's going to explode, Pais. Stop adding suspects."

I laugh because he sounds so ridiculous.

"Sorry," I say, and it's a rare lighthearted moment that actually makes me smile.

"I'm sorry. Can we back up a few minutes?" Harper asks. "Robert killed Camilla, who is his mom. We're sure on that?"

"They were talking before he stabbed her. They have the same last name, but we can't be sure they're mother and son. She definitely knew him, looked like she was trying to reason with him. You can't reason with a psychopath, and she found that out a little too late."

"This is *way* too much," Ava says.

"What happened to you? When we left, you were happy to

find something you could do to help," I say. "We needed those warnings. Reeve and Liam still do."

She bows her head lower, refusing to meet our eyes. Shame isn't something I thought she could feel.

Gibson scoffs. "Forget about her for now. We've got to get Reeve."

"And Liam," I add.

"They're not together. Well, they weren't when I left them, anyway," Harper says.

Gibson stiffens. "You said they both went into the house."

"They did. I saw them part ways just before the door closed."

I can't judge them too harshly, because Gibson and I got split up.

"Why would they do that?" I ask.

Harper shrugs. "There was a lot of noise in there. I couldn't figure out where it was coming from, so I guess they couldn't either."

Gibson scrubs his hands over his head. "Okay. First, we go for the jammer. Then we go for Reeve and Liam."

That's not at all what I expected him to say.

"You don't want to get Reeve first?"

He drops his arms by his legs. "Yes, I want to, but our best chance is to get a signal, Paisley. I know my battery is almost out. How's yours doing?"

"Gone."

"I don't even have mine, and Ava's died last night," Harper says. "We should get to the jammer, like Gibson says. We'll get the others after."

"They might even be there," Ava says.

"Shut up!" Gibson snaps. He takes a breath and puts a bit more distance between himself and Ava. "Let's go."

I shelter my eyes with my hand as we go back outside. The hairs on my neck stand on end even though I don't see anyone creeping around.

"Anyone else feel like we're being watched?" I mutter as we move swiftly, four pairs of eyes searching for one man. He could easily have gotten over here from where I saw him by the coaster.

"Don't go there," Harper says.

I don't want to go there.

She sticks close to me and lets Ava hold her arm. We haven't heard a thing from Ava since she tried to defend her actions in the restaurant.

I can't say I was all that surprised that she hid, but somehow it still feels like a betrayal.

Then again, is it right to expect her to risk her life for ours?

We all get to make that choice.

"No!" Gibson shouts.

I look around his shoulder and immediately see why he's so angry.

The jammer is gone, leaving behind a squished patch of grass.

"We're always one step behind!" I snap at the same time Ava cries out.

"He . . ." Before she can finish her sentence, she's running.

Robert is closing in on us. This time he has a goddamn *sword* from the lobby.

"Run!" Harper screams.

We sprint after Ava and almost instantly the killer starts to run too.

"We're . . . getting farther from . . . jammer," I pant. My lungs scream for more oxygen. I gulp air and push harder. Robert came from the opposite direction of where we're headed. He likely came back to the jammer from the haunted house and moved it.

"Range," I say as we fly across the park.

"What?" Gibson's reply is a breathy scramble.

There's no time to reply, though, as we run through the gate and follow Ava toward the cliff and the service jetty.

I run down the stairs and that's when I realize our mistake.

"The rowboats," Gibson says. He looks around as if they've just gone for a nice little sail. "They're gone."

"Asshole sank them too," Harper replies.

Would it even be safe to take them?

"Um. Guys," I say. "We're screwing ourselves here."

"He was coming for us. We couldn't stay there," Harper replies.

"We can't stay here either. It's a dead end!"

Robert's ski-mask-clad head pops over the top of the cliff and my blood turns cold.

He takes the first step down toward the jetty.

"He's still coming," I mutter, my stomach turning inside out. "And now we're trapped."

# 21

We back up along the jetty, getting farther away from Robert but closer to the ocean. Ava screams and grabs Gibson to use him as a human shield. He doesn't push her away.

"What do we do?" Harper asks, looking between Gibson and Robert. "Seriously, what do we do? He's *right there*!"

Yep, I can see that he's right there.

"Two choices," I say, and my voice sounds hollow even to my own ears. "We jump and swim or we stand here and get stabbed . . . with that long blade he has."

"Swim," Harper says. "I vote swim."

It's okay for her, she's basically an Olympian.

Robert holds the sword to his side almost casually. It's about as long as my forearm. I can't tell if it's a medieval one or a fake, but it really doesn't matter.

It can still kill.

"It'll take him about fifteen minutes to get from here to the other jetty. We need to swim faster than that," Gibson says.

Of all the terrible ideas we've had this weekend, this one wins. Hands down.

I look down at the water. It's calmer, the storm a distant memory, but waves still crash against the rock. The tide bringing you back to the island as if it's working with Robert, returning his victims.

There is still room for a lot of error. Like drowning.

"Gibson, have you ever swum it before?" I ask.

"Of course I haven't."

"Great."

"We can do it," Harper says.

Robert jumps from the last step onto the jetty. His thick boots thunder along the wood. He cricks his neck and lunges forward.

I'd rather drown than be stabbed.

Gasping, I turn. Gibson, Ava and Harper react in the same way. We run the last few steps to the end of the jetty and jump.

The ice-cold water steals my breath as I disappear under.

My clothes are soaked through in an instant. It makes them weigh a ton.

I paddle to the surface. I splutter as my head breaks up through the water. Kicking my legs as hard as I can, I swim away from Robert.

"He's not following," Gibson says, swimming beside me. Harper is just in front and Ava on the other side of Gibson.

I take a breath and dive back under, knowing it's much faster.

My hands cut through the water and shove it behind me. I propel myself forward as if I actually made the swim team at school. I wasn't fast enough and at the time I wasn't that bothered.

I now wish I'd gotten in and had a year's worth of practice behind me. A wave knocks me sideways. I kick above the surface again and paddle out so I don't slam against the rock that appears to be coming at me.

"He's gone," Harper says, taking a quick look over her shoulder.

They're all farther out than I am. In my haste to get away, I haven't swum in a straight line; rather, I headed toward the rocks.

Robert must be on his way to the other side.

In the blink of an eye, a wave snatches me. I don't have time to correct my course before I'm pulled under.

Panic seizes my body as I'm trapped in a current.

I break the surface and gulp a lungful of air. I kick and kick, my arms and legs moving much too quickly to be effective. They ache like hell.

The waves have me.

This can't be how it ends.

"Paisley!" Gibson shouts.

They're all so much farther now.

"Go!" I scream, choking as water splashes into my mouth and eyes. "Go!"

They can't come back for me. It's too risky.

"Go!"

Gibson turns around and swims, easily catching up to Ava. Harper is a dot to me now.

"Go," I whisper as a wave carries me away and I slam into the rock face of the island.

I grasp at the jagged surface and manage to claw into a lip. Water splashes around me, but the hands of the current fail to take me back under again.

Pulling myself up, I breathe through my nose until my lungs stop burning. I find a ledge for my feet and stand up, still holding on.

The others are out of sight now.

I pant and rest my forehead against the rock for a second. Robert might think I'm dead when I don't show up at the other jetty. It would give us an edge. But to get that edge, I have to not die.

If I follow the others, he will find me, but if I go back, I have a chance.

It's a good thing I chewed all my nails off, or they would have snapped against the rock. I place my foot on a rock, but I slide.

Dangling off a cliff, I clamp my mouth shut so I don't scream and alert Robert. My feet scramble to find somewhere to rest.

Oh god, come on.

I close my eyes when I realize it's not going to happen. My hands cramp up, and with shooting pains in my fingers, I drop back into the ocean.

*Fight.*

*Fight.*

*Fight.*

I duck under and kick off the cliff face. My arms and legs work in perfect synchrony as I swim for my life. I stop to let the wave carry me, and when it's done, I kick harder again. There's no point in trying to outswim a strong current. It never tires.

It takes me a while; my arms and legs burn with the effort. But I manage to do it. First, I swim out to sea to get out of the current that wants to continuously ram me into rock. Then I turn and swim toward the jetty.

It takes a long time. My muscles ache. My arms are on fire and my clothes weigh me down.

I manage to hold on to the jetty and heave myself up. Once lying down, I stare up at the sky and I give myself a minute to catch my breath and gain an ounce of strength back.

I'm exhausted and just want to stay here forever. I don't have long. It's too risky to stay still alone, so I force myself to stand.

My legs feel like jelly as I get to my feet.

Something tickles my face. I wipe it away expecting it to just be water, but my hand is red when I look down. I hit my head for a second time today and clearly I've cut myself.

I lift my dripping T-shirt up and use it to press against the gash on my forehead.

If I'm left with a scar, hopefully it'll be a cool one like Harry Potter's.

The wound doesn't bleed for long, so I walk along the jetty and climb the stairs quietly.

Crouching down as I near the top, I look around for Robert.

There is no one as far as I can see. Which is not necessarily a good thing.

For the first time, I feel so completely alone. I want to cry.

There's no one here to help me, to save me if Robert circles back. It's just me alone. One-on-one . . . and he has a sword. It would hardly be a fair fight.

Liam and Reeve are also out here alone. I have to assume that Malcolm is alive and by himself too.

Where would they go if they were looking for the rest of us?

Is it even smart to go running around searching for them?

Maybe not, when I know the general direction Robert was coming from after he moved the jammer.

Gibson was putting finding the jammer ahead of finding his best friend. I should do the same.

I run from the gate behind the entrance to a roller coaster.

Something is bothering me, and I can't quite place it.

I don't have time to sit down and make a list and work through it the way I usually do. What I need to do now is act.

We have to get service back to the island so we can call for help.

I move to a tree, and then another.

Every step I take I drip water, but there's nothing I can do about that now. It's cold. The sun is beating down rays of fire anyway. It won't be long until I dry and warm up.

I run from the tree to a food cart and crouch down.

Footsteps hit the asphalt behind me. I stand, spinning around, ready to confront whoever's coming.

"Paisley, thank god!" Liam says, wrapping me in a bear hug.

Relief floods my veins as I fall into his embrace.

"Hey, you're wet and you're bleeding. Jeez, what happened to you?"

I'm shivering as Liam lets me go. He doesn't seem to care that he now has a wet patch on his T-shirt. "Been in the sea."

He frowns. *"Why?"*

He asks as if he thinks I went for a nice dip. I shove my frustration away.

"Robert chased us down to the jetty and we had no other choice."

Liam looks around. "*We?* Where's everyone else? Oh, please don't tell me . . ."

"No, they're alive. Gibson, Ava, and Harper. At least, they were. They went ahead. I came back because I got stuck in a current and didn't have time to get around the other side. I don't know if they made it." My vision blurs as my eyes fill with unshed tears.

"They left you?"

He sounds furious and was a bit too loud. I look over my shoulder. We're still alone.

"They didn't have a choice."

"They're going to the other jetty?"

I nod. "Where were you?"

"Haunted house for ages, then looking for you. We heard screaming and found Kenna. She's dead."

"Yeah, I saw."

"You were there?"

"It was me and Gibson you heard in there. Not Kenna."

He shakes his head, brows furrowed. "Harper was gone when I got out. I lost Reeve in the house, so I went and checked on Ava. She was gone too, but I'm glad she and Harper turned up with you. Jesus, Paisley." He runs his hands through this hair. "I—I don't know where Reeve is or if he's even alive."

"He'll be okay. Have you seen Malcolm?"

"No," he says. "Why didn't Ava warn us?"

"Gibson and I found Harper when we got out of the house. We all went to check on Ava because she wasn't responding on the radio. She was hiding in the kitchen."

His jaw goes slack. "That little coward."

"It doesn't matter now. We need to get out of here, Liam. I don't know what to do anymore."

"I haven't seen the jammer."

"We found it, but Robert came for us. When we went back, he'd moved it. I saw the direction he came from and think it's got to be that way."

He blinks twice, taking in the information. "Okay, show me where. You're shivering. We can go to the hotel first."

I shake my head and start walking. Liam follows. "I'm fine. I don't need to get changed."

"He's wearing a creepy-ass mask," he says.

"You saw him?"

"Why do you think I'm hiding over here?" He winces. "Doesn't seem like a smart move to try taking him on alone. Not when he has a knife."

"Yeah, well, he's upgraded now. I got the knife when he grabbed me."

"What?" Liam asks a little too loudly, grabbing my hand. "I'm sorry, he got you?"

"In the haunted house, yeah." I blow out a breath. "So much has happened, Liam. My mind is spinning."

"Well, are you okay? Did he hurt you?"

"Physically, I'm fine. The rest . . . I'm sure a therapist will spend hours working that out in the future."

He blows out a sigh of regret. "I'm so sorry I left you. I won't do that again."

"You did nothing wrong. I was with Gibson, and we got split up in the house. I don't recommend going in there to hide from a killer, by the way."

Liam laughs and quickly covers his mouth with his fist. "Sorry. Weird time to find something funny."

"Perfect time, actually. Laugh or cry, right."

"How did you and Gibson get split?"

I shrug. "We were being chased, the killer was between me and Gibson. I couldn't get to the door where he'd just gone."

"So the killer was closer to Gibson at the time but came for you?"

"We were kind of in a triangle, each of us standing at one point. But yeah, he was closer to Gibson." I frown. "Why wouldn't he take out the biggest threat first?"

Liam slowly shakes his head. "No. No, he wouldn't. Would he?"

I give Liam a look. "We scratched Gibson and Reeve off the list when we saw the killer walking while we were all together."

"That was before we *knew* Camilla was in on this. I mean, she had to know Robert was behind it, and they were talking right before he decided she was in his way. That has to mean she was somehow involved."

"Maybe. Or perhaps she only suspected. He did *murder* her. Are you saying you think all four of them are in on it?" I ask. "Camilla, Robert, Gibson, and Reeve? No. Surely not all of them."

But it could be.

Why didn't I see this before? It could easily be more than two people. In fact, it would be safer for them to operate as a group.

"It doesn't make sense. Why wouldn't Gibson just kill me when he had the chance? Why get Reeve or Robert to follow us through the house? I've been alone with them both. I still don't think Reeve would do it."

"Er . . . I don't know. Pass. I've known the three of them for *two* days. That's not long enough to really know a person."

Wives and husbands, parents, families of murderers have all claimed to know the person who turned out to be evil. Two days. Twenty years. I'm not sure we ever know anyone.

"I get we're all relative strangers, but they've had multiple opportunities to kill us."

He pushes his hands through his hair. "I don't know! What the hell is going on here? What's this about. Why kill? And who do we trust?"

That's a lot of questions I don't have answers for.

I take a step back. "Honestly, Liam. I haven't got a clue."

Right now, I think the only person I trust completely is myself.

# 22

Liam and I walk back toward the Black Tulip. Neither of us crouches and hides this time. We're either brave or stupid. We do at least have the good sense to stick near buildings and trees.

I'm tired in every way possible.

Liam's eyes cover the whole park, his fists clenched, knees bent ready to spring. He's on high alert.

Part of me just wants this asshole to jump out and confront us. We could get it over with. Two against one. Liam is strong, and I'm so pissed off, I could take on a WWE wrestler and win.

"What's wrong?" he asks, sensing something is off.

"Where is this leading? What does Robert and whoever else want?"

"Well, we think it's about Malcolm, right?" he replies. "But why now and not when the park is open? More people to slaughter then. Why only us?"

"It's harder to control an island of hundreds of people. Eleven is much easier. He has more places to hide. One thing's for sure:

he knows the island like the back of his hand. Reeve and Gibson have been here long enough to know where to go, but to know the inside of every building and every ride?" I shake my head. "I'm not so sure. Gibson was outside most of the time."

"They could have explored on their off hours."

"We need to regroup and talk this out," I say. "There are questions everyone needs to answer."

"Does that include you?" he asks.

"If you have any for me, Liam, shoot. I've got nothing to hide."

"Nothing?"

"No. Why?"

He shrugs. "We all have secrets."

"I'm not looking at finding out anyone's hidden crush." Though I wouldn't mind knowing his.

"Right. Deeper questions, like: are you homicidal?" he says.

It's my turn to laugh. "Precisely."

"No one will answer yes to that."

"Not with their words."

His eyes slide to mine. "You're a human lie detector?"

I wish. "No, but I've listened to a lot of podcasts and watched a lot of true-crime stuff. I love the ones where experts pick apart a criminal's police interviews."

"You're the best we've got," he replies. "Do you feel confident enough to pick out the killer here?"

That would be a big *no.* I'm confident enough that I could tell who to trust after an honest conversation. That doesn't mean they're not guilty, though.

The hotel is ahead, and I can see Harper through the lobby window.

"They're there!" I say, breaking into a sprint. The doors slide open as I reach them; a second faster and I would've run straight into them.

"Harper!"

The three of them turn around and Harper runs to me.

"You're okay!"

We slam together in the middle of the lobby, and I hug her like she hugged me when we got back from the haunted house.

"Wait, you're hurt," she says, noticing the gash on my head.

"It's nothing." I manage a half smile. "Forgot it was there."

That's not a lie. Maybe it's the adrenaline, but if I hadn't felt blood trickling, I wouldn't even know I was hurt.

"Damn, girl, you've got more lives than a cat," Gibson jokes. He pats me rather awkwardly on the back. "How did you get out?"

I let Harper go. "I went back, figured the killer would be chasing you on the other jetty."

They're all soaked through like I am.

"I'm so glad to see you," Harper says.

"Let's all go change and then meet back here," Gibson says.

"The killer has a master key," I say. "We should go to each room together for safety."

There is absolutely no way I'm giving him, or anyone else, the opportunity to go off alone. If Gibson *is* in on this, he's not going to get the chance to murder anyone else.

"Yes, I like Paisley's idea," Ava says, her eyes wide.

Liam smiles at me, understanding exactly why I want us to stay together. "Come on, let's go up and let the girls change first."

Gibson looks like he's about to argue but Liam walks past him toward the elevator, not leaving it up for negotiation. So he follows us with a shrug, his clothes dripping water.

I cannot wait to get out of these jeans.

"Should we take the elevator?" Harper asks as the doors slide open.

"I don't think anyone is here. Robert is probably lying low and planning his next move. We should stay in the club room on the third floor. The windows in there cover most of the park. We might even be able to find Reeve and let him know where we are."

"We can also do that from the security room," Ava says.

"We've done that before. What if the power goes again? It's time to change it up. Gibson, do you think if we shone a light from the window someone on the mainland would see?" I ask.

He looks back as he steps out of the elevator. "Maybe. It's worth a shot. Have we given up on the jammer? That's still our best bet."

"If you think I'm going back out there, you're freaking crazy!" Ava snaps. She unlocks her door, and we go in. Her cases are lined up along the wall. It's like a clothing store has exploded in her room.

She grabs a few things and goes into the bathroom.

Gibson steps in front of me. "I haven't seen Reeve."

"He'll be okay."

Shaking his head, he replies, "After everything he's been through . . ."

"What's he been through?" Liam asks, raising an eyebrow. Everything about his tone tells me he thinks Reeve is guilty.

Gibson raises Liam's scowl with a glare. "A lot. He had a hard time, but he's doing really well now, getting his life together. After everything he's overcome, to die here now, in a place that's helping him get on his feet . . . He doesn't deserve that."

Liam arches a brow. "None of us deserves this."

"That's not what I'm saying."

"We're so not arguing over this," Harper says. "I just want to get changed and go to the club room. I'm hungry, thirsty, and pissed off. Screw the jammer, I say we go after the source."

"Okay, I love this Harper," I say.

She flashes me a smile. "I've had enough. I'm *so* over this, and I get that that sounds way cold, but that's how it is. We either run around scared looking for a magic box that will give us back our service or take this guy down."

"Yeah, right, but only one problem with that," Liam says.

Harper puts her hands on her hips, daring Liam to find a hole in her plan. "Go on."

"He killed his mom. He has nothing to lose, there's nothing he won't do, and he has a sword. How the hell do we compete with that?" Liam looks at Gibson. "We go after everyone who's missing. He's going to want us to find Reeve."

"So that's exactly what we're not going to do," I say.

"No way!" Gibson snaps. "We're not leaving my boy out there. He'd go back for you, Paisley, you know he would."

I hold my palms up trying to get him to calm down. "The

killer wants us outside running around, splitting up. We've done that and it almost got us killed. Some of us are dead."

"Are you forgetting that James actually was killed when we were together?" Liam asks.

Since when did he switch to Team Gibson? Two minutes ago, he thought that Gibson might be in on it.

I can't keep up.

Ava reappears from the bathroom. She's changed into jeans and a light knitted sweater. Her hair is up in a bun and her makeup has been reapplied.

Her makeup has been reapplied!

I breathe deeply.

"Are you for real?" Harper asks. "We're out here dripping onto the carpet, shivering, and in danger of losing our toes, and you're freaking contouring!"

I grab Harper's hand and tug her toward the door. "We'll go to your room next," I tell her.

"I'll be quick." She shoots Ava a dark look, but Ava doesn't even flinch. It was Harper's mistake to assume that Ava has any shame.

Harper is true to her word and changes quickly.

I can hear voices through the wall as I tie my hair up in my bathroom. It's still damp and will only make my top wet if I leave it. There's a small cut on my forehead, but nothing as bad as Reeve had.

My body is covered in bruises. I'm going to be an interesting shade of green and purple for a few days, but I'll live. I've bashed my head twice today and almost drowned.

To be standing here with only cuts and bruises is pretty good going. Maybe I do have nine lives.

It's not something I want to test.

I've changed into a pair of black yoga pants and a baggy T-shirt that says *I would rather be watching a true crime doc.* It's comfortable and won't be so heavy if I find myself in the water again.

My wet clothes are discarded in the bathtub. I'm never wearing those jeans again. Or any others. They've been off for five minutes now, but I can still feel the wet material chafing against my skin.

I grab a hoodie that was draped over the counter and tie it around my waist.

Who knows if I'll need it, but it gets cold here at night and we might be outside. Hopefully on a boat sailing away from the island.

The digital clock glowing in the bathroom mirror, below the TV, reads 3:02 p.m. My stomach growls. I wish we'd had lunch.

I leave my room with my cell charger, and we get back in the elevator. Gibson's room is off the lobby with the rest of the staff's.

"Maybe we should've packed more supplies," Harper says, clinging to her charger, a can of soda, and fluffy fleece pullover.

"Like what, a gun?" Ava asks. She also has her charger and a beige borg jacket.

"We can grab something in the kitchen after I've changed," Gibson says.

What I wouldn't give for all of us to be sitting down to Kenna's cooking and a normal weekend.

"I was kind of hoping someone would notice that none of us are online. Do you think that might happen?" I ask.

Liam shrugs. "I doubt my mom would. I posted yesterday. She'll assume I'm fine because I've been online. I'm just a shitty son and not messaging her directly."

Ava snorts. The sound isn't something I would ever expect her to make. "My parents wouldn't notice anything unless I'd been missing for a month. And that would only be because the credit card bill would be tiny."

"I'm sorry," I say.

She turns her nose up. "Why? At least I don't have to answer to anyone."

I can tell she doesn't mean that, not really. It must be hard not having your own parents care enough to check in with you. Never again will I complain that mine are all up in my business. Or at least I won't for a good few weeks.

"Mine are the same as Liam's," Harper says. "They'll see my online presence as proof of life."

"Yeah, that will only work with mine for a little while," I tell them. "If they don't hear from me by tonight, my mom will be the one escorting the police here."

"Well, that's good. We thought we'd have to make it to tomorrow, but we might be saved tonight. We just need to hunker down in the club room until then. There's enough furniture in there to block a door," Liam says.

For the first time since we realized Will went missing, Liam looks relaxed. And I realize that I may have given him false hope.

I would fully expect my mom to raise the alarm, but it's no guarantee. Liam is taking it as if it's a given.

"We need to make sure we can survive through Monday, just in case," I reply. "We have to be able to protect ourselves. Once Gibson changes, we should grab some food and drinks and take them up."

"If we're going with this plan and not taking him out, can we get some beer?" Harper says.

"No!" Gibson snaps. "The last thing we need is four tipsy teenagers giggling their heads off while some lunatic is trying to slice our throats!"

"That's what happened to Kenna," I remind him uneasily. "Why was that only Kenna?"

Gibson unlocks the corridor leading to the staff rooms. "Who knows, Paisley. Why does it even matter?"

He sounds thoroughly over me and all my "crime stuff."

"If you can figure out—"

"Enough, Paisley," he says between his teeth.

Liam holds his hand up. "Hey, she's only trying to help, man."

"It's not helping, though, is it? We know *nothing*."

"We know it's Robert. We know Camilla's death was the most brutal because he knew her. We know he's getting more efficient with his killing. Will had multiple stab wounds, James fewer, and Kenna only one across her neck. He's getting a feel for this. Whatever his reason for killing, he's starting to enjoy it," I say.

Gibson swallows audibly. "But that hasn't helped us stop him."

"No. I have a feeling only Malcolm could do that."

"Because this guy hates him? Why? He gave Camilla a job and a pretty well paid one."

Liam shakes his head. "Nah, did you see the knockoff bag she had? She wasn't paid much."

"How would you know that?"

"It's my mom's way of keeping up appearances too. We live in an area that's too expensive for us. She will never give up the zip code, so she pretends with the rest."

"You're not poor," Ava says as Gibson lets us into his room.

He grabs clothes and heads into the bathroom.

Liam rolls his eyes. "I never said I was poor. I said she lives above our means."

"Okay, so this is somehow connected to Camilla and Malcolm. Gibson," I call, knocking once on the door. "Do you know how long Camilla has worked for Malcolm?"

"She was on board before he bought the island, but beyond that, I don't know."

I pace the tiny staff room. "All right. So we have a killer who wants to destroy Malcolm's reputation, destroy him financially, and probably put a knife in his neck. Robert murdered his mom because, presumably, she was getting in the way. She had to have suspected but never tried to stop him before all this blew up. Why?"

They look at me and I stop pacing.

"I think Malcolm knows Robert or knows of him," I say. "We find him, we might just get some answers."

# 23

"Hey, detective," Gibson says.

I spin on my heel to face him. When did he get out of the bathroom?

Five pairs of eyes watch me like they think I'm having a breakdown. And I feel like I just might. The intensity of what's happening is overwhelming. It's one thing to watch a TV show or listen to a podcast—it's another to experience it in real time.

"Yeah?"

"What are you doing?"

I wave at him. "Going over things. Figuring it out. This is what I do. I'll admit, I usually get there quicker. The answer is in here somewhere. . . . We just need to think. Could Malcolm be Robert's dad?"

"He doesn't have kids," Gibson replies.

"No, he told you he doesn't have kids." Liam raises a brow at me, and I nod. He's getting it. Question everything. Come at it from every angle. Don't blindly believe everything you're told.

"Fine. He could've lied, I guess. But why?"

Liam stands taller, demanding our attention. He has a theory. "He's more interested in money than anything else? No wife or husband. No partner at all. He said he's married to his work. Robert would be pissed if his own dad rejected him and then paid his mom crap."

"That makes sense," Harper says. "Right? I wouldn't blame him for being angry. If my dad did that, I'd want revenge."

"Pretty sick revenge, though," Liam says. "Why not just out him as a deadbeat? Murder is a bit . . . well, overkill."

"Are you talking yourself out of your own theory?" I ask, smiling as I remember the number of times I've done that before. It's so frustrating to spend time and effort figuring something out, being sure, then doubting yourself.

I've since learned to trust my gut and follow my instincts with a story.

Liam's frown is adorable. "I don't know. My life was pretty simple before this weekend, Pais. I never had to think about this stuff."

"You never tried to figure out gamer plots? Or whatever you do?" Harper sounds skeptical.

"Not to this extent, no."

Gibson leads us along the empty corridor and into the kitchen. I half expected Robert to jump out. Gibson listens, not adding much to the conversation. I can tell from the vacant look in his eyes that his mind is somewhere else. Like with Reeve.

It's not looking good for Reeve. It's been ages since he and

Liam split up. Gibson needs positivity right now, so I'll never voice my concerns. Besides, it's not like he doesn't know there's a possibility that his friend is already dead.

In the kitchen, we raid the cupboards and fill bags with as much food and water as we can. Harper grabs more Cokes—no beer bottles—and a pack of candy.

She notices me watching and shrugs. "If I'm dying, it's with a belly full of candy and a sugar rush."

Who could argue with that?

"I'm with you."

We cram into the elevator and the doors roll shut. I'm holding a bag full of premade sandwiches that Gibson said Kenna and her team had been making for the staff. They're still good until tomorrow. Harper has the junk. Gibson and Liam have drinks. Ava has her charger and a princess attitude.

My stomach rumbles but no one seems to notice over the sound of rustling bags and anxiety. I feel a little sick at the thought of eating a sandwich made by someone who was just murdered, but I try to shake it off. Food is food, and we have to eat.

Gibson hands me the bag of bottled water when we get into the club room. "Chuck them in the fridge, Paisley. Liam, we need to get this door blocked off. Harper and Ava, please find Reeve."

A wave of nausea crashes against my stomach as I think about Reeve being out there alone. He would've been back by now if he was okay. If Robert hasn't gotten to him, what else could've happened? He hit his head. Maybe he did have a concussion and he's collapsed somewhere.

I stuff the drinks away and go straight to the window. "Reeve, where are you?" I whisper.

Harper looks over her shoulder. "He's probably dead. Soon we all will be."

"Don't say that. He'll be okay. He'll find his way back. I know it."

"You like him," she says.

My heart skips. "He saved me."

"Uh-huh."

I roll my eyes at her. She notices more than I thought. But the truth is, I don't know how I feel about Reeve. Or Liam, for that matter. They're both gorgeous and have been flirty, so I think they're interested. I don't know.

Scanning the park, I notice that we have a good few hours of daylight left and we're going to need every second of it. When night comes, Robert has an even bigger advantage.

"We should be able to see Robert from here."

Behind us, Liam and Gibson haul furniture about.

"Don't go over the top," I say. "Reeve might need to get in quickly."

Gibson's face pales.

If Robert's chasing him, we might not have enough time to let Reeve in before he's stabbed.

Over by the Waltzer, I notice something move. I step closer to the window.

"You see that?" I ask.

"Yes! There!" Ava says, pointing toward the Waltzer cars that practically tilt upward ninety degrees.

"Who is it?" I mutter.

Gibson and Liam discard a large piece of furniture they're moving and run to the window.

I strain my eyes, but I can just about make out the figure moving behind one of the black-and-white cups.

"That's not . . . Is it Robert? Wait. No, it's Reeve!" I say. "It's Reeve! He's okay!"

Gibson spins and sprints to the door.

"No, no, no," Harper says, grabbing a fistful of his hoodie just before Gibson leaves the room.

He yanks himself away. "Stay here if you want. I'm not leaving him to die!"

Gibson's words feel like bugs crawling all over me. I stood back and watched Camilla be killed. We did nothing to prevent it from happening. How can I do that again?

"He's going back another way. Why wouldn't he come here?" Ava leans against the window.

"I can't see him anymore," Liam adds.

Gibson comes back then and presses his forehead to the glass. "Where did he go? Which way?"

"Past the Waltzers," Ava replies. "He's getting farther away."

"Maybe he spotted something. Does anyone see Robert in the opposite direction?" I ask.

There's nothing but sunshine, shadows, and rides.

Reeve has disappeared out of sight, and the park is still.

The water isn't too bad if you're not near the cliff face, so I wonder what our chances of swimming away are—ignoring the fact that I could have easily drowned earlier. It'd take hours, but we might be spotted by boats closer to the mainland.

Minutes pass and we see absolutely nothing.

"Where would he go, Gibson?" I ask.

He shrugs. "I've no clue. He knows the park better than I do. Shortcuts, rides, hideouts, all of it. He knows it all."

"That means if anyone can survive out there, he can," Harper says.

"Yeah, but maybe he's already used his luck on not dying when he was hit."

Liam narrows his eyes. "Yeah. Luck."

"What are you insinuating?" Gibson asks, narrowing his eyes.

"That Reeve is the killer. Think about it. He's been alone every time this asshole has struck, he knows the island, he's the only one the killer didn't use a knife on. And you've just told us he had a troubled childhood."

Gibson squares his shoulders, ready to defend his friend. But there's something in his eyes that sends a chill down my spine. Doubt? "That's not what I said."

"Could whatever he went through lead to this?" Harper asks. "If he wasn't your friend, could you link the two things?"

Yeah.

Gibson grinds his teeth, and he looks like he's ready to tell us all to go to hell.

"His silence means yes," Ava says.

Harper rubs her forehead. "So we're saying it's not Robert. It's Reeve."

Ava waves her hand in front of her. "Both begin with an *R*."

"Are you kidding me?" Gibson mutters. "Do you hear yourself?"

"Reeve could be Camilla's son, though. She's, what, mid to late forties?" Liam guesses.

I nod. "Yeah, I'd say so."

"Paisley, we've been through this. You said you believed he was innocent." Gibson is irritated that I've flipped back, but I can't be sure of anything. The more I learn, the more confused I get. It's supposed to work the other way around.

From years of being obsessed with crime, I've learned that it can happen like that. Information stacks up and it takes a minute to set it in order.

"When did you two have that conversation?" Liam asks.

"Before we found you all again. Look, it doesn't matter. I go back and forth depending on what's happening at the time."

"Why don't we discuss you, huh?" Gibson says to Liam. "You've been absent when the killer strikes too."

"Hey, screw you. I ran into the haunted house because I heard you and Paisley screaming. I saw Kenna cut from ear to ear, so don't come at me with—"

"There! Reeve's on the move," Ava says. "If you want to stop arguing for two minutes. If he's the killer, we'll find out if we watch him."

"It's not him," Gibson grits through his teeth.

We watch Reeve crouch behind anything and everything that's bigger than him.

I place my palms on the glass and only realize I'm not breathing when the window doesn't mist in front of me.

"Please get back here," I murmur.

"Robert's not out there," Ava says. "I wonder why."

Gibson doesn't bite. He continues to stare out the window with frightened eyes as he searches for his friend.

I can't imagine how it must feel.

"He's making his way to the hotel, I think," Gibson says.

Placing my hand on Gibson's arm, I reply, "That's good. He's going to be fine."

"When we're all back together, I say we go together for the jammer. We can set something on fire if we can't find it," Harper says.

A large fire would be seen from the mainland. It's not something you'd expect to see on an amusement park resort. The fireplace in the hotel wouldn't kick out enough smoke to raise an alarm, so it's not like anyone would be used to seeing that from here.

"Harper, that's not a bad idea."

"What? The fire thing? Do you seriously want to set fire to the island?" Liam asks.

"Not the whole island," I reply, and I sound a little defensive even to my own ears.

Gibson, still watching Reeve, adds, "We could set fire to the check-in booths by the entrance. The fire would face the mainland. People would see it. Let's get to the restaurant and grab as much alcohol as we can carry. Matches will be in the kitchen."

"What about Reeve?" Ava asks. "We've only just got here, a place where we thought we'd be safest, and now you want to go back out there! You guys are all over the place!"

"So we should just stay still even if we've thought of a better plan?" I ask. "We're going to die if we don't get help, Ava."

"I'm just saying we should stick to one thing. Not ping-pong between *everything*."

"If you have a better idea, we're all ears," Liam says.

Gibson snorts. "Oh, you're on board now, are you?"

"Just because I had questions doesn't mean that I don't agree with plan two-point-oh or whatever number we're on now."

"Nine-point-oh," Ava mutters.

I move away from the window because everyone else is still watching. My anxiety is only getting worse the longer I watch Reeve, and I need to think. "It doesn't matter how many plans have failed. This is where we are now. Nothing else has worked, we've wasted enough time on the jammer. Robert has control of that, but if we set a fire, that's something *we'd* have control of. We take away his power."

"Do we wait for Reeve to get here?" Liam asks.

"No, he'll have to pass us in the bar to get up here anyway. Come on, let's get downstairs so we don't miss him."

We run out of the room. Gibson is first and he leads us to the stairwell. It's probably safer anyway.

There was no chat about being quiet so as not to alert the serial killer where we are. We thunder down the stairs like we're advertising for our own deaths. I hold the rail, so I don't fall on my face. My limbs are still seriously aching. It'll be a miracle if I can even walk tomorrow.

"Gibson?" Reeve shouts with no regard for his safety. Same as us. "Are you here?"

"Reeve!" Gibson yells back, throwing open the doors at the bottom of the stairwell.

I get through the door in time to see them do a half hug, half slap-on-the-back thing. Reeve laughs. "Damn, it's good to see you." He looks over Gibson's shoulder to see who's with him. Who's survived.

"You're bleeding," I say, stepping around Gibson.

He shakes his head. "It's not my blood."

# 24

"Of course it's not his. Half of the people who were here are already dead. There's blood all over the island." Ava's pacing back and forth in her pink Converse. "Can we just do this thing and get out of here?" She throws her hands up in the air.

Reeve runs his hands through his hair. The bandage we put on him earlier is seeped through with blood. "What happened?"

His eyes are wide like he's just seen something horrific. And he has. "Camilla's dead," he tells us. "Her body . . . she's lying in the middle of a path. I went to see if she was alive, but there was so much blood. No pulse."

He looks down at his bloodstained T-shirt.

Up close I can see that the stain is kind of a handprint, like he's had her blood on his hands, panicked, and tried to wipe it off.

I swallow hard and look at Gibson. Camilla was murdered in front of us and it's not something that I want to explain again. The cops will make me go over it more than once, I'm sure.

Gibson seems to understand that I don't want to talk and gives me a small nod.

"Paisley and I saw her die," he tells Reeve.

*Murdered,* I correct him in my head.

Reeve's jaw goes slack. He lets out a gasp. "You saw it. Are you okay?"

"No, not really," I reply. "But things have moved on since then. We don't have time to go over trauma."

Gibson takes over, putting his hand on my shoulder for comfort. He knows how horrifying it was to see Camilla being killed. "We found the jammer and Robert was standing near it. Paisley and I had a plan. I was going to distract him while she broke it. Before we could act, Camilla came walking up, hands raised. They spoke, she was trying to stop him, we think, and he stabbed her. He moved the jammer."

"The look on her face," I whisper. I don't dare close my eyes as I know I'll see Camilla's shock and devastation as she realized that her son had stabbed her.

The image flashes in my mind so vividly it makes me gag.

Well, I guess I don't need to worry about closing my eyes because I can see her anytime.

*Stop thinking about it.*

Gibson clears his throat. "She screamed something, we think Robert's name, but he just stood there, watching her bleed out and die."

I press the pressure building up in my forehead. "She bled out and we ran. We *ran.*"

"You love all this murder stuff, right? So this is probably just a regular weekend for you," Ava says.

Really? I take a breath and try not to let Ava add to the stress of this situation. I'm going to have one hell of a headache soon.

"Uh, hardly," I snap. "I saw a woman get stabbed right in front of me. I've seen Will's and James's and Kenna's bodies. We don't know where Robert is anymore, we don't know if Malcolm is alive, and we've got a fire to set."

That about sums it up.

Liam wraps an arm around my shoulder and gives me a squeeze. "It's okay."

I avoid eye contact with Reeve.

"I still think it's a bit suspicious that Gibson and Reeve have never seen Robert around," Ava mumbles. She glances over at Gibson and does a little half-shrug.

"Say that again," Gibson demands.

I move forward and push his chest when he goes to take a step, but he looks at Ava. "Do you know how many people work here? We're not fully opened, and we've never had every member of staff here at once yet. There are plenty of people who work here who we don't know. So shut your damn mouth."

Ava glares but she doesn't argue with him.

I'm not sure what to believe anymore. My brain hurts from constantly stressing about it.

"When did Robert start?" I ask. "Do you remember?"

Gibson shakes his head. "No. Reeve said there were inconsistencies with his file. But knowing that information isn't really going to help us with what we need to do now."

The others look at me for a second. They're all thinking the same thing.

"We have no idea where he is," I say. "We tried to watch out for him from the club room, but nothing. He could be anywhere. He could be in the hotel watching us."

"We'll be fine, Paisley," Gibson says.

"We can't wait around here for another night," Reeve says.

Ava rolls her eyes. "I'm not swimming ever again. We've ditched worrying about the jammer and you should hear the crazy new plan."

Harper takes a deep breath. "Will you just shut up."

Reeve scowls at Ava and turns to us.

"Hold on. What are we doing with fire?" Reeve asks.

"Before we tell him our plan, can we find out what the hell happened to him?" Ava asks.

And to be fair, it's a smart idea. I can't see how it can be Reeve, but it would be pretty irresponsible of us to not even find out.

"I lost Liam looking for you guys. I've been all over. The rowboats are gone, by the way."

"Yeah, we found that out earlier, right between finding Kenna dead and taking a dip in the ocean. It wasn't a surprise," Gibson replies.

Reeve swears under his breath. "Okay. What about this fire?"

"We want to set off the fire alarms, so we're setting fire to the check-in booths," I say matter-of-factly. "Without cell service, it's the best we can do. We have a shopping list, so let's grab what we need."

Reeve does a double take, trying to catch up with us, but he isn't quite there yet. "Wait, what?"

Gibson and Liam walk around the bar. Harper and Ava help by finding bags to carry the alcohol.

Reeve blocks my way with his arm as I go to help. "Wait a second. We're setting a fire and you watched someone get murdered. And you were in the sea?"

I give a firm nod. "Correct. You're all caught up now."

"Paisley, this fire idea is crazy."

"Yes. And that's why it's brilliant. Robert expects us to try to contact the outside world, fix the wiring, find the jammer, everything we've already been doing. What he won't expect is this. To beat him we need to surprise him."

"But this is arson," Reeve points out.

I blink at him. "To stop more *murder.* I think I can live with that. Malcolm has insurance, and our crimes pale in comparison to Robert's."

Ava picks at her nails, preoccupied with a chip in the pink paint. "We don't know if Malcolm's even alive," she says, not looking up from her manicure.

"Or if he's in on this," I add. "I get that this is his island, but think of the publicity if he's a survivor of a murderous weekend. Everyone would be talking about his amusement park."

Reeve runs his hand over his hair. "Would he go that far?"

Liam shrugs. "Do we try finding him? We're about to set part of his island on fire."

Gibson shakes his head. "Going after someone is another thing that Robert might expect. We've done that before."

So we really are giving up our humanity to save our lives.

Is it a fair trade?

I'm not sure, but I don't see many other options anymore. It feels like something I might regret, but at least I'll be alive to have regrets.

"Kitchen," Gibson says.

We follow him even though it's a bit ridiculous for six people to get one box of matches. We're also not doing the splitting-up thing again—like Robert expects.

"Why did you and Liam split up in the haunted house?" Ava asks Reeve.

He slowly tilts his head. "It wasn't a conscious decision. Anyway, who are you to judge when all you do is hide and expect everyone else to save you?"

Her cheeks flush bright red, but I think it's more from anger than embarrassment. "I'm just saying. You've been alone every time something bad has happened. Do you expect us to believe that's a coincidence?"

His dark eyes turn black as he stares at her like he could strangle her on the spot. "Watch your poisonous mouth. All I've tried to do this weekend is keep you all safe. I've risked my life running into buildings because I've thought you were in danger. I should've swum to the mainland this morning and left you to deal with it." He takes a calming breath through his nose. "I lost Liam in the haunted house. When he didn't answer me, I assumed he was coming back here. I've been working my way back since. Okay?"

Reeve looks at the rest of us as he's giving us the explanation. He doesn't care what Ava thinks about him, but he doesn't want us to think that he's a killer. Despite doubting him at times, I've always come back to what I feel. Reeve is a good person.

"That's a great story," Ava mutters.

"What's up with her?" Reeve asks, tilting his head toward Ava.

Gibson rolls his eyes. "Ignore her, man. We need to get outside and get this fire started. Keep trying Malcolm on the radio, Reeve. He's alive until we find a body."

"Would he really hide while we're out here dying?" I ask.

Reeve lifts my chin and for a second, I drown in his eyes.

This is *not* the time for a crush.

Ignore the crush!

"We're not going to die," he says.

"I bet Will, Kenna, James, and Camilla thought that too," Harper says.

"Can we please stop arguing? We have what we need, so let's move out," Gibson says.

When we get outside the hotel, it's like hours have passed. The sun is hidden behind a thick layer of snow-white cloud. There's no rain forecast, so nothing should interfere with visibility and our fire.

Reeve lets us through the gate separating the hotel and the park.

"Where's Robert?" I whisper.

Slamming the gate behind us, he replies, "I don't care. I've had enough of this. The bastard is going down. Now."

Okay, I care where Robert is.

I side-eye him and notice that Harper is doing the same. From the suspicion painted all over her face, I can tell that she's thinking the same thing. Reeve is angry.

As we get closer to the entrance, I can smell the sea. It's oddly comforting, and I hope it's a good sign.

Gibson and Liam walk ahead like they're on a mission. They look like guys in action movies when they're walking away from explosions. We're about to go start one.

Reeve hangs back with me, frowning.

"You all right?" I ask.

"Not sure. Something's off. I've felt it all day, but I can't put my finger on it."

"In addition to the murder spree that's going on?"

He lets out a wry chuckle. "Yes, in addition to the murder. Don't you feel it? We've only ever seen one of them, masked. Never Robert and Camilla together."

"I have."

"When he killed her. Was she dressed in black, then?"

Huh, good point. "Yeah, but it was the same black pantsuit that she was wearing this morning. If she was the one in the ski mask and cargos, she changed after."

"How have we not seen Robert more?"

"He doesn't want us to. I'd be sneaky if I was on a killing spree too."

He laughs again but he's not amused. There's not a lot to find funny here. "Yeah, I guess."

"He's alone now. Maybe he'll trip up."

"Camilla had a cool head. Before Robert started killing, anyway," he says. "This guy doesn't. You could be right, but do we really want him to go off the deep end?"

The skin on my forearms prickles with goose bumps. The thought of that happening makes my blood run ice cold. I don't want this guy to be any angrier than he already is. If we worry about that too much, we'll only end up dead.

"What we want and what we're going to get . . ." I trail off as we reach the booths by the entrance to the park. The steps leading to the jetty are just beyond that.

Gibson puts the bag on the ground and we each grab a liquor bottle.

The wooden booths have carved gargoyles and the name of the island set into them. Someone spent a lot of hours crafting this and we're just going to burn it to the ground.

A pinch of guilt works its way into my head, but I shake it off. This is necessary.

I'll burn down whatever I have to in order to get off this island. I can't spend another day here.

I unscrew the cap on the vodka, hold the bottle up, and pour it inside the first booth. The liquid splashes onto the floor. I shake it to cover as much of the walls as possible.

"This feels so wrong," Harper says, following my lead.

Her words don't quite match her actions, she's flicking the

bottle all over the place with bright eyes. I get it: we're about to take control here.

It's like going to one of those plate-smashing places. Blaine went to one of those with some friends on the last day of high school.

My heart aches as I think about my brother. Everything I'm doing now is so I can get home to my family. My parents are never going to let me out again after this. To be fair, I don't think I'll ever want to go out again anyway.

"Stand back," Liam says.

He and Gibson each hold up a lit match. I watch the little twin flames. With a flick of the wrist, they both chuck the matches into the booth.

A second later, orange flames rise and quickly take the first booth.

# 25

I watch, mesmerized by the fire, which seems to burn slowly at first but then spirals out of control. Huge flames roar up to the sky.

The first booth is almost completely gone; a shell of charred wood and metal that I assume was attached to chairs and a desk is all that's left now. The fire jumps, spreading to the second booth, and then the third. The acrid smell of smoke, not the salty sea air, is all I can smell.

"We shouldn't stay here long," Liam says, looking over his shoulder.

"We have to stay close to the jetty when help comes," Gibson replies.

"Yeah, but we're just advertising where we are right now." Liam looks over his shoulder again, anxiety etched into his face.

He looks scared now.

"What's he going to do while we're all together in daylight? He only strikes when he has the upper hand."

Gibson isn't wrong. Robert has only ever attacked us when

we've been in a group in darkness. We're not trapped in a pitch-black room, so what will he do now to split us up and get control?

It shouldn't be too long before someone notices the fire and realizes we need help.

Will he hide out or try to leave? The cops will search every inch of the island. What's his escape plan? Or maybe it's just to take as many of us down with him as possible.

That's what I would do. It'd really drive his point home. Whatever that point is. He's going to prison for the rest of his life anyway; he might as well make sure he makes the serial killer hall of fame.

Liam doesn't have a response for Gibson. What is there to say? We can't go running off now. Not when help will be coming soon.

The fire roars, growing quickly. I tilt my head up and, for a second, I'm petrified that it will spread beyond the booths.

"Is it getting out of control?" Harper asks nervously. "Does it seem too big to you too?"

"Uh-huh," I reply.

She's the only one near me. Gibson, Reeve, and Liam are around the back of the booth and Ava is along the side, only just in view. We've covered all areas in case Robert does come.

Heat prickles my skin and I take a step back with wide eyes.

"Seriously. It's burning up like crazy," Harper says. "Is that normal, Paisley?"

I block my eyes and take another step back when the flames double in size again.

"I—I don't . . ."

Without warning, an explosion bursts from the far booth.

I'm thrown backward by an enormous ball of fire.

Landing heavily on the ground, I curl onto my side. My skin prickles from the heat. Groaning, I try to move, but my body refuses to listen.

What the hell made the explosion?

Although I don't lose consciousness, my body is heavy like I've been up for days without a second of sleep. I don't know how much time passes, but I push myself onto my elbows and look around.

Groaning, I scan the area.

Someone in black walks in the distance. They're a dark blur, and for a second I think I'm seeing Ghostface with his long cloak. Am I in a *Scream* movie? I can't see the face clear enough to be sure.

The next second, he's gone and all I see is fire and smoke.

The flames are pretty.

I watch for a minute, mesmerized by the orange flames flickering up to the sky as if they're trying to burn the clouds. It's beautiful, like a kaleidoscope.

A thick crackling of fire drags me half back into the real world.

I'm on the island.

Why?

Robert. Murder. Fire. Escape.

"Run!" someone shouts. They sound so far away. "He's here! Run!"

I rub my forehead and blink away my confusion.

F*ire. Robert. He's here.*

Who's here?

I rub the ache at the back of my head and wonder if that's what's making my mind fuzzy. When I withdraw my hand, my skin is clear of blood. Thankfully, I haven't been seriously hurt. Or I don't think I have, at least.

Something flammable must have been in that booth to make it go up like that. It wasn't yet in use; the front window was boarded up. It must have had chemicals or something like that in it.

God, why is my head throbbing so much?

I push myself to my feet, dazed, and search for anyone else.

Sudden realization steals my breath. Gone is the confusion. It's replaced with ice-cold fear.

The words I heard while on the ground. Robert is *here.* I clench my fists as the words slot together and make sense.

After a heartbeat my vision comes back into sharp focus, and I can finally see the large fire and absence of my friends.

I look for danger. For Robert.

This would be the perfect time for him to strike.

He must be here—where?—and I seem to be alone.

I breathe, terrified, panting.

There's no sign of him as I look around and see someone stumbling my way.

"Paisley!" Ava shouts, running unsteadily to me from around the side of the booths. There's a shard of glass sticking out of her neck. Her hands tremble violently as they hover over the glass.

Leaping forward, I grab her wrists, preventing her from doing something stupid. "No, don't pull it. You'll make it worse. Look, it'll be okay, but we need to get out of here. Everyone else is gone, I think."

How long was I on the ground?

"I—I didn't see where they went," she says, her voice a couple octaves higher than normal. Her eyes are wide, pupils stealing the green and making her look wild.

Unfortunately, there's no time to check her over like I want to. We need to get out of the open.

I grip her hand and drag her along with me. We don't want to go too deep into the park and potentially miss a boat that comes. I want to stay where I can see the horizon, but we need to find someplace safe to hide until then.

"I'm cold," Ava says.

My heart skips. That's not a good sign.

"You're fine," I tell her over my shoulder and hope that I sound confident enough, so she believes me. I'm surprised that she's still standing.

We duck behind a park map. We're on the wrong side of the fence, but I don't want to cross over back into the park. I'm happier being on the outside of the perimeter. It'll be quicker to get to the jetty.

"Sit down," I say, pulling the collar of her sweatshirt to the side.

Up close I can see that the glass isn't in her neck but in the dip of her collarbone.

"Why is it so cold?" she says.

Her eyes are fixed ahead, and she looks like she might slip into shock at any second.

"Hey, I need you to breathe, Ava. In through your nose and out through your mouth." She seems to understand me. "Yeah, that's it," I tell her, trying to stay calm. "I'm not going to leave you. We just need to wait here until help arrives. Can you do that for me?" I ask in a whisper.

The crackle of the fire is loud even from over here, but I don't want to risk Robert hearing us.

Ava tries to nod but winces and her hand flies to her neck.

"Don't touch. It's all right."

"I—I want it out. It shouldn't be in there."

I'm holding her hand. "We will get it out, but we can't do that right now. It's not bleeding, but it will if we remove it. We could do a lot more damage."

There's a small amount of blood around the entry but that's it. She's incredibly lucky.

"H-how will I get it out?"

"They'll do that at a hospital. All you have to do is nothing, okay? We'll sit here together and wait."

"Where's everyone else?" she asks.

"I didn't see anyone. I was on the ground for, well, I don't know how long. They might have thought I was dead, or they might have just run. That was the plan now, right? We don't go back because we've proved that it's a real dumb idea."

"N-no, they wouldn't all just leave us."

"It's okay. We're all fighting for survival. Me and you are together and we're going to be all right."

"You really believe that?"

"Yes, I do. We've come this far." I peer around the side of the map. It's not the best place. We can be seen from certain angles, I'm sure.

I gasp as I spot someone moving and it makes Ava freeze.

But it's not Robert I can see through the fence. I sigh in relief.

"It's not him. It's not him," I say to reassure her. "Keep breathing, Ava. It's okay, it's just Harper."

Harper's crouched on the ground, looking around with wide, terrified eyes. I can see her chest rise and fall heavily as if she's hyperventilating.

I can't leave her.

I look around to make sure the coast is clear and then call out quietly, "Harper! Harper, over here."

She jumps, mouth wide as her head spins our way.

When she sees that it's just us, she puts her hand on her heart and gives me a nod, telling me she's coming to us.

We just have to get her here without being seen.

I look back toward the fire and there's nothing but flames and embers. "Go!" I mouth.

She needs to double back to get through the gate before she can get to us.

Swiping away tears, she nods.

"Go!"

Without a second thought, she leaps up and sprints to the gate. She's athletic, so it doesn't take her long at all to run back to the booths and through the gate.

I watch with anxiety curling in my gut as she sprints to

us. Robert is nowhere to be seen, but that can all change in a heartbeat.

She makes it to us after just seconds on her feet and drops to the ground in front of us. Lying on the grass, she tilts her head up and says, "You're alive."

"You thought I was dead?"

"When I got up and heard shouting, I looked around for you. It took a second, but I saw you on the ground. Your head was on the stone path, and you looked . . . I thought you were . . . I should've checked, I'm so sorry."

That explains why I have a raging headache.

"No, you did the right thing by running. Did you see Liam and Gibson and Reeve?" I ask. "I don't know if they're okay."

"Oh my god, there's glass in her!" Harper says with absolutely zero tact as she stares at Ava's injury.

Ava blinks heavily. "I'm going to have a scar, aren't I?"

"No, you won't. You'll be fine," I tell Ava. Who knows if she'll believe me. "Harper, did you see where the others went?"

She shakes her head. "Not really. I was passed out for a second too. I think I saw Liam and Gibson. They ran in different directions. I don't know about Reeve. I was so scared and confused."

"Someone said they saw Robert. Who was that?"

"I don't know. Everything happened so fast. The explosion, being thrown to the ground, the threat of Robert. The voice was deep, male. That's all I can remember."

"There's no way that our fire was missed on the mainland. Not after that explosion. Right?" Ava asks.

There's no guarantee that the explosion would have been heard. But a ball of fire and now the thick flames and black smoke will be seen. It's a giant orange scream for help.

"They'll come," I say. "The harbor will try to contact the island and send someone when they don't get a response."

"Are you sure?" Harper asks.

"They'll have to after that."

"Should we do something about the glass in her?"

Ava has her eyes closed and she's breathing in and out slowly, controlling herself. Tears roll down her cheeks, leaving a trail of black mascara behind.

"Not much we can do," I say. "We'll get her medical help when the boat arrives."

They might send medics anyway. I watch the horizon for signs of boats or helicopters.

"Please come soon," Harper whispers, following my line of sight.

I echo her prayer and squeeze Ava's hand.

For a minute, the island is quiet beside the roar and crackles of the fire.

It's peaceful and I'm tempted to sleep. Not that I would. I'm just so exhausted.

The calm abruptly ends when Harper falls against my back, screaming.

My face goes cold as it drains of blood. I turn around and see the dark figure approach.

He's found us.

Robert.

He walks toward us with a cocky confidence that is scarier than the ski mask over his face.

I leap to my feet, tugging Ava with every ounce of strength I possess. She's almost deadweight. Probably in shock.

"Up," I order. She lets out a strangled scream when she sees why I suddenly got up, and she cries harder.

"Run," Harper says, sprinting off.

I've been there with the swimming.

We're on the cliff's edge and the next opportunity to enter the park is a quarter of the way around where the service entrance is. And that's only if the gate has been left open.

Gibson and Reeve are the only ones with keys.

We'd have to climb faster than Robert can run.

Robert's footsteps thud on the dry grass behind us. They sound closer with every second and I don't know how long we can run for. We can go around and around the island on the outside perimeter but eventually he'll catch up.

Ava with her injury is slower than usual.

My heart pounds at the same rate as my head.

Harper is a little ahead of us. My arm is stretched behind me as I pull Ava along. Realizing that we're falling behind, Harper holds her hand for me. For a second, I contemplate not taking it so he can't get us all. But it's not just my life I'm playing with.

"Come on!" she says, wiggling her fingers. She doesn't want to speed off and leave us to die.

Gritting my teeth, I push harder and grab her hand. Together we manage to pick up the pace, running like a badass girl team ready to take on the world. Or in our case, escape a killer.

Ava rasps behind me, her chest rattling. The sound makes my heart squeeze. She's not just out of breath, she's finding it hard to breathe. What damage is that glass doing in her collarbone?

I don't want to think about what would happen if she passed out.

"Ava, keep going," I say, not daring to look back in case it slows me down or makes me stumble.

She whimpers, and I think she's trying to say something, but there's no time to find out what she wants because Robert is right on our heels.

We're yanked backward, my arms wrenched, the three of us going down like dominoes. Our screams mix together.

I look up and there he is. Tall, wearing black clothing, a short sword at his side. He's upside down, which seems to make it worse.

His eyes.

Familiar.

Robert raises that sword and the blade glows orange from the distant flames.

I scramble to get up and fall over Harper, who's rolling. I grab Ava's hand but it's too late.

Robert plunges the knife down into her chest.

Her eyes are saucers, her mouth forming a large O.

"No!" I scream.

Robert is frenzied. He retracts the sword and stabs again.

Over and over the knife disappears into Ava's torso all the way down to the handle. Blood splatters with each strike.

I can't watch. I have to move. I have to survive.

"Go," I say to Harper, pushing off from the ground like an Olympic sprinter.

# 26

We run as fast as we're physically able to, into the park and then back out of it. Something—adrenaline? terror?—enables me to keep up with Harper. Tears stream down my cheeks, but I manage to hold in the sobs I know will come eventually. Now isn't the time for tears.

Harper leads us back into the park. It's the last place I want to be, but we don't have much choice. Robert's boots thud loudly on the ground behind us.

After a minute, his steps fade. Neither of us slows at all. If he's playing with us, we aren't going down without a fight.

We run around the outside of the fence and Harper jumps up on the platform to the swings. I follow, holding her hand as tight as I can.

We both drop to our knees behind the center of the ride.

I slow my breathing and she puts her head between her knees.

After a few seconds, I crawl to poke my head around the corner.

I look up and scream when I see Robert's legs inches from my face.

He tilts his head, looking down at us. Harper scrambles to her feet, tugging me up with her. I slip but manage to get away as Robert's fingertips brush my arm. If I'd been any slower, he would've been able to grab me.

He's toying with us. Letting us run. Enjoying the game.

"Paisley!" Harper screams as we run toward the other side of the swings.

I stop dead as Robert appears in front of us, going around the other way. He lunges, swiping his sword through the air and narrowly missing Harper's leg. I manage to push her to the ground before he could strike.

I land on a swing. The chain rattles as I slip to the ground on top of Harper. We waste no time in kicking our legs as Robert attempts to move closer to us.

Screaming, I flail my legs like I'm possessed. Fear claws my throat as I fight for my life.

Finally, I manage to boot him in the shin, and he stumbles to his knees.

Harper and I leap to our feet. We shove swings out of our way. They fly back wildly. Maybe one of them will hit him. Stun him for a second.

I grab Harper's hand again. The small comfort of being together spurs me on. We don't know what's happened to Liam, Reeve, or Gibson, but at least we have each other. We need to fight for that.

Harper leads us back out the gate and I've never been so

thankful to not be in the damn amusement park. I never want to be back on that side of the fence again.

I look over my shoulder as we run through the gate.

"Gone," I rasp. "He's gone."

Harper gulps a breath, and we slow down.

We've lost Robert. Slowing, I collapse on the ground by the edge of the cliff.

"He almost had us," Harper says, sobbing.

I look down, and that's when I notice the blood on my hands. Ava's blood. It's on my hoodie too.

I scrub my hands against the blades of grass. "Oh god, it's all over me," I say, hyperventilating as I try to rub off the blood.

"Paisley, we have to keep moving," Harper says. "Paisley, stop! We need to go. He almost had us. He's not done."

"I'm covered."

"Hey." She sits beside me and grabs my hands. "It's okay."

"I tried to pull her faster but she . . ."

"I know. There was nothing we could do." She shakes her head, wiping a tear away. "We did everything we could to help her, but now we need to help ourselves."

"Which one of them is doing this?" I ask.

"I don't know. Gibson is the only one we've been with while someone else has been chased or killed. But he's way close to Reeve. I think he would protect him."

"Yeah. He does that a lot."

Her eyes shine with suspicion. "The childhood thing Gibson was talking about. You know what happened to Reeve."

I scrub my hands on my sweats. Blood is drying in the creases of my palms like red rivers flowing on my skin.

"Reeve told me. He served time in juvenile prison when he got into a fight protecting Gibson. No one would give him a shot after, but Malcolm did. That's what doesn't make sense to me. Why ruin the one person who's given you a chance?"

"He was in *prison*."

"Yeah."

"You didn't think that was important to share with the rest of us?" She winces, realizing her voice is too loud.

"I didn't think he was guilty! In the lobby when the lights went out, he was hit, and then James . . . How would he have had time to get over there, stab him, and get out before the lights came back on?" I say, keeping my voice low.

"Camilla could have."

"She was against the window, presumably trying to look outside for Robert. I don't think she could've."

"So you believe he's innocent?" Harper hisses.

"He doesn't hate Malcolm. If anything, he feels like he owes him. You wouldn't destroy the one person who gave you a job and a chance, would you?"

I look over my shoulder again.

"Do you think someone is trying to frame Reeve?"

"I don't know—maybe. Robert would've had to get into the files to check Reeve's history. I don't think he or Gibson would've told anyone. But Malcolm knew and it's safe to assume that Camilla would have too."

Harper shudders. "Robert's done his research on all of us."

I nod. "Definitely. I mean, I looked you all up and I wasn't even planning a murder spree."

"I did too. We all did." She lets out a long sigh.

"We all did," I repeat. I stand up and look around. "We all did. One of us. Oh god, he lives with his mom." My heart thuds harder in my chest as I piece it together. "His dad didn't want to know him. He's been hard on Malcolm and that makes sense because he doesn't have it all despite his mom pretending that they do. Oh my god!"

"Yeah, we know that much about Robert but—"

"No, not Robert," I say. *"Liam."*

"Liam." It's her turn to echo me. "Stop it. Are you serious? You mean Liam is the one doing this?"

"He's Robert."

Harper looks incredulous. "Paisley, come on. . . ."

"We trusted him because he's one of us and we thought he didn't know anyone on this island," I say, feeling the truth of what I'm saying with every breath.

"Are you telling me that Camilla is his mom and they pretended not to know each other? Why would Malcolm play along?"

I nod. "That's exactly what I'm saying, and maybe Malcolm wasn't playing. Why assume that Malcolm knew what Robert looks like?"

"Slow down. Malcolm is his *dad*?"

I hesitate. "I'm having trouble with that. If some dude knocked me up and left me to raise a kid alone, I don't think I'd take a job as his PA," I say.

"Unless this was their plan all along."

"Hmm . . . but Camilla's been working for him for a long time. It doesn't add up."

Harper pinches the bridge of her nose. "If Malcolm isn't his dad, who is he?"

"He's my uncle."

Harper and I both jolt. When we turn, we find him standing by the gate. Between us and the park. Behind us is the cliff's edge.

Liam—*Robert*—holds the ski mask in one hand. The sword in the other.

Now he's only wearing bloodstained black cargos, a long-sleeved tee, and a self-satisfied grin.

"You're good, Paisley, I'll give you that. A regular little detective. But how different things could have been for you if you'd just figured it out earlier. Maybe some of the others would still be alive."

My heart ricochets against my rib cage and panic spreads through my veins. I know I've got to stay calm. Focused.

Or we're dead.

Harper grabs my wrist tight. "Paisley," she whispers, expecting me to do something.

Like what?

"Liam," I say, raising my free hand, trying to think fast. "I—I just want to talk to you."

"You want to talk?" He sounds amused, like he cannot comprehend why I would ever want to have a conversation with him after finding out he's the killer. "Do you want it on the record, Paisley?"

He's joking, but it gives me an idea.

"That's what you want, right? Someone to tell your story. I mean, tell it from *your* point of view, not some detective or doctor painting you as a psycho. The troubled teen who turned to murder to solve his problems. What effect do videos games have on young minds?"

He turns up his nose.

No, I didn't think he would like that much.

"You know that's what they're going to say about you," I insist, trying to sound bolder than I feel inside. "It won't matter *why* you did what you did. Not if you don't get your side of the story across. You also know that. Think about it. A really great story needs survivors, witnesses. If Harper and I die and the rest of the world twists your truth, what will be the point of all of this, huh?"

I back up a little, taking Harper with me. She's fast as lightning, she could get away if I distract him. One of us needs to get off this island. He's not taking both of us down.

"Have a conversation with me for a minute. Let Harper walk away, and you and I can talk. We've done a lot of that this weekend already."

Harper gasps beside me. "Paisley, no. I'm not leaving you."

Liam waves the sword. "Yeah, come on. We're all tired of running around all over this island. Let's not spread the victims out again. I've done twenty thousand steps today."

Hearing him talk about his step count throws me for a second.

It's almost a normal conversation until I remember he got those steps chasing people down.

"Why, Liam?" I ask.

It's the only question I ask, but there are about a hundred more that are on the tip of my tongue. I don't want to overload him and make him snap—again—and I want to keep him talking to bide time.

"Malcolm," he replies.

It's the only thing he says, and he says it as if I should understand.

"Why do you hate your uncle?"

He smirks. "How long do you think we have until the cops arrive?"

I lick my dry lips. If he feels cornered, he'll react. "They might just send a boat out, not cops. Someone like Gibson."

It's a complete lie, obviously. The fact that we're unreachable and there's now a fire aren't great signs that all is well. Cops will come.

They have to come.

I hold his stare and clench my jaw. He's challenging me. Who will crack first? He wants to know if I believe my own bullshit.

Like a great reporter, I hold my nerve and stare right back into the eyes of a killer.

All he sees is my strength, not the huge waves of nausea roiling underneath.

"Liam, let Harper go. She needs to check on Ava. We don't need her here when we talk."

He snorts at my pitiful attempt to get Harper away. "Ava's dead, Paisley. You know that."

My stomach lurches. Her face flies into my mind. She was so scared. Poor Ava.

"What about Gibson and Reeve?" I ask, almost hoping that he won't answer. If I don't know, then I can pretend they're alive and waiting for the boat.

Liam shrugs, looking away. "Probably bled out by now."

His words knock the air from my lungs.

Could that be true? He probably had enough time if he went straight for them after the explosion, but then he would've risked one of us seeing. And he wouldn't meet my eyes when he said that.

He has for everything else.

"God," Harper whispers.

I can't tell her that they're probably not dead. Maybe they'll find us if they're still alive. Though we agreed to keep going forward, so why would they look?

"It's just us now?" I ask.

He shakes his head. "Malcolm isn't dead yet. Let's take a little walk before the cavalry arrives." He motions with the sword for us to move, and so we do.

The explosion must've been about ten or fifteen minutes ago. It takes twenty to get here, but there will be a period of time when they try to make contact before they leave.

We just need to survive a little bit longer.

# 27

Liam directs us to the seafood restaurant near the back of the park. We weren't far from it when he caught up to us.

He lets us in using the door codes we had no idea he knew. He says nothing, just raises the sword to show us who's still in control.

Clearly, I know I cannot beat him.

Not right this second, anyway.

The restaurant is clean and rather clinical-looking compared to the rest of the island. There are modern white tables and chairs, a sushi bar, and a stainless-steel kitchen that I can see through a wide hatch.

He opens a door off the kitchen and gestures with his chin for us to go in there.

There's nothing I want to do less than walk in there—a storeroom—but what choice do I have?

I go first, Harper only just behind me. She's plastered to my back, and I think I can feel her trembling.

Liam flicks the light on. I should get used to calling him Robert, I suppose.

It doesn't seem real that it's the same person.

But is it?

"What's your real name?" I ask.

"Robert Liam Jenkins," he replies.

"Camilla was in on it."

He walks around a tall shelf splitting the storeroom in half. It's stacked with products, like rice and sauces, in preparation for the opening next week.

That won't happen now.

"Hello, Malcolm," Liam says.

I step around the corner.

Malcolm is tied to a chair with a gag in his mouth, dried blood under his nose, and his right eye swollen.

With a painful-sounding groan, Malcolm lifts his head. When he sees Harper and me, he mumbles something around the cloth.

"Shut up," Liam—Robert—spits. "The girls were wondering why I despise you. Care to weigh in?"

He yanks the gag from Malcolm's mouth, and it falls down around his neck.

"Robert, please. You have to let me go."

"No, I don't. Tell them what you did."

"It wasn't my decision. Your grandparents' will was their—"

"Stop!" Robert spits. "Stop making excuses."

"What happened?" I ask. "Robert, tell us. You'll tell us the truth, not him."

Malcolm shoots me a death glare. There's a reason why I don't want to take Malcolm's side. Surely he can see that.

"My mom was older."

He's already using past tense.

Sick.

"Older by three years, but that didn't matter to my grandpa. He was a mean old bastard. Hated women. The heir to their millions was always going to be a male. If Malcolm had come first, my mom wouldn't have been born."

"That's terrible," I say.

"She worked her ass off every day to please them. She went to college, got a good degree, joined the family company at mid-management level. My grandpa made it clear that she would never get any higher. Malcolm messed around, got drunk, partied his way through college. He dropped out and was still left everything."

"I was young, Robert. The pressure of having to—"

"I really don't care how you felt," Robert says, not giving Malcolm the chance to get his side across.

"My grandparents were worse after I was born. My dad, whoever he is, took off and Mom had to do it alone. No one helped her, not even her brother. She was alone with a kid to raise and a shitty job she could never progress in."

He waves the sword at Malcolm.

"They died and you inherited everything. The whole estate was yours. Mom didn't get a penny, just a clause in the will that said she was to be kept on in her current role. And what did you do with this injustice?"

I can guess that he didn't split it with Camilla.

"*Nothing.* I was ten by this point, had no relationship with my grandparents because I was the bastard child who brought shame on the family. I'd met them twice and that was only because I was in the car when Mom had to run into the office. I don't remember you," he tells Malcolm. "Did you ever visit?"

Malcolm swallows audibly. "I made sure your mom had money."

He barks a laugh. "Uh, if you mean that you let her keep her job, okay. While you turned into an overnight multimillionaire, she got to keep her nine-to-five."

Malcolm's head is ducked, eyes low, cheeks red.

His sister. I knew there was something more to their relationship.

He's not proud of how poorly he treated his sister, but it took all of this to get there. That much is clear since he never divided the estate.

Camilla must have been heartbroken.

"My mom went from being controlled by her parents to being controlled by her brother. Everything she worked so hard for was worthless. You should've seen her pain when she found out she was getting nothing."

Liam clears his throat. "I was furious. She was devastated. Then Malcolm 'promoted' her to be his personal assistant. She was running multiple companies for him and earning a friggin' secretary's wage. Malcolm barked his orders, told her which direction to take the business, which hotels to buy, and sat back while she worked her fingers to the bone. Eight a.m. to seven p.m.

every day. Her wage increased by ten thousand dollars. For three more hours every day she got an extra ten grand a year!"

Liam's face turns as red as his uncle's.

He breathes out through his teeth in what almost sounds like a growl.

"I was fifteen and barely saw my mom. It meant I was alone in a house that was too big and too expensive for us. Everyone knew her parents were rich, so she pretended we were too. When Mom told me he'd bought an *island,* I lost it. It took a full year to get her on board."

Malcolm gasps, eyes wide, jaw slack, and he looks up at Robert with betrayal in his eyes.

"That's right, uncle. Your sister ended up hating you as much as I did."

"What did Camilla agree to?" I ask.

Her reaction in the bar when she whispered about Robert was real. She was scared and confused.

Liam smirks over his shoulder. "She agreed to sabotage the island. The influencer thing was my idea, she just needed to plant it with Malcolm. By that point I had an online presence playing video games. Nothing else to do since we had little money and my mom was always out. I worked hard to build my platforms. I told her we'd scare everyone who came and make the island seem unsafe. A broken ride here, a kitchen catching fire there was all we'd need. Once you all put it out there, he would be ruined. The worst amusement park in the US. I promised her no one would get hurt."

Malcolm shakes his head, sobbing softly, probably wishing he'd shared his sudden fortune with his sister.

Who, in my eyes, was just as entitled to their parents' money, considering all she'd done. What kind of brother takes everything for himself?

I feel Harper tug on the hem of my T-shirt, but I don't dare look at her. We can't escape yet. Robert isn't distracted enough. He'd catch up to us quickly.

I rest my hand on the metal shelving beside me. How easy would it be to pull that down? Harper and I would be prepared. We'd duck as we pulled it. Malcolm was just past where it would fall.

Robert would take the brunt of the hit.

I had to try.

"Why did you change your mind about hurting people?" I ask.

"He didn't recognize me when I stepped onto the island. His own nephew." Liam laughs. "It made me hate him more. I didn't think that was possible, but it was. Silly, really, since I counted on him not knowing who I was."

"Why did you kill your mom?"

Malcolm sobs a "no" and folds into himself as much as the rope will allow.

Just as I'd hoped, Robert turns to Malcolm while answering my question.

"She wanted to stop me. I've had *this* planned for a very long time. I started hating you when I was a kid, and it grew bigger and stronger every day. Sometimes I could barely stand it. I wanted to walk into your office and put a knife through your eye. God, I think about that so often. She knew I'd done something when Will went missing and she wanted me to stop. I couldn't have her getting in my way."

So his loathing of his uncle trumped his love for his mom. What a sick, sick person.

That explains Camilla's reactions every step of the way.

With his back turned, I look over my shoulder at Harper and silently tap the shelving. I bend my knees slightly. She nods, telling me she understands what I want her to do.

She places her hand on the same shelf as me.

I mouth *"One, two, three"* and we both yank the shelf hard. I duck and before I hit the floor, I shuffle back.

The shelf tilts. Boxes fly off onto the ground. Robert only has enough time to turn halfway before the shelf smashes him on the head.

I'm on all fours, backing up as fast as Harper behind me can go.

"Paisley! Harper!" Malcolm shouts as we stand up at the other end.

"No, we have to go," Harper says, tugging on my hand. The shelf is lying on top of Robert. He's still, but that doesn't mean he's dead.

"We can't leave him. He'll be dead if Robert gets up."

She swears under her breath and picks a knife from a magnetic strip over the countertop. I watch Robert as she cuts a trembling Malcolm loose.

I never thought I could feel sorry for him, but he's clearly shaken after learning that his sister is dead.

He stands, throwing the rope onto the floor just as Robert groans and pushes himself up as much as he can.

The shelf is caught on the wall an inch above him, so he's not even on his knees but all he has to do is roll.

"Come on!" I shout as the two of them run past the shelf.

Harper reaches me but Robert is too fast. He's rolled over and slashes the sword at Malcolm's calves. Malcolm goes down with a hell of a scream.

"Run!" Harper shouts.

The last thing I see before I'm out the door is Robert sticking the sword into Malcolm's back.

Just like Malcolm did to Camilla.

# 28

Harper and I burst outside and, holding hands, dart toward the jetty.

From here it'll take about ten minutes to get there and I'm just praying that help is waiting for us.

I haven't heard Robert following, but we're both breathing hard, and my pulse is loud in my ears. I wouldn't hear footsteps if they were right behind me.

He will follow us. What choice does he have now?

His game is almost over and there are still too many players left.

"Reeve!" Harper says, yanking me to a stop. "Behind the entrance to the big coaster."

I look to my right and see him too, crouched down, cradling his head in his hands. My heart squeezes at his anguish.

Oh god, he's okay.

We turn and I look over my shoulder as we run to him. I drop to my knees and the relief of finding him alive brings tears to my eyes.

He's startled, but his shoulders loosen when he sees it's us.

"Gibson," he mutters.

I don't see Gibson. "Reeve, are you okay? Where is he?"

Reeve stares ahead as if he's not heard us. Oh no.

I place my hands on either side of his jaw. "Hey, you're okay. Reeve, look at me."

His dark eyes slide to mine. He's haunted, and I don't need to ask why he was saying Gibson's name. His expression is clear. He's found his best friend dead.

No.

I swallow my horror and blink away tears. "It's going to be okay."

Reeve shakes his head. "He was the only one . . . the only one who . . ."

"I know. I'm so sorry. You still have me. Okay. We're getting out of here."

Now that we're here, I can't believe I ever thought I could like Liam more than Reeve.

The only one who had his back.

"He died in my arms. Stabbed. I tried to help, but I couldn't do anything. Before he died, he mumbled 'Help her.'"

"Help who?" I ask.

"I couldn't see anyone, but I was focused on trying to help him. I figured he'd seen one of you."

"It must've been Ava. She was wandering around in shock because she had glass in her neck," I say. "It's Liam, Reeve. He's the one doing this."

"Liam? Our Liam? No way. You can't be serious."

Harper and I look at each other. He hasn't seen what we've seen. The cold, callous side of Liam—Robert—who can kill and revel in other people's pain.

I take a deep breath. "His real name is Robert Liam Jenkins and he's Camilla's son. Malcolm's nephew. We don't have enough time to explain everything, but I assure you it's Liam."

I look around, waiting for Robert to make an appearance. He surely will soon. "We've got to get back to the jetty. Reeve, you need to get up."

It seems so callous to ignore his pain right now, to ignore the fact that Gibson is dead, but we can't afford time to grieve or process.

"Son of a bitch. I ran after him, I tried to protect him. He killed Gibson! Oh god, what do I tell his parents?" Reeve mutters. I don't know if he's asking us or just thinking aloud.

"We need to move, Paisley. Is he coming yet?" Harper asks.

"No, but he will soon," I say. "Reeve, please. I need you to be you right now."

His hands cover mine over his cheeks. "I can't leave Gibson here."

I don't know where Gibson is, but it must be nearby.

"You won't be leaving him. Help will be here any second. The cops. They'll take Gibson. But right now we need to get out of here. Robert was getting up when we left the restaurant."

"Getting up?"

"We knocked him over with a shelf. He killed Malcolm. We ran."

"He also stabbed Ava," Harper says.

"Maybe he followed Ava after stabbing Gibson and that's what Gibson was trying to warn you about," I say.

Reeve blinks. "Ava's dead and she had glass in her?"

"Seriously, can we move," Harper says. "We've been here for too long already."

"She's right. We need you with us if we have a chance at getting out of here."

He takes a ragged breath. "I'm going to *kill* him."

"Reeve, no. Let's just go to the jetty to wait for help."

He'll find us eventually anyway.

"He killed Gibson."

"I know, and I know it's killing you but if you don't help us, we all might die. Reeve, please."

I heave a reluctant Reeve to his feet. Harper scowls at him the entire time. I think she's about ready to leave him behind. It's not at all helpful to sit there and do nothing.

We're at risk while we're trying to help him.

But I get it. The death of his friend has left him shattered.

Reeve nods. "I'm with you. When you're safe, Paisley, I'm going back for him."

"Okay," I reply, knowing full well that I'm not going to allow that to happen. But I need Reeve to cooperate.

He takes my hand and we all sprint, not bothering to hide because there isn't time.

"I see a boat!" Harper cries as we get closer to the park's main entrance.

Our fire is still burning bright, our smoky SOS billowing up to the sky.

It worked.

In the distance, I see it too. Just a dot at the moment, but it will be here soon.

We're saved.

I hold on to Reeve as we run, partly because I'm scared and partly because I don't want him turning back and going on some revenge mission.

He's unarmed while Robert has a blade and a taste for blood.

We flee through the gate and almost fall over each other as we put the brakes on at the top. Because waiting for us is Robert.

He's standing tall, shoulders wide, sword by his side.

Reeve bares his teeth.

There are three of us and one of him. With a sword, though, the scale still tilts to his side. The dot sailing toward us takes on more of a boat shape, but Robert is now between us and safety.

He stares at us, waiting to see what our next move will be.

"Put that down, coward," Reeve says, stepping in front of Harper and me.

"Reeve!"

"I'm doing this, Paisley. That boat is minutes away. I'll keep him busy, you two go."

"We're not leaving you," Harper replies. "We've come this far, and the boat is almost here."

Robert begins to walk toward us. Each step on the jetty makes my heart accelerate.

"He's coming closer," I mutter.

"Good," Reeve says. He used to be scared, despite not really admitting it. That's all gone. Robert killing Gibson has changed everything. Hatred replaces fear in Reeve's eyes. "You two jump and swim to that boat. I'll deal with *him*."

A shudder ripples through my entire body. Reeve looks like he's about to tear Robert to pieces.

It's a glimpse of the Reeve the night he was arrested.

I need him to calm down.

"Gibson wouldn't want this," I say. "You know he wouldn't."

In front of me, I watch Reeve's shoulder stiffen. He heard me and he knows I'm right. Gibson wouldn't want Reeve to become a murderer.

It doesn't look like we're going to have a choice. Even if Reeve didn't want to hurt Robert—which he very much does—if Robert comes for us, we'll have to defend ourselves.

Robert chuckles as he walks along the jetty and steps onto the rock. "Wow, you still don't see it, do you? How could I have done all this alone?"

"You had the help of your mom," Reeve replies. "You're going to die for what you did to Gibson. It's three against one now, asshole."

Robert sneers. "Guess again, *asshole*."

I'm grabbed from behind. At the same time an arm pins me in place, something sharp pokes against my neck. A knife.

It takes one, two, three, four seconds for my brain to catch up and realize what's happening.

No.

*Harper.*

Reeve looks over his shoulder, his face full of shock and fear. "What the . . . ?"

"Harper," I whisper. "Why?" I feel my face getting hotter at how stupid I've been. "You all along?"

Harper laughs in my ear. "How did I do, baby?"

Robert smiles back, his features softening. "You're perfect, as always."

What the hell?

They're *together.*

The boat is clearer in the sea, maybe five minutes away now.

Something clicks into place, and it all makes sense.

God, no.

"Gibson wasn't saying 'help her,'" I say, and Reeve frowns. "He was saying *Harper.*"

She is the one who killed Gibson.

I gag at the thought of her hands on me after murdering Gibson.

Was he her only victim?

She laughs again. "You don't know how hard it was to keep a straight face with that one."

Bile rises in my throat and I gag again.

I thought I could trust her, that we'd get out of here and keep in contact. I thought I'd found a friend.

It was all a lie.

She must've been the one to take the boat, sink or anchor it at sea, and then swim back. She's been to Europe and swam the channel between England and France. This must have been like a warm-up compared to that.

"When did you two meet?" I ask, surprised at how calm my voice is.

"Two years ago. Online. We've spoken every day since then, bonded over our messed-up families."

"You said your parents are strict."

Reeve's gaze flits between us like he's unsure why I'm talking to her. He looks like he wants to murder them both.

Four minutes until the boat arrives, approximately.

"That's one way to put it. They controlled every aspect of my life. Every minute, every mouthful, every item of clothing I wear, every book I read. Until I met Robert."

Robert takes another step closer. "Harper was on board with my plan from day one. The real plan, not the bullshit one I fed my mom."

"We're going to be a modern-day Bonnie and Clyde," Harper says.

They've both consumed all the Kool-Aid. What are the odds of them finding each other? Both sadistic.

"Why did you have to kill?" I ask. "I don't believe you want this, Harper. You're a good person, you don't have to do this. You can stop."

"Shut up!" she spits. "Do you know how famous we're going to be?"

"I don't know why you'd want to be with someone who chases other girls," Reeve points out.

"Flirting with Paisley was part of the plan," she growls.

"We had to be one of you, earn your trust. Paisley was the one most likely to figure this whole thing out, so we needed to befriend her."

I'm drenched in shame over being duped by two killers.

I had a crush on one and thought another was my friend. I actually wanted to keep in touch with Harper after this.

How stupid I've been.

"Right, Paisley was planned. But was kissing Ava part of earning our trust?" Reeve asks.

I catch on the second he's said it.

Harper reacts. I can't see her, but her body stiffens behind me. Distracted, she lowers the knife a little just so it's not digging into my skin. Her attention is on Robert, who she now believes cheated on her.

Reeve and I waste no time in acting. I bend my knees and drop. Reeve leaps toward us.

Harper and Robert both shout out, but we're faster. Reeve barrels into us, and when Harper falls to the ground, I go for her knife.

Robert has to get up the steps. It won't take him long, but we have a few seconds to take one of them out and give ourselves an advantage.

Harper screams as I take the knife easily. Her surprise at Reeve's words and losing her grip on me sealed her fate.

This much she didn't think through.

I take the knife and without a single thought, stick it into her side. The blade meets a second's resistance but then slides easily.

Much easier than I ever imagined. My eyes widen as the blade sinks beneath her flesh like warm butter. I gasp and let go as if the thing has an electrical current.

That was too simple.

I blink, but nothing changes. I did that. The knife that's buried deep in her body is because of me.

Harper stares at me, jaw slack, hands frozen in midair. "Y-you."

*Yeah, I stopped you.*

Reeve jumps to his feet, yanking me up with him. He pulls me out of the way as Robert, screaming, falls beside Harper.

The knife is still embedded in her side, and she hasn't moved an inch. I don't know if it's a fatal wound, but I don't think she'll be able to get up.

The boat is almost at the jetty now. "Reeve," I say, hearing people on board shouting to us. I can't quite make out what they're saying. Something like *Put the knife down and stop what you're doing.*

It's as if he didn't even hear me speak. He launches his fist and cracks Robert on the jaw.

Shouting expletives, Robert tries to get up, but Reeve is too fast. He punches him again. Over and over, he delivers blows. Robert's lip splits, and blood pours from his nose like a faucet.

"Reeve!" I shout. I can't leave without him.

The people on the boat are so close, I can make out two men who are barking orders at us. They have no clue what they're about to roll up to.

"Reeve, they're here!" I grab his arm as he retracts it from Robert's face. "Come on!"

He twists, about to argue with me, I'm sure. Something in my expression makes him stop, though. He shoves Robert with his other hand and stands up.

"Let's get out of here," he says.

The boat is mere meters from the jagged rocks now. Still, Reeve and I run down the steps toward the approaching boat.

"Help!" I scream. My vision blurs as I try to see through tears. I want them to know that we're the good guys.

The people on the boat lean over the side. "What the hell happened to you?"

I burst into floods of tears, so Reeve tells them there are two killers and seven murder victims on the island.

Four teenagers, three adults. The owner.

So much death.

Through watery vision I see their faces fall. All four of them. Harbor patrol, who have presumably seen their fair share of death.

The boat slows as it pulls up to the jetty. Almost there. I'm tempted to leap for it, but I'd probably miss.

"We've made it, Paisley," Reeve says, kissing the side of my head. "You're going to be safe."

Like he promised when all of this started.

"Seven victims?" a large man with a thick mustache asks.

Reeve reaches up to grab the rope being thrown. I notice one of the men on the radio. One of the men is talking about being armed.

They're scared to step off the boat.

I don't blame them.

Reeve wraps the rope and we're just about to jump on the boat when something slams into me.

I scream as Robert grabs me from behind. His arms clamp around my waist.

The last thing I see before I'm dragged underwater is Reeve's horrified expression.

# ACKNOWLEDGMENTS

I first want to say a big thank-you to my family for making it possible for me to hide away for hours, days, and weeks at a time to hit a deadline. I love you guys.

Ariella and Amber, thank you for being the best team ever!

To every amazing person at Random House who has worked on editing, cover design, marketing, etc., thank you. Wendy, thanks for always believing in me and the ideas I come up with!

I want to say a special thank-you to booksellers, bloggers, vloggers, "booktokers," for shouting about my books.

My last but by no means least massive THANK YOU is to you, the reader.

*Don't be afraid.*

BE TERRIFIED.

# prologue

# FEAR

I watch the pathetic buzz of excitement from my car. The heavy snowstorm creates a kaleidoscope of color as students sprint into Rock Bay High wearing brightly colored parkas and the hockey team's letterman jackets. This school is all about hockey; if you don't like it, you can pretty much rule out succeeding in athletics here.

They all stare at their phone screens as they run. With my window cracked open, I can hear some of them over the howling wind as they pass me without a second glance—the way I like it. They debate the topic of the day: Who has the worst death fear?

My mouth twitches as I realize that it's working.

January through March is dead in this town, more so than usual, so I knew it would be the right time to begin my plan. My meme is spreading like wildfire. I never had any doubt that it would. Morbid curiosity, boredom, and a stream of serial killer documentaries on Netflix have made death and murder cool.

Now I have everyone talking about the most painful and gory deaths. They're sharing *their* most feared end.

I used a fake account to post the meme, some random girl's pretty face as the hook. I used it to friend-request Kason Risby. I knew he'd go for it; he's the type. As soon as he reposted the meme, I logged out of that account, and I haven't looked at it since.

The cops can trace the IP address, but it will go to a greasy truckers' café off the interstate. Far enough from our cruddy fishing town.

I watch everyone run up the steps, the jocks in a pack, the band geeks carrying instruments, the popular girls cackling. They disappear into the building quickly because of the weather, but I know what they'll be talking about.

High school is always the same. The thrill of a new challenge or dare lingers for weeks, and everyone gets involved, desperate to be a part of something.

Snow whips my face as it flies sideways through the gap in my window. My car is damp, my hair wet. I've been locked out in bad weather so many times over the years that it doesn't bother me anymore.

I think I could survive for days out in the snow.

That's one positive from my childhood, I suppose.

With a sigh, I close the window, get out of my car, and walk a few steps closer to the building. My heavy boots crunch in the snow.

They're all excited about sharing their biggest fear. Excited by something I barely made it through. It's a game to them, all laughing and debating whose death fear is actually the worst. Strangling, drowning, falling, hanging—the list goes on.

My hands curl into fists. This town must have known what I was going through, but no one dared look closer. Not one adult asked if everything was okay at home. My life was a game to the people who should have taken care of me.

Soon they will all know that *I'm* not playing.

This *isn't* just some stupid meme.

This is revenge.

Death *is* coming.

# one

# IZZY

Snow coats the ground like a fluffy blanket. It looks beautiful, like thousands of tiny crystals that glisten in the sun. But it also conceals what could be underneath.

Last winter it took two months—until the snow finally melted—to find my neighbor's dead dog. Two full months that little terrier had been lying there, just yards from their front door.

Anything could be lurking under the snow.

We have a couple of months left of freezing conditions, but the air has been warming. Not quite enough to make the snow melt or stop it from falling, but just enough so that I don't feel like I'm being punched in the lungs *every* time I step outside.

I walk to my car and immediately blast the heat. The roads are clear, as they're plowed regularly, giving the impression that they've been carved out of the ten inches of snow that frames them.

More storms are in the forecast.

The sun is up, but gray clouds stop it from making an appearance. January is perpetual nighttime in our little fishing town. When my car is warm, I flick the lights on and back out of the driveway. Luckily, my dad shoveled yesterday, or I'd be late to school.

I better get accepted into Florida State. No more freezing air, no more winter coats and woolly hats, and no more wondering if there's anything dead under the snow.

My sister, Lia, escaped to college in North Carolina last year, and she's enjoying the warmer climate—and the food—immensely.

It's senior year, and I still haven't gotten Justin Rae to notice that I exist or told my best friend, Sydney—Syd—that I don't really like going to parties, the mall, or any other place she drags me to.

We're supposed to be going to Mariella Whitmore's party tonight. Rich girl, wants to marry a billionaire, says "like" a lot—you know the type.

Lia calls me a shadow person because I follow silently and never stick up for myself.

I'd be offended if it weren't completely true.

My car rumbles as I pull into the parking lot. I park in the same spot as always, Lia's old one.

I check myself out in the visor mirror. My complexion is fair, clear skin and rosy cheeks that I'm so grateful for, because I'm terrible at applying makeup. My hair is naturally wavy, which suits me just fine, because I prefer to sleep in rather than waking early to style it. I have the same hazel eyes as my sister, though my left eye has a ton of green specks. Syd says it's cool, and I've grown to like it.

I close the mirror and grab my backpack.

Rock Bay High has been my home for the last three and a half years. The town used to be named Rock Bass Bay, but they dropped the "Bass" years ago in an attempt to sound less fishy. Now we sound much cooler than we are.

It didn't help, though. Thanks to bigger ports in the state, this still isn't a town you come to unless you live here.

"Izzy!" Syd says, pulling my car door open as if it's on fire. Frozen air hits me instantly. "What took you so long?"

Startled, I look at the time on my dash. "I'm actually earlier than—"

"Forget it. Have you heard? Justin dumped Gemma. He's back on the market!"

That would be awesome news if I had even a hint of a shot with him.

"I don't care," I tell her.

"Sure you don't." She rolls her incredible sage eyes and scrolls her phone.

Syd's tall, has smooth, dark skin, full lips, stunning shoulder-length curls, and the biggest smile. We've been inseparable since freshman year.

"You should go for it, Iz."

Justin has never given me a second glance with his pretty green eyes.

She gasps as if she's just remembered something. "Hey, have you seen this? It's everywhere right now."

She shoves her screen in my face as I get out of the car. I blink and rear my head back. "Well, I can't see it from three inches in front of my face, can I?" I push the phone back.

"See."

"A new meme? A game? Fear what? What am I looking at, Syd?"

There's a picture of a frozen red rose on a snowy dock. Some of the petals have broken off and are scattered around it. Text sits over the image:

**REPOST WITH YOUR DEATH FEAR!**
**If death came for you today,**
**what would be the worst way to go?**
**#thefear**

"That's not at all creepy—wait, is this a picture of *our* dock?" I look over my shoulder in the direction of the port, though school is nowhere near it. Then I look back at the picture. Yeah, it definitely is. The wooden post behind the flower looks just like the one at Puck's, the local diner. It even has the initials of the owner, Matthew, and a hockey puck carved into it.

No wonder everyone around here is going extra crazy for this challenge. They think someone we know created it.

"That's totally what I thought! Must be someone around here trying to go viral. How lame," she replies.

"They didn't leave their name. Looks like the original post comes from Janie Dow. Nice play on Jane Doe there. How long before this is flagged?"

She shakes her head and takes her phone back as we walk into school. "Who do you think it is? It screams high school, right?"

I shrug. "Probably someone who goes here."

Inside, it stinks like cleaning products and the repressed scent of feet. Our hockey team trains daily, and the smell proves it. So do all the shiny trophies from the glory days in the trophy cabinet.

Rock Bay High is *big* on hockey. RBH Blade Rockies banners hang above almost every door, with the sharkiest-looking Rock Bay logo I have *ever* seen.

Justin is captain of the team and insists on working harder so we have a shot at winning . . . *anything* this year. We actually might with him and Kason Risby leading.

I glance down the hall and notice that almost everyone is staring at their phones and muttering to each other. That's not about this meme, right?

"What's your fear? Wait, I know this. It's suffocating, right?" Syd asks, tapping on her phone as we weave between crowds of students.

"Yep," I reply. "And yours is being stabbed to death, a *million* times, like in a horror movie."

"I don't like pain, and that has to be such a painful way to go, right? I heard drowning is peaceful."

I bark a laugh.

Peaceful. The only peaceful way to go is in your sleep. That's what I'm hoping for—when I'm old and gray.

I can't believe I'm even thinking about this.

"Fire would be an awful way to go, too," Syd adds.

"I thought social media was where people went to brag about their perfect lives."

Syd links her arm with mine as we walk to homeroom. "That's so yesterday, Izzy. Keep up. Now it's all about challenges and serial killers."

"I'm not eating Tide Pods."

"That should be your death fear, Iz."

"Stupid people on TikTok or ingesting chemicals?"

She laughs as we enter the classroom.

"No way is being shot in the head worse than drowning," Kason says loudly, as if he wants the entire school's attention, and flicks his dark hair. He laughs and thumps Justin playfully on his muscular arm.

They're a good duo. Every guy wants to be them, and every girl wants to date them. Isn't that what they say? I'm sure that's what Kason thinks. He's a cocky asshole who's relying solely on hockey to get him into college.

Syd and I take seats at our usual desks.

Justin is . . . different. All right, he's super sure of himself and popular, but I've never heard of him treating anyone badly. He *is* a serial dater like Kason, though.

Another reason why I wouldn't go there even if I had a chance: I think he averages about three months with a girl and then moves on. Still, it's longer than Kason's three hours.

I'm in agreement with Kason on this one, though: drowning would be worse than getting shot.

Mrs. Grady takes attendance, and the bell for first period rings.

I overhear about a dozen horrible ways to die as we walk to AP English.

Mariella strolls past with her stand-in friend Jessie, as her real friends, Tayley and Debbie, aren't in her first period. "As if I'm going to die any way other than spectacularly. It needs to be, like, newsworthy, you know?"

I swear I lose a brain cell every time I hear her say "like."

In AP English, I take a seat near the back, next to Axel, a kid who could probably have his master's degree already and rarely talks to anyone. He always wears leather and a bored expression.

It wouldn't surprise me if someone said their biggest fear was "Axel staring at me to death with his threatening glare."

There's a rumor that he's older but got held back. Only that doesn't make sense, because he's a genius. There's another rumor that he intentionally failed exams to stay behind. But who would want to make high school last longer? No one.

I take a look around the room. I've never seen everyone so cheerful in the middle of winter before—especially halfway through January. And all it took was discussing the one way they'd never want to die . . .

Justin is in the last row with Tayley and Debbie. Tayley is hanging on his every word. It looks like she's begun her campaign to be his next girlfriend now that he's single again.

Mr. Morrison bursts into the room and clears his throat—he does that to start the lesson.

I try not to switch off at the constant drone of his monotone voice.

"How was your weekend?" I ask Axel.

His head twists toward me slowly. His eyes are such a light blue they're almost the color of the ice outside. They don't look real, but I can see that he's not wearing lenses. "Fine. Yours?"

I flip open my textbook. "Shopping and a movie night with Syd."

We have a very similar conversation almost every morning. I try to talk to him so that the period doesn't drag. He grunts one- or two-word replies. There is something new I can add today.

"Did you see that meme being reposted on Insta?" I ask.

"Yep."

I wait for him to expand, but seconds tick by and now I'm just looking at him like a weirdo.

"Okay," I mutter, my shoulders hunching. This period would go a lot faster if he weren't so hostile.

He gives me a half-hearted smile that's more irritated grimace and turns away.

Everyone else in the room talks, having quiet conversations and laughing under their breath. My table with Axel is always quiet.

Behind me, I can hear Tayley telling Justin that her biggest fear is being crushed.

Not a great way to go, but I think it would be over quickly. There wouldn't be a lot of time to think. Not like suffocating, where you'd know for minutes that you were fading. You'd fight and eventually realize that you're losing—dying.

I look up and see Axel turn his nose up. No, he definitely

doesn't seem like the person to take part in TikTok challenges or anything else that involves being a sheep. I know him about as well as I know a perfect stranger, but I don't imagine he does anything that he doesn't want to.

Not like me.

I wonder what his death fear is. It would probably be something like being shot with a huge military-style gun. One of those guns that goes on firing forever in movies.

Asking him wouldn't hurt. He could always tell me to go away or ignore me. He'll probably ignore me.

He picks up his heavy textbook and flips it open, the muscles in his forearms flexing. He's not on the hockey team, but I guess he works out. I avert my eyes, unsure if it's me making him uncomfortable.

"Izzy?"

I jolt at the authoritative tone in Mr. Morrison's voice.

"Sorry?"

"The partner project on Poe. You're working with Axel."

My stomach sinks in alarm, and I hope that I don't look as scared as I feel. "A group project?"

"*Partner* project," Axel replies.

Well, that's just great. How unfair is it to partner us with the person we're sitting with rather than letting us choose? I thought it was bad enough working independently beside him. We might have to meet up outside of school and say more than seven words to each other. How will he cope with that?

I peek to my side, and he's glaring at his textbook as if it's just flipped him off.

Well, it's safe to say that he's not loving the idea of working together either.

"Should we meet up after school this week?" I ask.

"Why?" he asks, as if it's not actually obvious.

"Um, to work on the project . . ."

Surely he doesn't think I want to spend time hanging out with him. I don't think I'd want to be alone with him.

"We can do it in class."

"Sure, but what if we don't finish?"

"We will."

I bite my lip hard so I won't tell him to get lost. It's not like this was my idea, yet he's making it seem like I'm forcing him into it.

"Fine. You're going to have to talk to me, though. You get that, right?"

"I don't mind talking to you, Izzy."

That's the first time in the three and a half years at this school that he's used my name. In fact, I don't think I've ever heard him use anyone's name. Also, he's lying. He obviously does mind talking to me.

We start work, or rather, I start work. I decide what we should focus on in our presentation, opting for how Poe's rather depressing life influenced his writing. Axel replies with his usual grunt to everything I suggest. I get the impression that he doesn't care what we do for this project; he just wants to get it over with.

So, I scribble lots of notes while he stares at the table like a serial killer.

When that wonderful ding of the bell rings, I sigh in pure relief.

"Axel," I say as he grabs his unopened notebook and stands.

He looks down and grunts, "What?"

Damn, he really is tall. A mountain of a seventeen-year-old, he could easily get away with being twenty-one. His square jaw, ruffled blond hair, and almond-shaped eyes make girls melt . . . until they meet him.

*Just say the words, Izzy.*

"What's your death fear?"

He turns his nose up in the exact way I thought he would. Yeah, he's definitely above all this meme stuff.

Still, I hold my ground, tilting my chin up and waiting.

Finally, he replies, "All of them."

"I'm sorry, what? All of them?"

He walks around the desk but keeps his eyes on me. "Falling, burning, illness, being buried alive, crushed, strangled, suffocated, stabbed, shot, beaten. They're all bad. Everyone is running around arguing over whose fear is the scariest, as if they have everything figured out." He shakes his head. "The truth is, when death comes, no matter how it comes, it's always scary."

# STAY UP ALL NIGHT WITH THESE THREE UNPUTDOWNABLE READS!